W9-BIG-353

Someone was always trying to goad me into a gun-fight, but somehow I forced myself to resist the temptation to take the fool up on it. And I was doing my best to resist now.

But this man Lipton was calling me a coward for refusing to have it out with his friend, and I couldn't help but fly into a rage. In an instant, all the teachings of O'Rourke, all of my good resolutions since leaving home, disappeared; suddenly I was back in Bostwick, with the chance of a battle opening before me.

"Are you armed?" I asked Lipton.

"I am," he answered slowly.

"Then draw your gun," I said. "If it's murder you people want, I'll start by showing some excellent examples of killing. Draw your gun now, Lipton, or I'll make the first move for mine!"

Other Paperback Library Books

by Max Brand

The Man From Mustang
Mistral
The Seven of Diamonds
Dead or Alive
Smiling Charlie
Pleasant Jim
The Rancher's Revenge
The Dude
Riders of the Plains
The Jackson Trail
The Iron Trail
Pillar Mountain
The Blue Jay
Silvertip's Search

Silvertip's Trap
Silvertip's Roundup
Outlaw's Code
Montana Rides!
Montana Rides Again
Outlaw Valley
Showdown
The Song of the Whip
Tenderfoot
Smugglers' Trail
The Rescue of Broken Arrow
The Border Bandit
Gunman's Legacy

For information on ordering any of the above books, please turn to page 256.

MAX BRAND

THE LONG
CHANCE

PAPERBACK LIBRARY
®
A KINNEY SERVICE COMPANY
NEW YORK

PAPERBACK LIBRARY EDITION

First Printing: January, 1972

Copyright 1927 by Frederick Faust

Copyright renewed 1955 by Dorothy Faust

All rights reserved

No part of this book may be reproduced in any form without permission in writing from the publisher

This Paperback Library Edition is published by arrangement with Dodd, Mead & Company, Inc.

Paperback Library is a division of Coronet Communications, Inc. Its trademark, consisting of the words "Paperback Library" accompanied by an open book, is registered in the United States Patent Office. *Coronet Communications, Inc., 315 Park Avenue South, New York, N.Y. 10010.*

CONTENTS

CHAPTER I

A Wrong Start

THERE has never been any doubt in my mind that what I was intended for by nature was a life in the great West, where the cattle run the range and where the mountains have a meaning that is not entirely scenic. I was born with the hand and the eye and the heart for it and, as for the reasons which took me part of my life from the West— well, most of them were so foolish that I am almost ashamed to write them down.

It began with my dear mother, the best and the kindest soul in the whole world, but nevertheless preëminently a mother, and therefore entirely blind where I was concerned. There was enough heart in her to have mothered ten; but I was her only child, and was enveloped in a cloud of intense feeling—worship it became later.

She had been simply a jolly, pretty range girl, in the beginning; but it was in a frontier district where pretty girls were a rarity and treated somewhat like saints. In a region of Indian wars, cattle and sheep feuds, wildness and outlawry, where the rough-handed outcasts of the world assembled to find new lives, there was a premium upon nice girls. And no doubt my father considered himself the luckiest man in the world when he was able to marry her. I don't think that he had much to commend him beyond stately good looks, and a very accurate rifle. He was fairly well known as a hunter and trapper and trader among the Indians; and, when he appeared at the fort in his suit of antelope skin, with the finest beaded moccasins on his feet and his long hair flowing down over his shoulders, of course he took the eye of the ladies. So he married my mother; I was born; and three months later he was killed by a drunken Comanche.

Ah, I'm glad that I was an infant, then, and not able to understand the grief of my mother! But as long as I knew her she could never speak of my father without tears in her eyes. He had died in the very height of their romance. He was still a great and glorious man, to her. And there she was, left with the only person in the world that possessed a drop of his blood, her baby boy!

It made that baby boy a sacred thing. She felt that she was far from good enough to deserve such a great treasure, and she began to make herself over so that she should be able to rear me as I ought to be reared. If my father had lived, I would have been turned out in his own pattern, a trader, hunter, and a jolly, happy fellow. But that would not suit my mother now. She began to read and study and improve herself. And, as I grew old enough for teaching, she began to teach me, desperately, and reverently, and endlessly!

I always had to have a book in my hands: I could read and write when I was four, when I should have been rolling in the dust and pulling the hair of the other boys in the fort. When I was six, I was quite a scholar. And when I was ten, I was really getting on with my books, and the priest at the fort had taken over part of my studies and was prepared to carry them on past the point where my mother could have taken them.

Then one day my uncle, Stephen Larkin, came into my life with a strong hand. He was a typical frontiersman. There was no real malice in him, but he could hardly speak without swearing, and he told my mother frankly that she was ruining me. She was amazed. She felt that what she had been doing for me should be the admiration of the world; and, though she didn't say so, she let my uncle understand her pride. He merely snorted.

"There's not a boy in that street," he said, "who can't thrash him."

My mother went to the window and looked out. The street was filled with children.

"Nonsense!" said she at last. "Isn't he the true son of his father?"

"Not a little bit!" said Uncle Steve. "The man you married was the straightest-shooting, hardest-riding, fastest-hitting man on the prairies. And you've got a boy that's only the son of a book. Open him up and what's inside of him? Just print!"

My mother turned around to me with fire in her eyes. She was a frontierswoman herself. She would rather have seen a man dead than shamed with cowardice.

"Are you afraid of any of those boys?" said she.

I was. Horribly! But I merely smiled. Of course I was not, I said.

"There you are, Stephen!" says she.

"Stuff!" said Uncle Steve. "It's easy enough to talk like that, but the little rat is getting blue around the gills. Look here, Sammy—"

"His name is Samuel," corrected my mother coldly.

"Sammy," said Uncle Steve, "you see that kid out there with the freckled nose and the black, stringy hair? Do you dare go out and slap his face? He's shorter than you are."

Of course he was. But a great deal broader, and ten times as muscular. He was the terror of the whole town. I closed my eyes and then I told myself that, after all, it couldn't last long, because the first blow would knock me out of time. So I walked out the door and slapped the face of the hero. He was too surprised to do a thing, for a moment, and then he started in and tore me to ribbons.

He knocked me into the fence, where my jacket caught on a picket and held me up so that I couldn't slip down into the dust, and there I hung and got a lambasting. I think that the second or third punch knocked my wits away. Finally my uncle came out and picked me off the fence and carried me into the house; and my mother, with a white face, began to sponge my cuts and bruises.

The first word that I could understand as I came to was my mother saying, "He didn't cry out once for help!"

"No," said my uncle, "he took his licking as game as ever I seen. As game as ever I seen! But, just the same, it was a licking."

My mother was silent, and with my swollen eyes shut, and a hundred pains darting through my body, I realized that the picket and the senselessness together had held me up and made a hero of me in the eyes of my family. I felt a guilty joy until I heard my uncle say, "We're going

9

to have this out of him. Honey, I'm going to teach that kid to fight!"

"Never!" cried my mother. "He's meant for better things."

"Fight like his daddy did before him," said Uncle Stephen.

And that won! My mother could never play a card over the mention of my father's name. Uncle Stephen declared that I had earned a vacation from studies and that he was going to take me for three weeks into the mountains, hunting.

It was five months before we returned. I went out soft and sappy and sagging at the knees. I came back like an Indian, on my toes. Every day I had to handle a rifle and a pistol; every day I had to do tricks with a bowie knife. And more than that, and worst of all, I had to box with my uncle for at least a half hour at the beginning of each day. He meant to be gentle, but he was twice as strong as he guessed; besides, he used to say, "I tell you three times how to block a straight left. Three times I show you and tell you. The fourth time, if you can't do it, you take it!"

Well I can remember standing up blubbering with rage and shame and pain and fear to be knocked down half a dozen times running. But the seventh time I learned the trick. Yes, Uncle Stephen was a brutal fellow. But he felt that it was better for me to get a beating from a member of the family than from an outsider.

"I don't want to have to die for you, kid," he used to say, "and unless you learn something, one of these days I'm going to see you a growed-up man, and shamed by some one, and then I'll have to step in on your side. Why, when I was your age, I could catch a wild cat by the tail and wring it off! There was nothing that I wouldn't fight and there was nothing that I couldn't kill!"

That was probably close to the truth. And for five months we hunted and he made a man of me. During four months of that time I moaned for home and mother. But before the end I had begun to handle myself a bit better.

10

And on my twelfth birthday I ducked a straight left and belted my uncle in the stomach with a neat right hook.

He gasped, then grabbed me in his arms and hugged me.

"Now wait till you get that freckle-faced little half-breed!" said he.

That was what I was waiting for too.

When we got home again, my mother held me off at arm's length and cried over her shag-haired, brown-faced, wild-eyed son. But when she took me in her arms she cried, "Samuel, darling, you've turned into iron!" And some laughter mingled with her tears.

That very afternoon I went hunting for the freckle-faced boy, and found him, and slapped his face again.

This time I should like to say that I thrashed him thoroughly, but the truth is that I didn't. I had learned a great deal, and grown strong; but in five months I couldn't pick up the vast, burning vitality which was in that youngster. I had the skill and fighting wit. But he took all that I could give him, and then whipped me terribly until I lay face down in the dust, bloody, stunned, helpless.

However, it was a grand go. It made my name in the town. And not a boy dared treat me lightly afterward, not even that half-breed, in spite of his victory.

Twice again in the next year I tried him, and then the third time I won. But by that time, to confess again, I had height and weight as an advantage, together with my greater skill. But when I came home, it was a great event, and my uncle swore that he was the proudest man west of the Mississippi, and I think he was. At least, I remember that he gave me a revolver to celebrate the event. It was a clumsy old Colt, but in those days any sort of a revolver was a curiosity and a treasure. Hand to hand, it could take six lives while the rifle was taking one. And Uncle Stephen saw to it that I began to master the weapon.

I don't want you to think that I was given up to fighting and brawling and hunting from that moment. No, mother kept me closely under her wing and at my studies until I was seventeen; except that every summer I was

11

allowed to go off trapping and hunting with Uncle Steve.

I came back from the last of those trips, eighteen years old, an inch over six feet, and with a hundred and eighty pounds on my bones. I had been trained to fight wild cats, as Uncle Steve used to say, and I felt quite up to it. I could handle a bowie knife like an expert; and I knew the intimate secrets of fanning a revolver and rifle work at short range and long. I could ride a horse as bad as they came; and I was just in the mood to conquer the world when I walked into my mother's house and found her lying dead with three women of the neighborhood weeping beside her bed.

Kneeling in the dimness of that room and crying over her cold, thin hand, I knew that my boyhood had ended and that something more serious than fist fights lay before me.

CHAPTER II

The Safety Killer

THERE was a pause in my life, after that. With all my heart, I longed to be off running buffalo, or trailing hostile Indians, or trapping beaver on the northern streams with Uncle Steve, but the stern voice of conscience told me that my mother had not raised me for any such destiny. She had intended that the culture she gave me should be put to a proper use, and therefore I must lead a quieter life.

Well, what sort of a quiet life could a youngster find in a frontier fort? I looked about me and tried to find the best way out, but all that I could get to do was to keep an account book in a trader's office. I became a clerk and for three years I remained in that position, learning how Indians can be made drunk and stupid, while their goods are filched away from them, and how cheap beads can be used to buy fine buffalo robes. I learned other things, also. My boss never lost his keen wits, but sometimes he lost the use of his hands and feet from too many potations of the poison which he sold as whisky. And on those occasions I had to take my place with him at the work of trade. For when he was a bit under the influence of liquor there were grave chances that some man, white or red, would try to take advantage of him and loot the place. On those days there was apt to be a call for a revolver shot, or a bowie knife thrown with an accurate hand; but most frequently, there was need for a well-placed set of knuckles on the point of another man's jaw.

For three years I carried on this intermittent war against my fellows. Each year my salary was increased. I began to share some of the profits of the store. I was a valued man. And then one day the marshal of that district walked in and had a little chat with me.

I've never forgotten him. Long afterward he made name and fame for himself; but, even in those old days, he was already a known man along the border. He was short, thick-necked, deep-chested, with a pair of pale, sad eyes.

"Do you know me, Mr. Cross?" said he.

"Yes, sir. You are Marshal Shane O'Rourke."

"I'm glad you know me. And I trust that you know me as a fellow who likes to keep young men straight?"

"I know that, sir," said I. "Will you sit down here?"

"When I have to say mean things," said the marshal, "I'd rather stand up and look a man in the eye."

That took me back a little.

"If you've heard something against me," said I, "I can tell you that you're on the wrong trail."

"Are you sure?" said he.

"Sure, sir," said I.

"What makes you sure, lad?" he asked.

"I've never stolen a penny in my life, never 'borrowed' a horse or a dollar. I've never been drunk and disorderly. I've stuck to my work and never bothered a soul that would leave me alone."

"That sounds good," said the marshal, "and I think that it's true enough. I think that it's true enough." He nodded at me while he talked, and then he went on, "Nothing happened to you the last few days?"

"Nothing," says I.

"Think close," said he.

"Not a thing. Everything's been quiet and as usual."

"H'm!" said he. "I thought that there was some trouble yesterday?"

Frowning, I recalled the record of yesterday, and fumbled with the edges of a pile of buffalo robes that had just been brought in by a party of Piegans that had come away down from their ordinary hunting grounds to trade there.

"Nothing yesterday," I told him, "except for a fool of a Negro teamster who insisted that he had been short-changed."

"Did he make much excitement?"

14

"No," said I, "we had to take him away from the post, that was all."

"So drunk that he let himself be led away, I suppose?" said the marshal.

"No, sir," I retorted. "He was a big surly brute, and he drew a knife on Mr. Chandler. I had to knock him down and carry him out to the shed. He sobered up and went away quite peaceably."

"All right," said the marshal, "and what about the day before yesterday. Anything happen that day?"

"No, sir, not a thing."

"Think close."

"I am thinking."

"No other drunken Negroes?"

"No, but the day before that there was more of a commotion. A couple of Piegans filled themselves with raw alcohol and a very little water. They decided that it was a cold day and started to set fire to the store. Of course we had to stop them."

"I didn't know that any one here spoke Piegan," he commented.

"No, sir," said I, "of course we didn't have time to persuade them with words."

"Then what did you use on them?" the marshal asked.

"You would have laughed at it," said I. "I didn't want to hurt them, so I just took this ox whip, you see? Loaded handle and a lash that cuts like a knife. I gave them a taste of that."

I could not help laughing as I remembered.

"You whipped them away, then?" chuckled the marshal, very sympathetic.

"Yes. They scampered, and howled like fiends. Except the chief. He came for me with an old pistol. Luckily I managed to knock him down with the loaded butt of the whip before he murdered me."

"Didn't kill him, though?"

"No, the doctor thinks that he'll live—or did think so yesterday. I haven't heard since," I replied.

The marshal turned away a bit and looked through the

15

window. The snow was beginning to fall, and spotting the surface of the pane with splotches of white.

"The day before the Piegan party?" he asked.

"What about it, sir?"

"Any trouble that day, if you can remember that far back?"

"Nothing of real importance. Wait a moment! Yes, a gambler from the river boats came here asking for a gun. We showed him the best we had and asked a fair price. He was very hot about it. Used foul language. Mr. Chandler asked him to leave the store. Then he declared that he was a gentleman and that he had been insulted by being ordered off the premises. He was one of those Southern hotheads, Marshal O'Rourke."

"Yes, I know the type," sighed the marshal.

"He finally whipped out a pair of dueling pistols and told us that he was going to teach us a lesson in courtesy that would last us the rest of our lives. Absolutely mad, marshal!"

"I hope that he didn't do any harm?" the marshal remarked.

"No, sir, I managed to get in a shot from the hip that dropped him."

"Well, well! That was lucky, eh?" he commented.

"Wasn't it!" I exclaimed.

"And what's become of him?"

"Mr. Chandler paid the funeral expenses very handsomely," said I. "Mr. Chandler is never niggardly about such things, sir."

"True, true!" said the marshal. "So I've heard! But the day before the gambler. Do you recall that day?"

"It's rather dim. Let me see," said I. "I believe that I do remember something. Yes, as a matter of fact, a trapper came in and swore that some of the outfit we had sold to him last year had been faulty. Mr. Chandler asked to see the faulty traps. The man cursed us, swore that he would have his money back, and declared that he wouldn't put himself to the trouble of carting worthless traps all the way back home. Mr. Chandler told him that in that case there was nothing to be done, of course. You can appreciate that, sir? Business rule!"

"Naturally. A business rule!" said the marshal. "Well, such things have to be! Of course! How did the affair turn out?"

"He jerked up his rifle to the ready," said I, "but there was really no hurry. I could take my time, so I shot him through the right thigh. A bullet there drops a man just as well as one through the heart, for that matter. Excuse me if I tell you a thing that you know perfectly well, marshal."

"What is your job here?" asked the marshal suddenly.

"Why, I'm the clerk, sir," said I.

"How many hours a day at the books then?" he pursued.

"Why, sometimes two or three at the accounts."

"Sometimes, but on an average?" he insisted.

"Well, perhaps less than an hour."

"And what is your pay, Cross?"

"Mr. Chandler raised me last month. I'm now getting fifteen hundred dollars a year," I told him.

"Fifteen hundred!" cried the marshal, and stared at me.

Remember that those days were in the long ago. A dollar was a dollar, at that time, even on the frontier.

"Mr. Chandler is very generous," said I.

"Darned generous," said the marshal bluntly. "Fifteen hundred for an hour's work a day! That's about five dollars an hour, isn't it, not counting Sundays?"

"Why, sir, about that, I suppose I never thought of it that way!"

"No doubt you didn't," said the marshal, with a hidden meaning in his voice. "And now, tell me. It can't be that Chandler is paying you for anything other than bookkeeping?"

"Why, no, sir!"

"It couldn't be, for instance," said the marshal, "that he has you here to do his fighting for him?"

I stared at him.

"Mr. Chandler can take care of himself with any man," I told him.

"How many fights has Chandler had in the past year?"

I merely stared. There was no answer. I began to "think close."

The marshal went on: "You tell me first that everything has been quiet here lately and that nothing has happened. Then, in the course of your memories of five days, I hear about a fist fight, the flogging of a party of dangerous Blackfeet, one man shot dead, and another dropped with a revolver bullet! Is this an ordinary program, young man?"

"Why, sir," said I, "as a matter of fact, sometimes we run on for ten days at a time without a particle of trouble!"

"Exactly!" said the marshal. "And I'll tell you why! The strangers around here know no better than to make trouble, but those who have the proper information take care to keep away from Mr. Chandler's hired mankiller!"

CHAPTER III

Good Advice from the Marshal

IT was a tremendous shock to me. It made my world spin around before my eyes. Who was it that said none of us know ourselves?

The voice of the marshal cut in on my bewilderment. "Give me that gun!"

"What gun, sir?"

"The one you have your hand on!"

Sure enough, I had automatically laid a hand on the butt of my revolver. I grew very hot.

"I meant nothing by that," I explained. "Just an instinct sir. You've been talking very frankly, sir!"

I gave him the gun; he frowned down at it.

"How many men has this weapon killed, young man?" he asked.

"It is a new gun, sir," said I.

"New, eh? Were you wearing it when you shot the gambler?"

"As a matter of fact I was, sir."

"And that's one notch that might have been filed. You don't file notches, Sammy Cross?"

"Why, sir," said I, "when a man is out on the trail of an Indian war party, I can understand his filing a notch for every dead man. But, as for the nasty little things that happen in a quiet trader's store, of course I couldn't claim any credit for that!"

"Bah!" snorted the marshal.

I turned cold.

"Mr. O'Rourke," said I, "I've taken a great deal from you. May I be allowed to say, sir, that I won't take another word of any kind in the way of—insult?"

"And what will you do, eh?" said the marshal. "I have your gun!"

"You haven't my knife, though!"

And it glimmered in my hand that instant.

"A gun against a knife?" said he.

"It's just as quick!" I told him. "And it will kill nearly as surely!"

He looked at me out of narrowed eyes.

"You cold-blooded young—" he began.

Then he paused.

"Marshal," said I, "I'm glad that you didn't finish that sentence."

"You are, eh? About the war trails that you speak of. I suppose that leading a quiet life like yours, with your books to keep up, you haven't had many occasions to ride on the war path?"

"No, sir," I confessed with a sigh, "I lead a rather dull life, on the whole. Terribly dull. There's very rarely any excitement. In the past three or four years I've only joined 'vengeance' parties half a dozen times."

"Humph!" said he.

"Seven times, to be exact."

"You were carrying other guns on the war trails?"

"Why, yes sir."

"Lemme see them!"

I brought in two rifles and a pair of revolvers. He snatched them from me. He didn't look at the mechanism, but only at the under part of the stocks of the rifles and the handles of the revolvers.

"Young man," said he suddenly, "there are eleven notches on these guns altogether."

"Yes, sir," said I.

"And these are the only guns you have?"

"One very old one I sold last month," I told him.

"Any notches on it?"

"Only two, sir," said I. "It was a stupid brute of a gun. Bore horribly to the right."

"Only two!" said the marshal. "Only two! *Only* two human souls sent to eternity by you with that old gun that 'bore horribly to the right,' eh? And in three years you've *only* been seven times on the war path! And on those trails you've *only* killed eleven men! And besides those, there are the men uncounted who were knocked over

20

in the quiet matter of 'business!' The lives that didn't count!"

And he added fiercely, "You young murderer!"

The knife shook in my hand. But I checked myself with a frightful effort, for he let the muzzle of my revolver hang toward the floor and made no move to protect himself.

"O'Rourke," I said through my teeth, "I've given you a warning before, and now you can act on it."

"Shut up!" said the marshal. "Oh, shut up, Cross. I tell you, it makes me heartsick! I knew your mother! And what would she think of a son like you? Answer me that!"

The knife glided out of my hand and stuck point down in the floor. I slumped down on an empty whisky barrel. And from that position I stared up at the man of the law.

"Marshal O'Rourke," said I suddenly, "tell me the truth."

"What truth d'you want?" he asked me, savage as ever.

"Tell me what men really say about me?"

"They call you a safety killer!"

I had heard that expression before, used to describe the men who made their business and their pleasure the killing of others, but who would never fight unless they knew that the law was sure to protect them. Of all the men on the border, they were the most loathed, and the out-and-out gun fighters, who slew from an irresistible passion for fight, were considered infinitely above the "safety killers" in morality.

I writhed under that accusation.

"It's not true! It's not true!" I groaned. "O'Rourke, I'll swear that it's not true!"

He remained there, looking down at me, searching me, with a sort of cruel understanding and compassion in his eyes.

"Lad," said he, "how old are you? Twenty-six?

"No, sir, a shade under twenty-two."

"Twenty-two!" he echoed.

"It's perfectly true."

21

The marshal turned away and began to stamp up and down the floor.

"Chandler is a fiend! A hound!" he said aloud, but addressing himself. "And a blockhead like this fool of a boy, throwing his life away!"

Suddenly he turned and pointed a stiff arm at me.

"Do you know what they ask at the other posts when they inquire about this fort?"

"What do you mean, sir?"

"I mean, do you know what's the first question they ask concerning this place?"

"No, sir, I've no idea. Unless they ask how the fur trade is going."

"Forget the fur trade! They merely ask if anybody has yet been able to kill Butcher Cross, the safety killer!"

"The cowardly hounds!" I shouted. "Give me the name of one of them, and I'll teach him how safely he can call me—"

"Aye, aye, aye!" broke in the marshal. "There's the murder streak cropping out, a mile wide, and red as scarlet."

It silenced me effectually enough. And, as I glared at the marshal, I couldn't help remembering his reputation, which was great and bright along that frontier. There were others who had their enemies, and plenty of them; but there was no man who could point a finger at Marshal O'Rourke and call him anything other than an ideal man of the law, flawlessly honest, brave, gentle, resolute, and with a kind heart beating in his breast. No man was slower to draw a gun than O'Rourke—and no man was slower in putting it up, once drawn. And suddenly I was filled with horror to think that this man, of all the world, should have had to denounce me so bitterly.

"Marshal," I said to him at last, "I never guessed at these things!"

He was silent.

"Mr. O'Rourke," said I, "I want to ask you something more."

"Fire away."

"Why did you come here to-day?"

"To look you in the face and see how old you were. And to tell you that the next man that dies under your gun serves me as a notice to come and get you in the name of the law as an habitual and merciless killer. And no matter how safe you may play the game, there are courts on this border where you would be made an example!" he concluded.

I shuddered.

For I well knew what some of those border courts were, institutions especially designed to keep peace and a fear of law intact throughout some enormous sweep of prairie and mountains. Courts where the stern judges judged by common sense and not by the letter of the law.

If I were known as an habitual killer, what would happen to me in such a tribunal?

As an habitual killer? And suddenly, looking back over the years which I had lived through so innocently, as I thought, I could recall a procession of strained, agonized faces, beginning with the freckle-nosed boy on that day when I had finally beaten him to his knees and made him confess that he had had enough. And there were other faces of men, young or in the hardy prime of life, rough-bearded, unkempt, whole-hearted fighters, heated with liquor almost all of them, while I was sure to be cold and steady of nerve. They had rushed into quarrels. They had thrust themselves forward like fools, and my gun had brought them down!

Oh, I had no remorse for the honest fighting of the war trails. And even in this fighting within doors, God could witness that I had never taken an unfair advantage. But now I could remember that when the other man made a motion toward a weapon, my heart had never failed to leap high with joy!

God forgive me for it!

"Marshal!" I gasped.

"Well?"

"If you were me—" I began.

"What would I do?" the marshal interrupted.

"Yes."

"How much money have you?"

23

"About four thousand dollars."

"A fortune! You've had no bad habits to spend your money on!"

"No, sir," said I.

"Never drank or smoked, even?"

"No, sir. Smoked a very little."

"My lad, I would leave this part of the country and never show my face here again until I'd proved myself the right kind of a man in a new part of the country! I'd go, and never come back until I'd washed my hands clean with honest living!" the marshal advised me.

CHAPTER IV

All Aboard!

I THOUGHT of Uncle Steve Larkin, first of all. I thought of the way in which he had trained me for a life on the plains, and it hardly seemed possible that he could have made such a terrible mistake about me.

"I want to believe you, marshal," said I.

"And what keeps you from it?"

"Steve Larkin, is he the right kind of a man?" I demanded.

"You don't have to glare at me when you say that," and the marshal smiled. "As a matter of fact, Steve Larkin is one of the best fellows in the world. I see what's going on in your mind. Why doesn't Steve see that you're wrong? Because honest Steve can hardly suspect any one of being anything except what everybody ought to be. How could he suspect you? I know what he's done. He's had the schooling of you. And the fine old chap grows maudlin when he tells how you hit a running antelope at long range; I've seen tears in his eyes when he told about the way you crawled into the cave of the mountain lion last year and dragged the brute out, dead. I've seen him stand up before a room filled with men and describe with gestures how he taught you to box, and knocked you head over heels until you learned the tricks. And I've seen him show the wrestling holds you had to practice until the day when you laid him on his back! But, my lad, he didn't watch the faces of his audience, or else he would have stopped talking!"

"He would?"

"Yes," said the marshal. "He only knew that they were interested. But there are different kinds of interest, and those frontiersmen set their teeth and watched him through narrowed eyes while he talked. For every man was saying to himself, 'That's the way that young Sammy Cross was turned into a safety killer, was it?' "

"Don't use that word!" I shouted. "If they want to see killing, I'll step out and—"

I stopped myself.

The marshal was squinting at me. And he was nodding in the way that I had come to hate.

"Why, lad," said he, "I understand, of course. You're not the first gun fighter that I've had to study. I've seen crowds of 'em and of all kinds. But I never saw one with a handier start in the wrong direction. Don't you see? You've got the killing lust in you. Some men like to shoot buffalo, and some like to trap beaver. But you like to kill and trap men, and you've made yourself so expert that to you it isn't really a danger. It's only a game with you! Don't argue and back-talk. Admit that it's the truth. Fighting is your game!"

I started to give him a quick and hot reply, but checked myself in time. For suddenly I could see that there was truth in what he said. I had been deluding myself into the belief that in staying on with Chandler I had been fulfilling the wishes of my dear mother; but, as a matter of fact, I had been kept there simply as a sort of watchdog, enjoying the chances for trouble!

"Sit down by yourself and think these things over," said the marshal. "I don't want to press you. I have no right to talk to you as I have talked. But I think that you're too good a youngster to stand by while you throw yourself away."

With that, he walked out of the store; and a moment later Chandler came in, a little tipsy, and singing to himself. He slapped me on the shoulder and asked me how things were running.

"We're going to have some fun to-day," said he. "That Canuck trapper that bought the rifles last year is back in town and he swears that you cheated him. They were those old army guns, varnished up to look new. You remember?"

"I didn't know that they'd been varnished up to look new," I confessed.

"Well," said Chandler, "you never suspect anything. Let *me* do the thinking, and you do the selling, my lad. That's the best way. But that Canuck is foaming and raging all over town. Be ready for him, old boy. I wouldn't miss the party when he comes in to stamp on the 'keed,' as he calls you!"

"Chandler," I said suddenly, "I'm going to quit."

"Hey! What?" he shouted. "Quit what?"

"Quit the business. I'm leaving Fort Bostwick!"

He leaned back against the counter and gaped at me.

"It's O'Rourke," he said softly to himself. "That hound always has hated me. It's O'Rourke!"

He said more loudly, "Sammy, what's wrong?"

"I'm tired," said I, "of being the watchdog. I'm going into another line of business."

Well, his face blackened wonderfully fast and wonderfully dark, and then he said sharply, "I understand. The pay isn't enough. But tell me what youngster you know of that's been making the income that you have, and salted away so much coin?"

I didn't answer. I simply shook my head.

"But you're valuable to me," said Chandler. Why, boy, I look on you the way that a father looks on a son! Who could I leave my money and my business to except to you, eh? And I'll tell you what, I'll raise you, Sammy, to two thousand dollars!"

Two thousand dollars! It was a lot of money in those days.

Perhaps if I had been a little older, I would have been more tempted but, to a youngster, money is hardly more than a name. I said, "There's no use talking, Mr. Chandler, I've made up my mind," and with that I started to leave the room.

He shouted after me, "Sammy, you've gone mad. I'll raise you higher! Why, it's like losing my own boy! I'll give you twenty-five hundred a year!"

Well, that offer did stagger me a bit. And yet, when I came to think of it, I could remember how many thousands he was taking in each year. He was growing rich, or would have grown rich if he could have kept away from monte and faro. But the gambling took his coin away almost as fast as he took it in.

"Money doesn't talk to me," I told him, and went straight to my room.

There I took out from the mattress the whole four thousand dollars that I had saved. I subtracted two hundred and fifty dollars for expenses. The rest I put in a big envelope, and wrote this note to Marshal O'Rourke:

DEAR MR. O'ROURKE: I'm not taking much time to think things over. You're an older and a wiser man than I am, and I believe that you've talked to me for my own good, and the result is that I'm going to follow your advice at once. The first thing I'm doing is sending you the money that I've saved here. I feel that it's been a dirty business, and that I don't want the coin I've saved here. I want you to take this money and spend it where you think it will do the most good. There's the Widow Callahan, whose husband I killed two years ago. I know that she's been having a hard time with her family, and she's been steadily in want. Well, give her some of this. And there are a lot of others, who have suffered on account of me. God forgive me for the evil things that I have done! I just begin to realize them, and it makes me feel like a lost soul.

Keep a good thought for me, yourself, and I shall try to live up to what you may hope.

Faithfully yours,
SAMUEL CROSS.

I had just finished that when Mr. Chandler rapped at my door.

"It's no good, sir," I said to him. "I'm not going to argue the matter with you."

"Sammy, Sammy!" he shouted through the door, his voice trembling with earnestness. "I beg you to think it over a little bit!"

"I've thought it over and I won't change."

"Just open the door!"

"No, Mr. Chandler. I'm saying good-by to you, now," I told him.

"Sammy, I've decided that I'll impoverish myself in order to keep you. I wouldn't know what to do with my life, if I didn't have you here. I'll pay you three thousand dollars a year, my lad! That's just the same as making you the senior partner!"

I could hardly believe my ears. Three thousand dollars a year! And then a burst of rage came hot over me. I must have been making this man rich, and yet he wouldn't pay me a tithe of my value to him until I put my thumb down and squeezed him. Three thousand dollars a year!

"Mr. Chandler," I said, "ten thousand a year wouldn't keep me here another day!"

"You ingrate," he screamed in a fury. "This is my reward for taking you out of the gutter and making you a man! This is my reward, is it? Well, I hope that you live to repent your ingratitude."

And he turned and stamped down the hall and down the rickety stairs.

I was rather glad that he had flown into a tantrum. It soothed my feelings about leaving him in the lurch so suddenly. I packed a big carpet bag, put on my best suit, with a couple of revolvers dropped deftly into the clothes in holsters that were slung under the pits of my arms. Then, so equipped, I walked down the stairs and out the back door.

I stopped at the hotel and left my fat envelope for the marshal. After that, I went on toward the dock, half-running, because I had remembered that the boat was due to start down the river that morning. The snow was falling in gusts and flurries that pressed like white moths' wings, softly and coldly, against my face; but I headed straight on until I could see the tall shadow of the steamer's smokestack through the snow-mist.

I took a ticket at the office and walked aboard. I had the last berth in the last stateroom; and, thirty seconds after I got aboard, the moorings were cast off, and we warped out into the current.

That moment the snow stopped falling, and on the

dock I saw Chandler hurrying up and down and waving his arms. He sighted me at the same instant, and he shouted, "Sammy! Sammy! Come back! I'll make it all right for you! Everything shall be the way that you want it!"

I stepped to the rail and thundered back at him, "Mr. Chandler, I thank you for your kindness. But I've had my eyes opened. I'm through. Good-by!"

"You fool! You fool!" he screeched at me, "you'll be inside a prison inside of three months! And I hope that you are! I hope that you are!"

I saw some of the passengers looking quizzically from him to me, so I turned my back and walked to the farther side of the steamer; and the roar of the engine a moment later cut off all the sounds from the shore.

CHAPTER V

A Long Shot

HOWEVER, as the boat pulled down the stream, cutting along fast with the current behind her, Fort Bostwick came into view again and I looked the place over hungrily, wondering if I should ever forget it.

No, I have never forgotten. I remember perfectly the square shoulders of the fort itself rising above the huddle of houses, which surround it like children pressing to its knees for protection. Protection from the nakedness of the plains that slipped away on all sides. Protection from the dangers of the mountains that piled rough castles of blue in the north and west. I think that I could sit down and draw the whole thing now, if I had any craft for such an art. I could put in the special color of each roof, and the degree of blackness which weather had given to each unpainted shack; and I think that the last thing that I saw was the major's favorite gray mare on top of the hill near the river, for the snow had not yet driven her in to seek shelter. Very bleak and desolate she looked on the crest of that hill against the dark, smoky, rolling sky—bleak and desolate as my own heart felt in my breast.

And it was well that I remembered the fort so perfectly, for I was never to be able to refresh my recollection. I never laid my eyes upon it again; no, nor upon the whole section of the mountains around it. Other portions of the West I was to know, but my immediate past was wiped out. A new life lay before me.

How new and strange that life was to be, I hadn't the slightest guess at that moment. But I knew that my soul had turned to the thinnest sort of air when a man paused by me. I looked at him and saw that he was smiling. And then I saw the clerical collar which he wore, and the black hat, and the robe.

Though my religion was not his, yet I could not help

31

feeling that there was a wonderful understanding and kindness in his eyes.

"A year from to-day, my boy," said he, "you will wonder if you were ever really unhappy in your life! What has sorrow to do with your broad shoulders? Shrug it off! Shrug it off!"

He walked on. I found out afterward that he was nursing a sick companion, so I didn't see him again in the whole course of our trip down the river. But those words of his remained with me.

That night was wretched enough. But in the morning, the sun was glistening outside the stateroom window. Through the port I saw that we had passed beyond the area of the storm; and the familiar brown fields stretched away on either hand, for the banks of the river were very low here, and the tide more than reasonably high.

My good cheer came back to me at once and, after I had washed and shaved, I walked up and down the deck, ready to smile at the world, if need be, with no qualms of spirit.

About mid-morning, we ran into a section of buffalo herd, swimming the stream. They swam sluggishly and, according to their nature, paid not the slightest heed to the big boat which was steaming down on them. The captain had to reverse his engines and, backing water all the time, he let the current steal us forward inch by inch through the crowd of swimmers. The passengers were in a great state of excitement. And I saw a tenderfoot fire bullet after bullet into the herd, and yell with joy as he saw the dead ones go down. He couldn't use the meat, he couldn't stop to take the robes. It wasn't even sport. Simply contemptible butchery. But no one spoke to him. A few of the true plainsmen shrugged their shoulders, but that was all.

In the meantime, there was another commotion on the bridge of the boat, and I heard some vague words about a white buffalo. I had seen two white robes. And I had watched the Indians pay fabulous prices for them; for, of course, the tribe which can sacrifice a white buffalo robe to the sun is sure to have good fortune in war and hunting for years to come! But I had never seen a white buffalo, and so I ran up to the bridge without asking permission.

The captain was in a great state of excitement. And, looking in the direction in which he pointed, I was able to see the big bull, a beautiful dazzling white, for he was fresh from his bath in the river. He was rambling on across the plains, with hundreds of his fellows around him, but his color, or perhaps it was his great size, made him stand out above the rest.

"I'd give five hundred for that robe!" cried the captain. "I'd give nearly that much for the mask alone!"

And he stopped the boat and ordered the skiff to be lowered over the side.

It seemed to me odd that no one attempted to shoot the bull. I pointed out to the captain that, by the time the skiff reached shore, the bull would probably be out of range, and the men had no horses with which to follow. He agreed, with a groan, and then, leaning over the rail, he begged some one on board to take a chance at a long-distance shot to bring down the quarry.

"There's Sam Cross standing beside you," said a passenger. "He's about as good as the next one with a rifle."

The captain whirled around on me, and he didn't have to ask me twice. I got them to bring me three rifles, loaded. Three of exactly the same make and weight and caliber. Uncle Steve had taught me the trick. You get your aim with the first bullet as nearly as you can; then, if you make an error, you can try to correct it a little with the second shot, and the third one gives you a really good chance, even at a great distance.

If only the bull didn't bolt!

I took a careful aim, with the captain dancing about me and begging me to shoot quickly, because he pointed out that the bull was moving away every second. The first shot was fired, and the captain groaned, and so did half of the passengers. There was such interest in that queer hunt.

But the white bull wasn't touched. I thought that I had fired a little to the right and short; and, sure enough, while

33

the white bull remained unconcerned, a cow near him whirled around and started plunging and fighting.

I corrected my aim quickly, and setting my teeth I slammed the second shot. Straight at him, but a little short, I suppose. The third time I tried and, by this time, I was holding the piece in the air at such a sharp angle that it seemed impossible to strike the mark. It *was* impossible— had not Uncle Steve given me a tremendous schooling in range-finding.

At any rate, after I fired the third shot, everything went on as before. I was shooting from such a distance, and the banks of the river so shut in the noise of the explosions, that the buffalo paid no attention, except the wounded cow. The white bull walked straight on after the third shot, and the captain yelled, "Man the boat!"

Just then the white chief paused, swung his head from side to side, and dropped suddenly to his knees.

"He's hit!" screamed a hundred throats. And then, "A kill! A kill!"

For, sure enough, the white bull had toppled over on his side.

Well, it was a great shot, and I was as vain and as flattered as could be at having managed it. But of course there was a whacking lot of luck about the thing.

You see, that bullet had been fired at such an angle that it caught the bull just behind the horns and, glancing down, broke his neck. He had gone on a few automatic paces. But when he dropped, he was stone dead.

They rowed ashore, got the hide off, and the mask, and brought them back to the boat; and the captain wanted to pay me anything that I would name. But I didn't want money. I felt, somehow, that any money I made out of skill with weapons was poisoned. I thanked him and told him that it was the best sport I had ever had.

I want to be forgiven for having insisted in such detail on the way I shot that buffalo, because I freely admit that it sounds a great deal like boasting. However, as a matter of fact, I have to tell about the thing, because it has a bearing on the moment which was the turning point of my life, as you'll learn later on.

At any rate, my not taking money from the captain was a pretty good thing for me in a great many ways. After that, there was nothing that he wouldn't do for me, and all the passengers were extremely cordial. On the third day after the shooting affair, an old, nut-brown fellow took hold of my arm, gave it a squeeze and said to me: "Kid, they been lying to me about you back there at the fort. You ain't no safety killer, and you never could have been. I know the type too well, and you ain't it!"

I couldn't give him an answer, of course, but it almost choked me with anger and with shame to hear him say it. I wanted to go back and murder the whole civilian population at Fort Bostwick. And yet, another mean moment of reflection told me that the report had been right, and I had been the lowest hound in creation.

Now we drifted down the river, making pretty good time. It was a jolly company, because people who go West are apt to feel a little desolate and dreary; but people going back East are like country folks headed for town. They expect fun and excitement.

So we all became jolly and comfortable, and the men were calling each other by their first names, and the few women aboard were very friendly, except to one another; and, as for me, I grew so good-natured that I wandered into a game of monte, and lost every penny that I had except a souvenir five-dollar gold piece.

It made me gloomy for a little while, but the very next day we came to the end of our trip; and I was so excited over seeing the waters of the Mississippi for the first time that I forgot all about my bad luck.

The captain made me take fifty dollars. So I left him one of my rifles as part payment for the loan, and went through the town to see the sights. I woke up in the morning broke again and ready to admit that Chandler had sheltered me from a great many of the dangers of the world—and kept me from a great deal of knowledge of it, too.

In fact I was as raw a greenhorn as ever came out of the wilderness, when I first looked at the muddy, sliding current of the Mississippi.

I had intended trying to press straight across the continent and get to one of the big Eastern cities: Philadelphia, Boston, New York, they were only names to me, and I really didn't care which one of them I landed in.

So I went down with my bag to the edge of the river where the boats were at the docks, and there fortune took the game in hand and sent me in a direction of which I had never thought.

CHAPTER VI

A Baleful Influence

THERE was a great deal going on along the wharf, especially the loading of the last of the cargo into the hold of a ship. The cargo, of course, was chiefly bales of buffalo skins; tons and tons of them still had to be worked in. Sailing time was close at hand; the baggage of the passengers was being brought aboard; and the passengers themselves were going up the gangplank, now and then.

Every once in a while, a red-faced man with an officer's cap would come to the rail and shout down to the dock: "Rogers! Rogers! Where's that Rogers?"

And then, from somewhere in the knot of toiling Negroes and half-breeds who were doing the labor, a great voice would bellow: "Aye, aye, sir! Here!"

"Rogers, confound you, why do you let those lazy hounds go to sleep like this?"

And Rogers would call back, "Sorry, sir, but I'm trying to do my best!"

"Your best ain't good enough!" the captain would thunder back. "I won't stand for this, Rogers! Stir up those rascals!"

And the mate would turn and berate the men with the most terrible words.

And what a vocabulary he had! I had heard some of the most eloquent cursing in the world done in the open plain, where the language was as free as the men; but I had never, I am sure, heard such talk as flowed from the lips of the mate of that Mississippi steamer. He had a word for every shade of rage and disgust, and an intonation that made his oaths ring far and wide through the confusion. The lash of his tongue whipped every one of those panting workers. I watched, and laughed, and watched again. And suddenly the mate rushed from the turmoil and bellowed to the line of onlookers, "Will any of you men lend a hand here, for Heaven's sake? A dollar for one hour's work from any of you!"

There was a mere shrugging of shoulders in answer, for those were "free" plainsmen, and they were not apt to mix with Negroes and half-breeds in such labor as this.

But I remembered that my purse was empty, and I could not help starting forward. "I'm willing," I told the mate.

"Bear a hand, then!" he shouted and, turning his back to me, he hurried away.

Afterward, when I came to know matters in the South and the whole slave territory better, I could see that I had done a thing sufficient to brand me in the eyes of the upper order of society forever. But at that moment, I was thinking only of the fun and the dollar.

I plunged into the work with all my heart. And soon I was getting such results that even the mate bellowed a word of approval, as he saw me go steaming by in a gang of Negroes, all grunting with their task.

The last of the cargo was rapidly cleared from the dock. In the meantime the passengers had gathered and lined the deck to watch; and, as I went aboard under a staggering burden, I heard a man say, "You have poor white trash even this far up the river, captain?"

I glanced aside and saw a tall young fellow of my own height and age, but a bit slenderer, I thought. A small mustache and a bit of pointed beard, glistening black, gave him an air of distinction. I was too hard worked to hate him even with a glance; but still I felt in him the presence of a new civilization. Now and then, I had had glimpses of the gentry of the South at Fort Bostwick but, on the whole, they had been pretty thoroughly reduced to Western ways and habits before I had an opportunity to grow acquainted with them. This tall and splendid youth, with all his white stock wrapped up almost to his ears, his fine coat, and his languid, haughty manner, made me feel that I was a rough barbarian.

However, I lost sight of him in the press of the work. I was enjoying the tussle with the great bales of robes. God had given me muscles, and Uncle Steve had seen the developing of them; and, as a result, I was clad from head to foot in a tangle of power which was a joy to use.

One bale stood on the dock.

"Confound you, Rogers!" shouted the captain, "you've held up these gentlemen and ladies for forty-five minutes!"

No doubt the captain was throwing as much blame as he could on his mate in public, in order to apologize to him in private. But he had been rubbing Rogers the wrong way too long, and finally the mate shouted back: "I've done two men's work in handling the crew of loafers that you hired for me!"

"Proper handling gets results!" answered the captain. "I've seen a five-hundred pound bale carried by one man!"

"Nonsense!" cried the mate. "A bale of skins?"

"The same!"

"Can't possibly be done!" the mate declared.

"Guard your language, Mr. Rogers!" called the captain. "There's a man there that ought to have carried in a bale each trip, if he had the proper handling! *I* would have had him do it!"

Mr. Rogers glared and snorted and turned purple with rage.

"By heaven, sir," he called, "there's one bale left, and there's the man, and you just step down here and make him handle it, now!"

"I have half a mind to!" answered the captain.

"I'll lay you five hundred dollars, captain, that the man can't budge the bale," cut in a voice perfectly cool and good-natured.

It came from one of the black-coated, somber-mannered gentry of the passenger list.

"I'll add another five hundred on my own account," said the mate, "if he can pick up that bale and put it on his back!"

"Wait one minute!" cried the captain. "I'll see about this."

He hurried down from the deck. There was no talk about delay, now. Not a soul among the passengers demurred, because in those days there was something sacred about a contest that carried bets. It had a measure of pre-

39

cedence given it such as people to-day will hardly believe.

Approaching the bale of buffalo robes, the captain laid hold of a corner of it and gave a tug. There was hardly a stagger of the bale in response, though the captain was no stripling.

"I suppose that's about enough for you, captain?" asked the gambler.

And a little chuckle followed.

The captain glared at them. His blood was up. He was from Alabama, where blood is easily heated; and, in such a moment as this, with the eyes of his crew and his passengers upon him, with money ready to be wagered, he was half desperate.

He glared at me.

"Speak up!" said he. "Can you shift that bale?"

I shook my head.

"Try, man, try!" said he.

It made me smile to hear such language. Back in Fort Bostwick, where they had called me the safety killer for so many years, certainly no one would have talked quite so freely to me; but, here on the dock, I didn't mind. I gripped the bale and pulled, and it heeled a bit under my grasp.

"I don't know," I said to the captain. "I could lift this bale. But, as for getting it on my back and carrying it into the boat, that's quite another—"

He didn't wait for me to finish. He turned and roared, "Rogers! I'll take your bet. And you, sir. That five hundred of yours is covered!"

There was a little bustle of excitement. In half a minute every soul was rushing from the boat onto the dock to watch the contest. And a thrill of weakness went through me when I thought that I could hardly hope to accomplish this thing. Little things are sometimes strangely greater in importance than in significance. I felt that I wanted to win that wager for the captain more than anything I had wanted in my life since I knelt by the bed of my dead mother.

As for the captain, he was made of good stuff, for now

he came to me and said quietly, "Let the crowd gather, lad. Let them come around and see the fun. Take your time, now. You're a bit shaky with the idea. And whether you win or not, there's twenty dollars for you. You get a hundred if you take the bale on board."

I pushed back the twenty.

"I'm trying this for the game," I told him.

His critical eyes flickered up and down my face.

"Have it your own way," he said. "You're a cut above what I thought."

He turned back to the others. "I have another thousand dollars free to bet on this friend of mine," he said to the crowd. "Is that money covered?"

Two more of those black-clothed gamblers hefted the bale and covered the captain's money instantly.

"You were in a hurry to get started, captain," said the mate. "But don't let's hurry you now!"

A little chuckle greeted this sally, but the captain barked, "That'll do from you, Rogers. Are you ready to try your hand, sir?"

"Ready," said I.

There was another whisper at the captain's use of the word "sir"; but I overheard him explain an instant later, "This gentleman will not take a penny. It's a game, to him. And if I had another thousand, I would bet it. But I haven't."

I wanted to protest and tell him that he was mad to wager so rashly, but somehow, I knew that no argument would help. Besides, the money had been placed. And it would have taken a strong hand to get a cent of it back from one of the professional gamblers.

I gave word that I was ready, a way was cleared to the gangplank, and I tested my strength on the bale, I heeled it easily over and that brought a shout from the crowd. Then I got a careful grip and brought the bale up hip-high before it slipped and fell back.

After that, I sized it up with more care. It was heavy enough, of course. But any one who has seen expert piano movers at work has seen men bear fully as great a burden

41

as the one I wanted to carry that day. It was simply the clumsy bulk of the thing that made it so hard to carry.

The fall of the bale had brought a groan from those who sympathized with me; and I heard the tall, pale-faced youth with the mustache and short beard saying, "I'd like to place a wager against that man. Will anybody take me?"

I didn't wait for the answer. The calm and haughty superiority of this soft-handed youngster angered me so much that I swore to myself that I would open his eyes that moment. I leaned, took a new grip, and swung up the edge of the bale with all my might.

There is a knack to the handling of anything; and at Fort Bostwick, in the store, I had grown accustomed to the shifting of great weights in skins. I got the bale up hip-high, rested it there until I had my breath and the ache had gone out of my shoulders; and then, with a twist of my body, I brought my shoulders under the edge of the mass.

It slipped and, once down, I knew that I could never raise it again; but I managed to take a finger hold on the edge of the bale that projected over my shoulders. And, by doubling far forward, I was able to keep the bale balanced. It brought a crushing burden on my hips and behind my shoulders. My wind was fairly pressed out of me, but the yelling of the crowd gave me strength, as did the hoarse, triumphant voice of the captain, yelling. "I told you so! Who's betting against him now?"

I went on to the ship well enough until I got to the gangplank; and there the sharp upward slant threw an agonizing strain on the muscles of my legs with every step.

Besides, that gangplank was a slender affair; and each time I stepped forward it sagged with a great groaning. You must understand that the freight gangplank had been drawn in before this! Half way to the edge of the boat, I paused and got my breath back. My legs were beginning to shake crazily under the terrible strain, and there was a sense of numbness from the knees down.

"He's finished!" shouted some one as I paused.

"Shut up!" called the captain. "Give him a chance." And then he added, as I made another painful, sinking step forward, "Lad, don't kill yourself for a bit of foolish money! You're worth more than this bet. Let the bale drop!"

His words gave me a sudden strength. I made the four or five steps that were necessary to reach the edge of the boat and, turning a bit, I tumbled the great bale onward. It fell with a heavy thud, and a little cloud of dust rose from it. Relieved from the burden, I gripped the rail and stood with hanging head, wondering if the blood would burst through my temple—such was the thundering of my pulses!

CHAPTER VII

A Knife in the Dark

THAT had been a dirty job, wrestling with the bales of hides; and one could understand why white men stood back and left the work for Negroes and half-breeds. But having been raised out on the plains, color didn't make a great deal of difference to me. On the long trails hunting, it was a small matter what color skin a man wore; but it was a great matter to find a man at all and exchange the time of day with him. Around a camp fire one was as apt to hear pleasant yarns from an Indian brave as from any white man. So what difference did it make to me that the other whites along the wharf had stood back and refused to work on the dock at the moving of the hides? I had gone in for it head over heels, as you may say; and now I stood on the deck grasping the rail, perspiration pouring down my face, covered with the dust and filth of the hides, and their none too fragrant odor in a cloud around me.

Sun-blackened by the life on the plains, I suppose that I looked as much like a Negro, or a half-breed at least, as any man ever looked in this world. But nevertheless, it made me rage when one of the gamesters who had lost money betting against me strolled past with a sneer on his lips and a shrug of his shoulders.

"I thought I was betting against a white man," said he.

There were others coming close around me, men, and women, too, and the captain shouldering through the crowd with a happy face. I reached out through them and caught the gambler by the arm.

"You can't talk to me like that," I told him.

He whirled around at me with a snarl.

"Keep your hands off me, you black dog!" he snapped, and reached for the butt of a pistol which showed under his armpit as he swung about and his coat flapped open. It

44

would have been an easy thing to beat him to the shot for, from his first movement, I knew that he was no such expert as my Uncle Steve had made me through long and cruel hours of practice. But, after my talk with the marshal, I had determined to change my attitude toward fighting. I would never take life if I could avoid it. And here there was no need at all. The jaw of the gambler was just within good arm's length, and a clenched fist can beat the fastest gun that was ever pulled. My left was back, so I let him have that neatly on the button, and the blow drove him backward through the crowd and sent him rolling under their feet.

There was only a grunt from the captain as he came up. "That served the puppy right. You come on with me, my lad," he said.

He took me through the gaping crowd into his own cabin, which was finer in its furnishings than the best room I had ever seen in my life, which was the major's quarters at Fort Bostwick. The mahogany desk seemed to me like a precious red-brown jewel, it was polished so brightly. There was a gay rug on the floor, too; the steamboat man made enough money on his trips to satisfy his flamboyant tastes.

He sat me down and dragged out a bottle of whisky. I took a mere nip, and my eyes opened.

"Aye, aye," grunted the sailor. "That's real, eh? It ain't the kind of thing that you've had out there on the plains?"

"Alcohol and quicklime is what they give you out there," said he. "But this is good for you. Take another drink. Take a real one."

I wouldn't do that, and I explained to him that I'd formed the habit of being a one-drink man. You had to form that habit around a trader's store, unless you wanted to be robbed outright by the first sharpster that came along to make a trade. And besides, the whisky on the plains was such filthy stuff that I'd only been able to down it now and then. The idea of drinking, you see, had never been made attractive to me.

"All right," said the captain. "Then here's a go to you, and looking in your eyes, my beauty!"

He tilted the big bottle at his lips, and I swear that I thought he would never take it down. More than a half pint of the raw stuff must have flowed down his throat before he lowered the bottle again. Yet there was not even a moisture in his eyes. He smacked his lips, corked the bottle with a sigh, and put it away in a drawer of his desk. That drawer closed with a promising clinking of more glassware.

"That's real," he repeated. "But for me, I never take a real drink before six in the evening. It ain't safe. No, not safe at all, with a ship under your command. That's the disadvantage of a captain's life on this infernal river. But now about you. I've cleaned up a tidy sum on your bit of work. And I have five hundred dollars for you here."

He started counting out the gold in handfuls. I stopped him at once.

"I don't want it," said I.

"But you earned it," he protested.

"No, I don't want it. It would really spoil the fun of the game for me."

"Will you shake on that?"

I smiled and shook hands with him. He turned my palm up.

"You never got your strength out of manual labor," he said at once. "Then how in time *did* you get it?"

"I don't know," said I. "Chiefly it came by nature, I suppose."

"Tell me," said the captain suddenly, "where you are bound for."

"Somewhere East," I answered.

"New York?" he suggested.

"Perhaps."

"What would you do there?"

"I don't know that, either," I told him.

"And then, why not South?"

"There's no reason, except that I hadn't thought about it."

"Think about it now. Come down the river with me to New Orleans. I like you, my boy. And I think that I could introduce you to some men who would push you

46

ahead into a good position. Understand, I've no old family, and I got no great lot of money, either. But I know some real gentlemen, fancy stuff! They could use a man like you."

I turned the matter back and forth in my mind.

"Why not?" said he, urging me.

"There's no reason against it," I decided.

"Then stay aboard this boat."

"Wait till I get my bag," I remarked.

"Cut and run for it. We're an hour late!"

I ran for it, willingly enough, bounded down the gangplank, and was back in a trice with all my belongings. The last moorings were cast off, the big paddle wheels began to beat the water, and out into the current we shot and headed down the river.

I was rather glad of it. The world seemed just then a friendly place to me; and I hardly cared in what direction I floated, for I felt that to make one's way was an easy matter.

I idled on the boat from stem to stern and from top to bottom. As I sat by the engineer, it seemed to me that there was nothing in the world quite so wonderful and splendid and such a proof of the gigantic powers of man as that old river scow. Wherever I went on the ship, I was made welcome, because the people had seen the lifting of the big bale, and they were glad to talk to me. I had supper with the second engineer and the second and third mates, who were all very kind and promised to show me the sights of New Orleans, when we finally arrived.

Afterward, I went out into the darkness and sat near the prow, listening to the rushing of the bow wave, and watching the lights along the shores slip softly back behind us into the deep darkness of the night. Finally, I stood up with my hands clasped behind me, and let the wind comb against my face and through my hair. It was a glorious, free feeling. And suddenly I asked myself why I should not be a sailor, and learn the great wide seas and the huge steamers that traversed them?

There was no reason. The world was mine, and I was foot free to go wherever I chose!

The idea fascinated me more and more; and, with a smile and a light heart, I was committing myself to a life on the bounding waves, when I heard a sharp cry behind me, and whirled in time to see the dark outline of a man not two steps to the rear of me, with the light from the forecastle glimmering faintly on a bowie knife which was gripped in his hand.

CHAPTER VIII

A Sum in Subtraction

IT was not a question of making a swift move in self-defense. One lunge of that long arm and one thrust of that keen-edged knife would have ended my days at that instant. But the figure in black was not making any effort to close on me. Instead, he turned about and confronted a man who stood behind, and there I saw the youth of the beard and mustache with a pair of pistols shining in his hands. It had been his voice that I had heard, and his voice that had stopped the other on his murder errand.

Of course you have guessed who the would-be assassin was. It was my friend the gambler, now with a great lump on his jaw where my fist had chugged home that day. He had seen me standing there in the darkness and decided that it would be a simple matter for him to put me out of his life and out of the world. He had been disgraced and beaten by me, and there are some men who always nourish their revenge with just such a thoroughgoing spirit as this. Kill the fellow who has exposed you; it comforts your soul!

There was no doubt that he was in a good deal of danger now, for the young fellow who was walking toward us seemed in a high state of excitement.

"You low dog!" he said fiercely. "You contemptible, murdering cur! Can you give me one reason why I shouldn't send this pair of bullets through your heart?"

The gambler stepped back toward the rail.

He had dropped the bowie knife, and thrown his hands above his head in token of surrender.

"Mr. Granville!" he gasped.

"Yes, I'm Granville!" said the youth.

"For Heaven's sake, Mr. Granville, have mercy on a poor—"

"I'll have no mercy," said Granville. "I'm going to

march you back to the captain of this ship and ask him to turn you over to the mate to put in irons, and when you get to New Orleans, I'll see to it that the finest lawyer in the city prosecutes you for attempted murder!"

"Mr. Granville," whined the gambler, "I want to tell you, sir, that I only intended to startle this young man—frighten him a little—"

"About face and march," said Granville. "And go softly, and keep your hands above your head every step of the way!"

"One moment, Mr. Granville," said I. "I think I know a better way. You stand by to see fair play, and I'll teach this puppy a lesson with my fists."

"Why," chuckled Granville, "that's not such a bad idea. Suppose you do it!"

"Very well," said the gambler, "will you let me take off my coat?"

"Take it off, then."

For a fraction of an instant Granville lowered his weapons, and in that instant the other whirled and leaped over the rail.

We ran to the side of the ship, and a moment later saw the head of the rascal come above the water, with a light from the ship glistening upon it. Then he was lost to view.

"He preferred to drown like a rat?" said Granville.

"No, sir," said I, "he'll make that island, just ahead of us. If he can swim a quarter of a mile with the current—and any child can manage that—he'll be safe—just a bit wet and cold."

"I should have pistoled him, I suppose," said Granville almost regretfully. "I shouldn't have let him go without paying him off. But perhaps he's had a lesson that will take some of the starch out of him."

He came straight up to me, putting away his pistols. He held out his hand.

"I've come to offer you an apology for the insulting remark which I made to you earlier in the day, Cross."

"Hello!" said I. "You have my name?"

"Yes," said he. "One of the passengers suddenly remembered at dinner that he had seen you pointed out on a boat coming down toward the Mississippi from the plains. He has told us a great deal about you and made you out quite a legendary figure, Mr. Cross."

I had been made out a safety killer, too, no doubt! And that thought made me set my teeth. However, I heard him say, "You haven't called it quits between us, Cross?"

"I do, though," I said, taking his hand. "Good lord! man, if it hadn't been for you, I would have had that knife in my back, and then a toss over the rail into the river! I owe my life to you, and——"

"Tush!" said he. "Tush! It doesn't balance a feather's weight against the ugly thing I had said about you before. Not a feather's weight!"

He asked me to come back with him to his cabin. And I went, rather confused, and unwilling to have this fine young man see me in my dirt and rough clothes by the close light of a lamp. He had the largest and the finest cabin of the ship and he made me comfortable in a chair at once, and offered me whatever I would have to drink.

"Tell me, Cross," said he, "if it's true that you've left the plains and that you are heading across the world with nothing in the way of a worry on your mind? And no family behind you?"

"That's true," I answered.

He nodded, and fell into a brown study for a moment. A very queer study, for his eyes were fixed steadily upon my face, but blankly, and he said not a word.

I began to grow red and uneasy after a moment. Finally he said, "Look here. Will you let me ask you to do some foolish things?"

I said to him solemnly, "Mr. Granville, you can command me the rest of my life."

"Where did you learn to talk like that?" he asked me suddenly. "Excuse me if I'm sharp."

"I don't mind," said I, "if you'll tell me what's odd about my speech."

"A very broad strain of old-fashioned formality," he said.

"My mother was a very old-fashioned woman," said I.

"She pruned your grammar for you, I suppose?"

"Yes. She taught me at home, very carefully."

"Well, it would do. By heavens, the more I think about it, the more I see that it would do wonderfully! Wonderfully!"

"In what way?" I asked.

"Not that I had the plan in mind when I went out there on the deck," he continued, paying no attention to my question. "Not a bit. But I'd noticed that gambler trailing you about the deck. For an Indian fighter you're very careless about leaving your back unguarded, you know. I went to keep an eye on the dog. Very lucky I did! Very lucky! Now tell me if I seem to be talking queerly?"

"I simply don't understand it all," said I.

"I hardly understand it myself. I hardly understand it myself," said he. "It's just gradually dawning on me by degrees—the possibility—but no—it isn't possible, and I'm a fool and a dreamer. I always have been one!"

He was immensely excited. Now he jumped up and began to pace the floor.

Suddenly he said, "Look here, Cross. Take that coat, will you?"

He had opened a case, taken out a long-tailed coat, and now he threw it to me.

I took it.

"Slip it on, will you? And don't think that I'm going to offer you a suit of old clothes," he went on with a laugh, seeing the redness of my face.

I put on the coat obediently. It was a good deal too tight, but he didn't seem to think so.

"Just a shade snug, but almost a perfect fit. No, you're just as long in the arms. Well—by gad! By gad! Who would ever have thought it? You're six feet and one and three eighths inches tall. And just a tiny shade over.

"Just a tiny shade over," I confessed, "but how in Heaven's name could you have guessed that?"

He had turned from flushed to pale, and now he stammered, "Don't ask me how I knew. I begin to think that Fate has a hand in this! Why else should I have been sent

52

up the river? Why should I ever have determined on such a thing as this trip?"

Of course, I couldn't answer. I began to have an uncanny feeling that all was not right in the mind of young Mr. Granville. And then he snapped at me: "Do you much care what happens to you in the next few months?"

I admitted that I didn't.

"Have you a mind for adventure?"

"I think I have," I told him.

He lost his enthusiasm for a moment and frowned at the floor.

"You've killed men, they say," he murmured. "That's true, I suppose. You've killed men. Rifle work, they say. And revolvers. A great deal of revolver work!"

I was silent. He seemed to know about me as much as he needed to know.

"I've heard," said he, "that there's no one quite as quick and deadly with a revolver as you are."

"That's nonsense," I told him. "Of course there are men who are a lot faster and a lot straighter, too. I've known some of them, and I've heard of others."

"How could you tell, really," he asked, "unless you met the fellows face to face and tried out your skill with them?"

I had to confess that that was the only way in which the test could be made.

"I knew it," said he. "I would bank on you. I would bank a great deal on you. I have met fellows something like you before. In college, in sports. You could tell the champions by the look in their eye. Hold on—I seem to be flattering you a good deal."

He was, and I was red under it.

Then he said, "Do you think me quite a crazy man?"

"No, sir," said I.

"That's the way that they would like to have me talk," he said with a sigh, "using a great deal of formality. And living up to my position. Damn it—I despise my position! I despise it!"

He jumped up and stamped on the floor.

Then he whirled out of that humor into another one.

"Look here," said he, "may I talk plain business with you? No, it isn't plain at all. It's the wildest thing that any human being ever conceived, but it begins to grow on me. It grows and grows. It gathers. I see farther into it. I can look into the future of this idea, and by Heaven, it seems nearly possible! Will you please listen to me?"

"Yes, Mr. Granville."

"Ah," he sighed again, "there you are, talking like a man in a book. Well, I could never talk in that manner. Never! I've tried it, you know. No good!"

He went on: "Money's some object with you, I suppose? I mean, it is with everybody."

"No, sir," said I. "Will you let me tell you what's in my mind?"

"Go ahead, go ahead," he snapped rather pettishly. "Though you haven't heard what's in mine, for that matter!"

There was something almost feminine about the humors and the changing moods of this chap. I wrote him down as the spoiled darling of some rich Southern planter. The son of a vastly wealthy and vastly idle family.

I said: "Chiefly, I've been looking for fun. I hardly cared what kind. I've done some years of what I thought was work. And then this evening I came within an ace of getting enough adventure to last me to the end of time. The reason that I'm not floating down the Mississippi feet first is because you took a hand in my affairs, and now, sir, my hope is that in some way I can make some manner of return to you. I don't care in what fashion. I wish to leave it to you. It seems to me that you have some scheme in mind in which I could be useful. If so, please consider that I am simply a tool in your hand."

When I finished, he stared at me, his lips parted.

"By the eternal!" he said at last, in hardly more than a whisper. "Exactly like a book. Perfectly like a book!"

"I'm sorry," said I, breathing a little hard, I suppose.

"Hold on!" he exclaimed. "I don't want you to go off on the wrong foot like that. I don't want you to do that, you know! But just tell me—if you can forgive my infernal rudeness—just tell me if you could really subtract a year from your life? Not for nothing—but for a pretty good round sum. Anything you want—say—a hundred dollars a week while it lasts—"

"Mr. Granville," said I, "I can't take any such salary from you. I want only to serve you. Will you tell me how I can?"

"That's the devil of it. How am I to tell you? It's so mad that I can't. Can't say a word about it. Besides, it might not pan out. But we'd have to try it, first. Gad, you're decent to listen to my ravings! To begin with, I could put it this way: I'd want you absolutely at my disposal for the course of a year. To go and come and rise and sit down exactly as I bade you. What about that? Not able to really call your soul your own, I mean?"

His eyes glistened at me. And I considered the idea with a growing excitement. Every young man is tempted by whole-hearted, extravagant affairs. And this was a little more whole-hearted and extravagant than any that I had heard of before. Although still I didn't know what he could be driving at.

"I'll make one reservation," said I. "I'm not to be asked to compromise my honor."

"Out of the book again!" he shouted, and threw himself back in his chair in a fit of laughter. "By heavens, Cross, you're marvelous beyond words!"

I could hardly hear what he said at this point. I should have told you long ago what was really the most peculiar thing about this young man. His voice was extremely husky and low, and after this excitement and burst of laughter, one could hardly understand a syllable that he spoke. He recovered after a moment, and taking a sip of wine, he said, "No, I don't think that one could say that it is a dishonorable affair that I have in mind. I only know that it's a necessary one! Terribly, vitally necessary to me! Life and death to me! Life and death!"

He sat gaping at some very dreadful idea.

"Life and death," he whispered huskily again. "And now tell me, Cross. Are you my man?"

He waited with the moisture standing on his forehead, his hands clenched.

I recapitulated slowly: "I put myself in your hands for a whole year?"

He nodded. He seemed too worked-up to speak. The muscles of his big throat were bulging in and out.

"And for an entire year, you are to do the thinking for me, and I'm to submit to you?"

"Yes, yes, yes!"

He managed to speak, then, but he was hardly audible.

"Yes," I said suddenly. "I'll do it."

"Thank God! Thank God!" cried Granville. "But wait —wait! It isn't enough! Swear it. Swear by whatever's sacred to you. Your mother, say. Swear that you'll stay with me through this entire year and do as I tell you to do!"

That made me hesitate. And his suspense was so great that I almost feared he would faint. He leaned against the door of the cabin, as though to keep out a possible intruder, and his face was utterly colorless, and his eyes bulging, as he stared at me.

"I swear by my mother," said I at last.

"Living, living?" he snapped at me with a terrible eagerness.

"Dead," said I sadly. And I looked gloomily down to the floor.

"All the better," said he. "With a fellow like you, that will be more binding. By gad, by gad, shake hands with me to round it off. Not so hard! Good God, you've crushed every bone in my hand!"

CHAPTER IX

I Start on a New Adventure

I FEEL that I haven't given to you a very accurate transcript of the scene as it actually occurred. Something has been left out. Of course, my memory is at fault after these many, many years, and I have omitted something of the unusual atmosphere which grew so marked before that interview was over that I almost felt myself bewitched.

I was glad to stumble out onto the deck after a time, and look at the cold, sane faces of the stars. And as I saw the dark, glistening water shooting by the side, I felt that I was embarked upon one of the wildest adventures that any human being ever had undertaken.

And yet all my forecasts and fancies could not hit on the strange truth!

I slept well enough in spite of the excitements of that extraordinary day. The next morning, I remembered my appointment to see Mr. Granville forward near the big coil of cable. Just before noon I was waiting there, half expecting that he would not appear, or that if he did appear, he would laugh at me for having taken him seriously the evening before.

Indeed, that odd interview appeared like a dream to me as I looked back upon it. All except the oath which I had taken. No, I felt that that had been a most serious and important thing, and if young Mr. Granville had been making a mere fool of me, I would teach him to regret tampering with such a sacred subject as my mother's name.

But, just before eight bells, Mr. Granville came sauntering out on the deck, and wandered gradually, aimlessly toward me. When he came closer, he broke into quick talk:

"You're to get off the boat at Hardin, on the left bank of the river, and then row across the river and down to St. Pierre, fifteen miles below. You understand? When the boat gets to Hardin, you get off. Say nothing to the captain or to any one who expects you to continue on to New Orleans. Take only what you actually need and can carry on your person, and sink most of your belongings in your carpetbag over the side some night before we get to Hardin, so that there'll be no baggage in your hand when you go ashore and no trace of you left on the boat in your cabin. Is that clear?"

I told him that it was and asked him what I was to do at St. Pierre. He said, "Just before you get to the town, you'll find a creek. Row up that creek for a mile and a half or thereabouts. There isn't much current in it at this time of the year, and you'll find the rowing easy. Keep on until you get to an old wrecked mill at the edge of the stream. Between midnight and morning, I'll meet you there and tell you what to do next. In Hardin, buy a boatload of food—and whatever else you need—perhaps ammunition—rifle and revolver ammunition!"

He added, "Here's something to pay for expenses!"

He gave me a little envelope and hurried away, saying as he left, "Don't be seen near me until we meet again at the creek."

It left me in a good deal of a whirl, as you can imagine. For now I found myself face to face with the mystery—with midnight—a false landing—a boat trip across the river—a stealthy night passage up a creek—why, these words alone dinned into my ears like a threat of death.

When I had a chance to do so covertly, I opened that envelope and found inside an even thousand dollars. It took my breath a little. If I had any doubt about the concrete importance of the things which I was about to attempt, this large sum of money removed it.

And I was rather touched by the faith which this young fellow had placed in me. I felt, in fact, as though he were a boy. For, though I guessed that we were nearly of an age, I had spent my life on the plains, and he had spent his in a sheltered home. So I naturally felt that I was more aged by vital experience.

However, I had definite things to do, and looking forward to them filled my mind. That very next night I took from my carpetbag all that I needed, and then I sank the bag over the side of the ship. And when the boat touched at Hardin the next day, I told the captain that I was going on an errand into town, and slipped down the gangplank with the other landing passengers.

I looked back from the edge of the dock, and at the rail above me I saw the tall form and the pale, tense face of Granville. I thought that there was a gleam of fire in his eyes, and I promised myself, as I walked up the main street of the town, that I would go as far in this adventure as he would ever dare to go.

I took the first alley and got out to the edge of the town, and there I waited in a shrubbery, and shivered a little as I heard the hoarse hooting of the whistle. I knew that the captain was calling me back to the ship. And I felt like a truant boy for not going.

Finally the whistle sounded again, downstream, and I knew that the paddle wheels were driving the boat on toward New Orleans, and toward St. Pierre, nearer at hand.

After that, I went into the town, and down to the river's edge. From an old fisherman I bought a battered skiff for a few dollars; then back to the main street I went and at a hardware store I purchased a rifle and a great quantity of rifle and revolver ammunition. So much that the storekeeper followed me to the door to bid me good afternoon. I made two trips between the town and the boat, carrying down supplies of one sort or another, as if preparing for a regular siege. And then, remembering that I had no fishing tackle, I went back to get that.

I had hardly entered the store when a fat man came wheezing in behind me and tapped me on the shoulder.

"Young man," said he, "where did you get that money you're spending?"

And he showed me a constable's badge inside the flap of his coat!

CHAPTER X

An Encounter I Didn't Bargain For

I WAS badly frightened. I suppose that every ordinary man usually *is* frightened when he hears himself arrested. But I had more reasons than one for being afraid.

For how could I explain that I had a thousand dollars given to me by young Granville? Why should he have given me that money? And might it not get Granville into trouble? More than that, suppose that he cared to disclaim having given me any such sum?

Well, to the poor and the friendless justice is apt to have a face and a hand of iron. I said to the constable: "Why, sir, where should I get the money except out of my pocket?"

"Smart, eh?" said the man of the law, glowering at me. "One of these bright young fellers from up North—a Westerner, he looks to me!"

I thought of pushing my hand in the face of the constable, running over his body, and straight down the street to the boat which I had left beside the river.

But to discourage that notion, he pulled out a great horse pistol that must have been thirty or forty years old, but which looked quite sufficient to blow half a company of men to Hades. And, at the same time, I saw half a dozen idlers gather in the doorway of the store.

He seemed to have read the expression in my eyes, that wise old fox of a constable.

He said: "Don't run, my boy, because no matter how fast you go, I have a messenger who's sure to tag you!"

And he shook his huge pistol in my face.

"All right, sir," said I, "I don't intend to try to run away. I don't want to be buried at your cost. But what have you against me, I'd like to know?"

"You got a lot of money there, ain't you?" he asked me.

"A little," I said.

"About seven or eight hundred dollars, constable," said the storekeeper who had sold me the groceries, coming panting and wheezing into the place that moment. "Or maybe more!"

"Hey, what?" gasped the constable. "That much? And his age?"

"You're right," said the grocery man, coming up and squinting at me, with the perspiration running fast down his face. "You're entirely right! It's stolen money, I take it. Wasn't there Mr. Tom Acton murdered and robbed five days back over in St. Pierre?"

"In St. Pierre Tom Acton was robbed!" exclaimed the constable, falling back from me a little as he considered the terrible nature of that crime. "In St. Pierre he was robbed, just five days ago. And here's the man with the money still on him! What's he been doing?"

"Wandering through the back-country, of course!" said the grocery man.

"Hold on," said I, "does it stand to reason that I would have murdered a man at St. Pierre and showed up here five days later to spend some of the money?"

"It sounds queer, at that," said somebody standing by.

"Aye, and does it?" roared the grocery man, who seemed to be a great person in this community. "And ain't none of you read books wrote by them that know, saying that every man that commits a great crime is really more'n half crazy?"

That seemed to silence all argument. I began to feel that I would have to name Granville, and yet I hated it worse than being scalped, very nearly! I gritted my teeth and said: "Is there any one here who will listen to a bit of common sense?"

"Hoity-toity!" shouted the constable. "He's talking about common sense, and a good thing for him if he'd thought about common sense and common decency before he sneaked up behind poor Mr. Acton and bashed out his brains—the dog!"

"Right, right!" echoed a number of voices. "A coat of tar and some feathers would improve the looks of him a good deal!"

"Tar and feathers," echoed another.

And a whoop and a yell ran through the store and was repeated up and down the street, where a crowd was gathering.

"Tar and feathers!"

That made up my mind on the spot. If I were to be tarred and feathered, they would take their pleasure on a dead man and not on a living one, and some of them would have to die before they could catch me.

"March for that door, young man!" said the constable, waving his pistol. "Open that back door, Rogers, will you? I ain't going to take him down the street but through the back yard to the jail. It ain't safe to expose him to the crowd, murdering skunk though he is!"

He waved the pistol toward the door again as he said, "Get out! And thank your lucky stars that you've fallen into the hands of a constable that'll protect you from the mob the way that I'm doing."

"Wait a minute, constable," broke in a tall, rough-looking fellow. "We're gunna have a say in this! This here is a murderer, and worse'n that, he's a damn Yank. We're gonna have our chance with him before you take hold on him!"

He pushed in between me and the constable—a whale of a man, with the little, red active eyes of a wild pig.

"Tom Yellowbee," said the constable, "you step away from my prisoner, will you?"

But the constable was afraid of that big man, and took a step back from him.

Yellowbee merely laughed.

"It's all right, constable," said he, "there'll be something left of him when I get through! Here, boys, come and take him!"

And he turned around on me, with a grin on his face—a grin of cruel mischief, like the mischief of a boy who has grown up in body but never in mind.

However, so doing, he put himself squarely between me and the constable's big pistol, which for minutes had been yawning at me like the mouth of a howitzer. I didn't need to ask myself what to do. I told myself that if I snatched out both my revolvers, I could shoot my way through that room in five seconds, but there would be nothing but a tangle of dead bodies before I got outside. However, I still could remember my talk with the marshal, God bless him! I didn't touch a Colt, though the tips of my fingers were fairly hungry for them. Instead, I reached for the middle of Mr. Yellowbee's stomach. There was a grease spot on his waistcoat that I used for a target, and I tried to drive that grease spot through his spine.

I think that I nearly did. He doubled over as though a hinge had broken in his back, and let out one ghastly yelp and moan as the last of his wind was driven out of his lungs. I pushed his hulk over against the crowd nearest the street door, and stepped past Yellowbee into a more real danger. That was the old constable with his pistol, for he meant business, that old codger; and now he fired straight into my face. I made sure that my right ear and the whole right side of my face hadn't been blown away; but I hit straight at him to pay him back, and I felt his nose flatten and squash like the rind of a watermelon under a heel.

A gangling, lofty man made a smash at my head with a chair just then, but I ducked the blow, took the chair from him, and knocked him back into the crowd toward the street.

I had intended simply to slip out to the rear door of the place, if I could, but now my blood was decidedly up, and I didn't care to dodge any trouble that might be in my way. That was a good homemade chair, of the toughest hickory, and made to last its life supporting heavyweights. It felt grand to my touch.

Three or four brave and determined townsmen had made their way to the front now, and they charged me shoulder to shoulder, like fine citizens. I pushed the legs of that chair in the faces of two of them, and as the third man tackled me around the knees, I jabbed the top of the chair on his head, and he hit the floor with a screech and lay writhing.

There was enough groaning and yelling and cursing in that room by that time to have represented a vast battlefield, I think. But it was nothing to what came, for I lit

63

into that crowd of idlers and beat that heavy chair to kindling wood over their backs and shoulders and legs as I herded them out of the store. They wavered and fought back for an instant only, and then they turned and bolted as if wild cats were scratching their hearts out. In the doorway they jammed, which gave me a chance to get in some of my best licks, and then the whole lot of them bulged into the open air. Those who could sprinted for safety, yelling for help; but a good many who couldn't run, staggered or crawled after them, howling too.

There was no one left of that crowd of heroes except Yellowbee, who was still gasping and choking on the floor. And I went past him into the back yard, and saw a fat-sized gelding in a corral behind the store.

There was a sea of noise running up and down the street, and just as I picked up a piece of string from the ground, a rifle clanged and a bullet hummed over my head. I turned, saw the puff of smoke and the shifting form of a man through the cracks of a tall fence. It was a bad target, but I fired a bullet shin-high and came close enough to make the marksman yip and run.

That gave me freedom to slide through the rails of that corral and get the gelding. I got on its back, fixed the string over its nose, and went through the bars of the corral in another moment. Not more than a second too soon, though, for I saw about ten men, every one armed with rifles and shotguns, rushing down the alley between the store and the next building. They hardly had a chance to open up at me, for I galloped the gelding around the store, and broke into the open street. Then up that street and for the woods to which its farther end pointed.

I think that forty or fifty shots must have been fired at me as I rode, but they were all chance shots, poured in as I whizzed by at a racing speed. Or else they weren't shots from behind, and I wasn't an easy target to hit, because I kept swerving the horse from side to side. And all the way I yelled like a Blackfoot Indian fighting a whole tribe of Comanches.

It sounds dangerous, as I write about it now, but at the time I thought it was the best bit of fun that I had ever had. When I reached the trees, I looked back and saw a herd of riders beginning to streak out after me from the town.

That was what I wanted. I mean, I wanted attention to start that way from the village.

When I was a quarter of a mile inside the woods, I turned to the left and cut in a wide semicircle back for the shore of the river. As I rode, I could hear the hunt go smashing and zooming past me, and the men shouting cautions to one another to shoot straight when they sighted me.

But while they were beating up the forest for me, I got to the river and there, what do you think I saw? An empty shore, with not a soul in sight! Not even a child or a dog!

CHAPTER XI

Eavesdropping

I TURNED the gelding loose and gave it a slap on the hip that sent it cantering good-naturedly away; and no doubt headed straight back to its home pasture. Then I went down to the landing place and found that not an article had been damaged in my skiff. Everything had been handled, but not even the rifle had been stolen, for I suppose that there had been too many witnesses for any one to dare to steal, until the hubbub from the town called everyone that way in a crowd.

I was too happy to ask many questions why or wherefore. I sat down in that skiff, grabbed the oars, and made them groan in the locks as I shot the little boat upstream.

Upstream? you may ask.

Well, in the ebb current along the shore there was hardly a down stir of the river. I could make practically as good time in this direction, and I felt it would be the very last direction in which people would care to look for me. They would think of me on the river as fleeing down the stream to get the greatest possible number of miles between me and the pursuit. But it was not mere distance that I wanted to gain, but time.

For two hours I pulled up the shore, under the shadow of the overhanging boughs most of the way. Then I pulled inshore, beached the nose of the skiff, and lay down in a tuft of grass to think matters over.

There were still several hours until darkness should come, and all of that time the townsfolk were fairly sure to spend searching for me. But I decided that I had come far enough away from Hardin, because I wanted to be in striking distance of St. Pierre and its creek, according to my promise to Granville.

This was what I did, therefore. I got some hard-tack and fresh apples from my supplies in the skiff and ate them, and drank some cider that I had brought along in a jug. Then I lay down on my back and watched the pattern of the trees against the sky. Only for a moment, and then I was soundly asleep.

God bless sleep! I was clear-headed and as fresh as a daisy when I woke. I thought it was deep night, but when I got to the edge of the trees I saw that the face of the river was still faintly purple from the sunset light.

However, I was not exactly the most cautious man in the world, and I had a great deal of work before me if I wanted to reach the mill on the creek bank before midnight.

I pulled the skiff into the stream and rowed out fairly into the middle of the current. By the time I got there it was dark enough for comparative safety, and then I turned the nose of the skiff downstream and rowed as I never had rowed before. It was an old boat, but a light one, and the oars were long enough to give me a fair leverage. I had rowed up and down the much faster current of the stream at Fort Bostwick many a time, so the art was familiar to me. And I fairly walked the skiff down the broad, lazy face of the Mississippi.

The lights of Hardin patched the left shore with yellow and streaked the surface of the water. And now, with night well begun, I hummed along with a steady pull, setting my mind fully on my work.

What a good time I made you can guess when I tell you that it was a shade short of eleven o'clock before I reached the mouth of the creek—and below the creek the clustered lights of a very considerable town.

That must certainly be St. Pierre, I thought, so I muffled the oarlocks, and turned the nose of my little boat into the stream. I began to doubt before I had become well committed to the work, because Granville had assured me that the current would be almost nil at this time of the year, and as a matter of fact I found a stiffish one to pull against.

However, a freshet up in the back-country might have sent down a flood, and so I stuck to my work stubbornly, and saw the trees walk slowly past me on the winding banks. And leaning hard to my work, with every back swing of my body I had a glance up at the thin, bright faces of the many stars.

Now and then, as I rounded a bend, the current would swish about the bows. And several times the bottom scraped loudly on a snag, but on the whole that was a fairly silent trip up the creek. For the bubbling and the boiling of the currents entirely covered the noise of the rowing, and I felt that I would have to be seen before I could be detected, and seen in the midst of a pitchy darkness, with the trees reaching out straight over me most of the way.

Just before twelve, I felt that I must have covered close to the required distance, and I began to search the shores more carefully. Around the next bend I found what I wanted: the squat and tumble-down body of a building, with the mill tower at one end of it.

There under a tree I moored the skiff and climbed up the shore. I went very carefully, partly because I had just come from great danger, and partly because my appointment was such an odd one, and partly, too, because the outline of that mill looked like the setting for a midnight murder, if I have ever seen one in all my days!

I hadn't more than got up the bank, which was very steep, before I thought I heard a light stir of voices before me. I crouched close to the ground, as Uncle Stephen had taught me to do so many years before, and then I thought I could hear the voices still more distinctly—two men, talking rapidly together, but at such a distance that I couldn't make out what was said.

I stood up again, with my rifle at the ready, and slipped along through the woods, doing my best not to make a noise. I had had enough training of that sort, for though most of my hunting days had been on the open plains, still there had been plenty of still hunting in the woods, and still hunting of the Indians as well as game! It takes a keen teacher, a good deal of patience and time, and a sort of instinct for the work, in order to walk softly among dead leaves and fallen twigs, but eventually one will come to have in the soles of one's boots a sense like the sense of touch in the tips of the fingers. Yes, almost a sense of sight, also! I had never become an expert like my uncle, and certainly not like any one of fifty Indian warriors I could name—but still I was more than skillful, and I got through that copse without raising a whisper.

Then, through the trees, I saw a light glimmering from the open window of a small shed which was a part of the mill. I stole up to the window, stopping to take my bearings every moment or two for fear that there might be a lookout watching, and so I came close enough to hear everything that was said, though I could not maneuver so as to see the faces of the two men. The window was not low enough for that. I could see the shadow of one head sweep occasionally across the farther wall of the room, but that was all. However, the voices sounded young; one of middle register, and one quite deep.

The deep voice was talking when I first came up:

"However, I've really finished arguing, and if I can't persuade you, we'll give the thing up."

"I haven't said that I can't be persuaded."

"No, but you sit glowering at me. I'm not asking you to do any favor for me."

"Don't be ugly about it, Lorrie."

"I'm not ugly, Dick. But I tell you that I've done enough and talked enough. Now—will you commit yourself?"

"How far?"

"As far as you please. I don't want to drag an unwilling or a half-hearted partner along with me."

"Well—I don't know."

"Make up your mind, then. He'll be here in a few minntes."

"He's probably here already, listening."

"Tush, man! Who could come near us, here, without making a noise over all the rotten wood and dead twigs that cover the ground?"

I smiled at that.

"Now talk up, Dick. What shall we do?"

There was a long silence.

69

"I'd rather wait until we meet him and have a chance to talk with him."

"You mean to decide after he comes?"

"Exactly. My blood isn't up to this thing, old fellow."

"You have no cause, I presume," said Lorrie sarcastically.

"Well, perhaps I have and perhaps I haven't. There really aren't any proofs against him."

"Enough incidental proof to convince a thousand jurors, I should say. But that's a matter to leave to your own conscience. I can't make your decisions for you!"

"Of course not! Of course not! But what I say is—let's meet him here and talk with him. Let's take him down the road and talk. And if I can make up my mind—"

"Confound it, Dick, if he's right and not wrong, why does he ask us to meet him here in this deserted shack? Will you tell me?"

"I don't know. But he's queer. He's a romantic devil, you know. He may have nothing but a fishing trip to propose to us."

"Dick, that's a bit childish."

"I suppose that it is. But let me have my way about it. After we've talked, if I agree with you about him, I'll say —oh, any exclamation! I'll say, 'In the name of St. Pierre.' Would that do?"

"Yes, of course. You could work that into the course of the conversation and he would suspect nothing, but I'll be listening!"

"That's finished, then?"

"Yes."

"I'll have to be content with that, I suppose, but I rather hate to be! Let it go. Hush! Here he comes, I think!"

I could hear nothing, but apparently they had made out something from the farther side of the shed. And now I heard a faint footfall, far away, and then:

"Hello!"

"We're here, Will. Come in."

"No, you fellows come out. I don't want to go inside that dark rat-trap of a place!"

I was glad to hear the stranger talk like this, for as far

as I could make out, the pair in the house had been plotting against his safety. And there was less chance of their doing him a mischief in the open air than in the gloom of that broken-down building.

They didn't argue, but walked outside with "Will."

"Shall we talk here?"

"No," said Will, "let's walk along, and I'll open my mind to you. I've been thinking it over. I'm full of the scheme. Are you willing to walk back toward my place?"

"Yes, of course."

And even as they spoke their voices began to fade away. I started to follow them; and then I remembered my appointment and halted.

CHAPTER XII

I Turn Student

IT was one of the hardest things that I ever did in my life, because I felt that Will was in the darkest sort of danger from the two young men whom I had overheard in the shed. I wanted to trail the three of them, and if foul play was attempted end it with a bullet from my rifle. For the voice of Will was so crisp and manly I felt sure that if I put away one of his enemies, he could deal with the other.

On the other hand, I couldn't be sure. Neither of the two had appeared to be a low-bred ruffian. They spoke with a good accent, and they seemed to be gentlemanly fellows. Somehow it was hard for me to reconcile such voices with midnight murder.

What else they could have in mind when the signal "In the name of St. Pierre" should be given, I could not guess. But in the meantime, I had pledged my word that I would meet Granville in this spot, and I felt that the oath which I had given to him was so sacred that it extended especially to every word I spoke to him, and to the slightest agreement that I might make with him. I had made him my absolute and complete master for the space of one year. And because I owed my life to him, I did not grudge the compact.

So, with a gloomy eye, I listened to the footfalls departing. Then I took up my vigil again.

It was a damp and gloomy one. The ground was half marshy and I could not sit down. I did not want to move about too much for fear of being overheard—by whom I knew not. But I began to feel, from what I had overheard, that this old mill was a treacherous and dangerous spot, reeking with evil of all kinds. It cast a darker shadow over my coming interview with young Granville. If he had wanted my services for any good end, would he have chosen such a spot for the meeting place?

I think that I moved slowly from place to place around the old, ruined building for more than two hours before I heard the clicking hoofs of a horse on the roadbed, and saw a rider outlined before me. He drew rein, paused a moment, and then a husky voice called softly, "Are you there?"

I stepped out from the shrubbery under the very nose of his horse, for I had recognized the odd voice of Granville. No one else ever possessed such a speaking tone.

He reined his horse back with an oath when I appeared. A gun glittered in his hand, and then when I spoke he uttered an exclamation of relief.

"You're there, Sam Cross?"

"It's I."

He flung himself down from his horse and clasped my hand with a real warmth.

"I should have known that you'd manage to get here," he declared, "but after the affair at Hardin I doubted so much that I almost decided not to come here to-night for the appointment!"

"You know about Hardin?" I asked him.

"I listened with my heart in my throat," said he. "And of course I recognized your handiwork in the description they gave of you. Except that they made you out a giant. And sort of a wizard, too. There are a dozen men that swear they fired rifle balls straight through your body without ever stopping you. But you weren't wounded, old fellow?"

"Not touched. Bear hunting is the same thing. Every hunter knows that he put a bullet through the bear's head. But the grizzly doesn't drop, you know!"

He laughed at that.

"You were the grizzly, right enough," said he. "The doctors in Hardin are taking care of twenty wounded men; mostly bruises and several broken bones."

"I had to defend myself," I told him, "because—"

"Tar and feathers. I heard about that. And the brute Yellowbee. Of course! I wish that you'd broken his back. A hard, stupid, brutal lot, they are in Hardin. But how did you get away? Was it the boat, after all?"

"Why not?"

"They searched the river up and down."

"Not far enough up."

"Well, Cross, if I had any doubt about you before, it's gone now. There's not one man in the world who can help me except you. And now I almost know for sure that you can do it!"

"I'm here to serve you," said I. "I have the stuff in the boat in the creek, there. What am I to do first?"

"Not rob a bank immediately," he said, chuckling at my eagerness for work. "No, you have a dismal enough duty to begin with. I'm sorry for that!"

"Never mind. Just tell me what it is."

"Telling won't do. I have to show you. Wait till I've tied up my horse."

He tied the horse in a cluster of saplings, and then went with me to the skiff. He sat in the stern and told me how to row, and I worked the boat another half mile up the stream, and then down a slough that branched off to the left. Trees and shrubs grew densely around us. A dozen times we were snagged and had to back water to push clear. Winding this way and that, through a passage that seemed to be growing constantly narrower, Granville at last gave the word to beach the boat on the right. And we climbed out and I found myself before a little, squat shack. Granville led the way into it. He lighted a match, and I found inside a heap of straw and a few old blankets.

When the ducks were flying, he explained, the place was sometimes used for hunting, but otherwise no one ever came near it.

"Now," said Granville, "I want you to spend a considerable time in this place. Just how long depends upon Mother Nature and God Almighty, very largely. I'll make it as short as I can. It's no pleasure to me to have you locked up here when I need you in another place so badly. But here you have to stay at present."

I asked no questions, but looked around me and stifled a sigh. However, in the great West, where distances are enormous and travel is slow, one learns patience.

"You have your guns?"

74

"Yes."

"And plenty of ammunition?"

"Yes."

"I'm glad I thought of that, because it'll keep you amused. You can go around here and practice at targets, or you can shoot birds, or whatever you please. But never be more than ten minutes from this island. When I come for you, I need to find you here; and when I come, I shall never have time to hunt. I should be starting back, now. And if my horse should be found there at the mill—who knows what would happen?"

"I wouldn't make rendezvous at the mill any more, if I were you. Too many other people use it for the same thing."

"What makes you say that?"

"Nothing that I care to talk about."

He lighted another match, and then ignited the lantern. By its glow he examined me.

"You're a curious fellow, Sam," said he. "Uncommonly curious. I won't ask you why you say that, but I'll take you at your word. In the meantime, do you like to read?"

"Yes."

"Here are a couple of books. I'd like to have you study them word for word—like a history lesson, if you don't mind."

"Thank you."

"No, you may not thank me. They're dry stuff. I'm away, now. Perhaps for a week. Perhaps for two weeks. I don't know. Will you stay here?"

"I? Of course!"

He shook my hand with a sudden enthusiasm.

"You're the right stuff!" he exclaimed. "God forgive me for dragging you into this mess!"

He was about to leave, and then turned back.

"Have you a razor?"

"Yes."

"Will you let me see it?"

I took it out of its case and presented it to him. He gave it hardly a glance but said, "Look here, may I take this along with me?"

75

"Yes, of course, except—"

"I think that I need it more than you do," he told me, and I would not argue so small a point. Plainly he didn't want questions at that time, and I was willing to leave him alone. His will had to be my will, and I might as well begin to accept that state of things at once.

We carried the load from the skiff up to the shack, and deposited it on the floor; then he said good night, and, stepping into the boat, he rowed away with long, strong sweeps of the oars, and I saw him weaving in and out along that narrow passageway with a deftness that showed he knew the waterways here by heart. That began a long watch for me.

By night, I slept as much as the mosquitoes would allow. By day, I roved here and there on the little island on which the shack stood, and murdered small birds with rifle or revolver shots. Or else I sat and read the two books which he had brought me.

They were even worse than he had promised. They were family histories of the Granvilles; the first dealing with the old records of the family when they were in England, and the second continuing the tale after a Granville came to Virginia, and then on to Louisiana. There were numerous pictures, from the stiff-necked cavaliers of the older days to modern times. The book had been printed only three years before, and I found pictures of my friend Granville and his whole family scattered through the last few pages. I scanned the faces of his father and his mother curiously, and of his sister, also, a beautiful girl of sixteen or so, as it seemed.

And, after that, I went through the two volumes carefully. When one has nothing to do except a bit of hunting and with all the day before one for study, it is odd how much can be accomplished. Before those two weeks were out, I could name all the faces in both the volumes with the greatest of ease, and, furthermore, I knew every minute detail of the family history as it was described in the books. My mother had kept me at my books for so long that it was not hard for me to study. I had developed the muscles for that sort of work, as you might say.

But, on the whole, they were very weary weeks that I passed on the island amidst the marshes until young Granville returned.

CHAPTER XIII

Showing That I Studied to Some Purpose

Two weeks to a day, the bow of the skiff pushed around a corner of the nearest waterway—for the marsh was honeycombed with narrow, twisting alleys down which five hundred canoes could have thrust and disappeared from the eyes within thirty seconds—and in it sat Granville, his strong back sweeping the oars vigorously through the water.

When he sprang out of the boat onto the shore, he looked around anxiously. But I had hidden myself in the trees, and he could not find me. He hurried into the house, and then he called to me in a guarded fashion. But I wouldn't answer.

"Gone!" I heard him say. "Gone, by gad!"

He started off at a run to search the island, and when he came back I was unloading from the skiff a number of things that he had brought over with him. He greeted me with a shout, and then with a volley of good-natured abuse, but we could afford to laugh with one another.

A moment later he was laughing at another thing, and that was the growth of red fuzz over all my face, for my whiskers grew at a prodigious rate, and had done so ever since I was a youngster. If I went to a dance in the evening at Fort Bostwick, I had to use a razor at night as well as in the morning. And now there was a fair cloud of short, bristling hair about my face.

"Give me back my razor," said I, "and I'll make myself feel a lot cleaner and look a great deal less than a monkey, I hope."

"Later, later!" said he, with a shrug of the shoulders. "But now tell me how the two weeks have gone?"

"They've gone at last," I told him. "It wasn't as bad as it might have been."

"But the mosquitoes?"

"They were a nuisance."

"Yes, I've brought over some yards of netting that will keep them out. It was criminal to bring you over here without providing that. You look pale, though. Have you had a touch of fever?"

"No, not a trace of it."

"It's simply living in the steam of the marsh," he nodded. "It's like being in a steam bath, isn't it?"

I shrugged my shoulders. There was no use in whining.

"And what about the books?" he asked suddenly.

"I've read them."

"Do you remember them at all?"

"Yes, I think so."

"Suppose that I were to pop out at you: 'Who was Sir Edward Granville?'"

"I should say: Sir Edward Granville was the second son of Baron and Baroness Granville, and in 1681 he was knighted by Charles the Second because of his services in exposing informers during the time of the—"

"Gad!" broke in Granville. "You seem to know it! Wait a moment. Let me try again. Who was Sidney Gresham?"

"He was a rich Liverpool merchant who in 1732 advanced fourteen hundred pounds to Oliver Granville in order to buy a share in a ship trading to the West Indies, with Oliver Granville as master, and after the voyage he—"

"You know it. Hold on! Do you know the whole of those two books as thoroughly as that?"

"I hope that I know them fairly well."

"You studied them?"

"Yes, word by word."

"Look here!"

He picked up one of the books, cracked it open and held it up.

"What's that picture?"

"That's Charles Leicester Thompson, who was killed in a duel with Gregory Granville in 1803 at Montgomery. They fought because of a—"

"That's enough! That's enough! How infernally thorough you are, Cross! Look here, I begin to really feel for the first time that my idea is not a stroke of madness but a stroke of sense—a possible thing!"

I was silent, of course, because I still hadn't the slightest idea of what he meant.

He walked up and down for a moment and then he faced me in his sudden, startling way.

"I'll tell you what, Sam Cross, I might as well show you my hand right now!"

"Thank you," said I.

"When I've told you my idea, then you can do as you please—but I suppose that you'll want to chuck the whole thing. That's up to you, and you'll have the right to refuse."

"No," said I, "for one year I haven't a right to refuse anything."

He stared at me.

"Well," he said, "as a matter of fact, that was the agreement. But we'll see—I mustn't drive you too far! In the meantime, will you take that razor—no, I'll have to be your barber, this once. Sit down on that box, will you?"

He brought out a razor and some small bottles, and commenced to work like a barber, shaving off my growth of whiskers. It was a pretty painful process, for though he meant well and tried to be careful, he couldn't help that it took him more than an hour, altogether, before he was finished, and most of that time I was sitting with my eyes closed and with a towel around my neck while he combed liquids into my hair. After that, there was clipping, trimming, and brushing, and finally he gave me a hand-mirror and told me to look at myself, while he stood back with his eyes sparkling with satisfaction and surprise.

But when I looked, I give you my word that my head swam. For I felt that in some mysterious manner another head had been clapped upon my shoulders!

I saw black hair, and a short black mustache, and the beginnings of a black beard. And were it not for the shortness of the mustache and the beard, I should have thought that by some trick of the conjurer's art I had been transformed into Granville! Yes, even my fine thick tan was largely gone; and I was almost as pale as he, from my life in the steaming marsh.

"Good heavens," cried I, "what have you done?"

"It works! It works!" said Granville. "And if it works with you, it'll work with the rest."

He grew so excited that his husky voice choked up and he could hardly whisper.

"And now you understand?" he asked me.

"I understand nothing!" said I.

"Then listen to me!"

"I am listening."

"You're ready for a shock?"

"Yes, I suppose I am."

"Very well! Then what I want to say is that you're to go to my house and take my place in my family and wear the name of Charles St. Maurice Granville, just as though you were me!"

CHAPTER XIV

I Become Another Man

I LISTENED to him with a horror that must have showed on my face.

"You take it hard!" said he.

"I can't do it, man," said I. "I can't do it—and yet, hold on! It won't be so bad if there's no living member of your family there."

"No living member?" he cried. "Why, you have seen the pictures of my mother and father and sister?"

I stared at him.

"Can you ask me to do such a thing?" I said to him.

"And why not?"

"To take the place of a son to his mother—when I've had a mother of my own and understand what it means?"

"Don't be too excited about small things," said he. "The fact is that you're a decent, honorable fellow, and probably you'll be a much better son to my parents than I could ever have been."

I shook my head.

"I can't do it," I told him. "You'll understand, if you think for a moment. I'm ready to serve you in any other way, but to step into the body and the feelings of another man! Why, man, suppose that your mother came to kiss me good night, as my mother used to do!"

"She'll do that," nodded he. "She always does, poor old dear! But you'll be happy as soon as you get used to it!"

"Or suppose that your father opens his heart to me? What of that?"

"Well, what of it?"

"To tell me everything that's nearest and dearest to his heart? I would feel like a more than contemptible eavesdropper!"

"You simply won't do it, man?"

"My whole heart revolts against it, Granville. Ask me any other thing, and I'll willingly try it!"

He was silent, staring moodily down to the earth. Then he said, "You gave me an oath, Sam Cross."

It stiffened me, of course, and made me look coldly at him. I began to like this young man less and less.

"I gave you an oath, yes."

"And doesn't that mean anything to you?"

"Yes, I'll redeem that oath, if you keep me to it!"

"Then I'll hold you to it! Man, man, I have to, and why, I'll explain later!"

I couldn't answer. What was there for me to say? But certainly I would never have given him my promise in the first place if I had dreamed that he could have had in his heart any plan so deep and so wildly strange.

"But though you could command me to do this thing," I said to him, "you will see, after a moment, that it couldn't be pushed through, Mr. Granville."

"You needn't be so formal, old fellow. I'm Charles to you, I hope; as you'll soon be Charles to the rest of the world!"

And he laughed, but broke off his excited laughter to ask me why it was that I felt the plan couldn't succeed.

"Because," said I, "though there's a certain resemblance, still there isn't nearly enough to deceive the eyes of one's own family!"

"That's exactly what there is, though," said he. "No, I've thought all of that out. I've thought it out in every detail! You see, I have to go away on a trip before long and when I supposedly come back—it will really be you! Now, I've noticed that whenever I go away—even for this trip up the river, for instance—on my return, my family always say, 'Why, you've changed so that we would hardly know you! You're not a bit the same!' And so they'll say and feel when you come back in my place; but when they see that we're exactly the same height, and when they see that you know all about the little intimate details of the family, and know their pet names and their nicknames, and all the servants and the horses and the dogs and what not—why, they'll soon get to feel that nothing could be wrong. And besides, we'll arrange to have you return at night. Everyone's prepared to have people look a bit strange by lamplight. Isn't that so?"

"That's reasonably true," I had to admit.

"Go on," said he, "pile up all the objections that you want. I don't mind. Now's the time to hear every objection that can be made, and to meet them one by one, because if I can't convince you that the thing is feasible, then I can't convince myself, really! Go ahead and raise objections!"

"The very first one," said I, "is that our faces are a good deal the same, but still there's a lot of difference."

"I don't think so," said he. "Your face I've studied like a book. When you sat in my cabin, I had a photograph of myself—a big one—standing behind you, and it seemed to me that there was only one difference, and that was around the mouth. You're a bit—well, stronger and stiffer in the lips, but this mustache changes you enormously in that respect. Then there's the nose. My nose is just a shade thinner and less arched, you know. Well, I admit that. But who'll be able to hit on that detail after I've been away for a few weeks? I should say that your whole face is a bit larger than mine, and if we were dressed exactly the same, and sat side by side, I suppose that people wouldn't think us doubles. They'd rather write you down as my older brother, you know. However, I think that the thing is close enough. Why, heavens, man, even when your hair was red and you had no mustache at all, I still saw the wonderful similarity! It made me dizzy! And I know how I look. I'm a self-conscious fellow. I've been proud of my rather handsome face—you see that's an indirect compliment for you, too. I've studied myself and tried to make the most of my advantages. And so I could tell when I saw you. The idea struck me like a thunderbolt. Wasn't it a startling, wonderful thing to conceive, old fellow?"

He was very childlike, in many ways, as you have been able to tell for yourself, of course. And I couldn't tell whether to pity or to be angry with him.

"It was strange enough," I had to say.

"You won't admire it, because you hate the thought,"

he said, "but that's all right! I can't ask you to be very excited about my own plans, when so much of the danger of this falls on your own head. My father's a hot-tempered fellow. And if he were to guess that there was the slightest doubt about you, I know he would have you tarred and feathered and then torn to pieces by the hounds! He's that way—savage as a bear. I've seen him. But listen to me! I'm trying to discourage you! Trying to make the thing harder for you in your own estimation. But as a matter of fact, there'll be no danger. None, really. If my father sees you, he'll accept you. There'd be more danger of my mother suspecting something, but as a matter of fact, her eyes are very dim."

"You have a sister, though."

"A sister? She's a name, and not a fact. Confound that girl, she hasn't looked at me more than once and a half since she was fifteen. We were rather thick when she was a youngster, but as soon as she grew old enough to find out that other men could shoot guns and ride horses—why, she stopped paying the slightest attention to me. I give you my word that she never looks at me at all. She yawns when I begin to express an opinion. And she gives me a black look when I come into the room. She doesn't really like me very well. I'm not dashing enough to suit her. She would like to have a hero of the hunt for a brother—a dashing, crashing duelist—a wild, strong man, you understand? She can't get on with the idea of me, because I'm only ordinary in all of those ways. You know, a prophet has honor everywhere except in his own country, eh? No, you'll be in no danger from Nancy, because she's grown so ridiculously pretty that every young buck in the countryside is making himself a fool about her. She hasn't any time for her own family, and least of all for me—which would mean you, too!"

He rattled along in this way, you understand, fully convinced in what he said, and rather convincing me, too. But still I was filled with doubt. I couldn't rate this fellow as an extremely accurate observer. There was nothing very steady, or accurate, or deep about him. In fact, he was rather a weak brother.

I said, "Setting all that aside, I don't see why I didn't make the strongest point first. And this point there's absolutely no getting around—the dye on my hair. Why, dye is always known, sooner or later!"

"Do you think so? Well, you try it! You'll find that you're wrong. I'll tell you how I learned about this dye. There was a black-haired fellow came into our neighborhood, settled down, and lived among us. For ten years he hunted, shot, rode, and gamed with all of us. Very jolly, keen sort of a man. And at the end of ten years or thereabouts, it was suddenly discovered that he was not a black-haired man at all, and not even a Southerner—though he'd seemed to have the accent down pat. As a matter of fact, he was a rascal who had run off with a lot of money from a bank in New York—trimmed the Yankees properly! But detectives finally trailed him—through something, I forget what—and he had to disappear. Now, doesn't that make you think better of the black dye? After he disappeared, everything was found out in his house. Yes, and he'd even worn a bit of a wig! Oh, I'll tell you, I think that a great many people could do with disguises, if they would only have the nerve to try them! Criminals do it all the time you know!"

There was a certain amount of truth in that.

He went on. "Then there's the matter of the difference in our voices—"

I started. Wasn't it singular that I hadn't thought of that most patent matter?

"There you are!" I cried with relief. "That ends it. The voices certainly could never be disguised with a wig, or any such thing!"

He grinned at me most cheerfully, and kept nodding his head, very pleased with himself.

"I knew that you'd feel that way, but as a matter of fact," said he, "my odd voice is the very thing that will make it all possible."

"I don't understand," I said.

"Well, of course you couldn't. For the reason that one man can't pass for another is always a question of the voice, isn't it? Because, as you say, a voice can't be imitated?"

"No, of course not."

"And since the beginning of the world no two voices have ever been the same?"

"Exactly!" said I, wondering at the way in which he built up the argument against his own idea.

"But listen to me! Ever since I was a youngster, there's been a growth of some sort in my throat. It's grown worse and worse. And recently I went to the city and had a doctor examine my throat. He declares that he can cut that growth out and that it'll probably not return. And he declares that I'll then have my normal speaking voice!"

I stared at him, beginning to understand.

"It's a foolish little operation," said he. "In three days I could be up and about and back home. But I intend to stay away longer than that. And, when 'I' return, it'll be you, Sam Cross, who walks into Granville House!"

I waited; I was hardly able to speak, because the excitement of the idea kept growing in me. And, indeed, you can see for yourself that the thing seemed more and more possible.

"Your friends?" I said. "And all the servants?"

"I've always been enthusiastic about photography, and I have been taking pictures for years. I think that I have pictures of every man and boy and woman and dog and horse on the place. And I've brought the entire collection over here, with a mass of notes. I've been up past midnight every night, writing out the information that you need to have about every one. And here you are! Friends and all. All their peculiarities and all the stories of the ways in which I was connected with them."

And he added, "You seem to have a sort of camera eye. You can remember things well. See how you've mastered the whole family history in these two short weeks! You'll have all this stuff by heart in another two weeks, I should say. Gad, the idea sounds more and more promising!"

Difficult, yes, but more and more possible. That was plain!

"And then there's the handwriting."

"Yes," said he, growing very serious. "I know that that's a ticklish point, and I suppose that it's the hardest of all. But I've never been a great letter writer, and I suppose that you could let the correspondence drop. Not entirely. No, you'd have to do some writing. Confound it, how could the thing be done?"

And he added, "Have you ever done much pen work?"

I looked back on the long years of work on the ledgers of the store in Bostwick.

"Yes," said I, "I suppose that I'm a pretty fair master of a pen."

"Are you? Then thank God for that! There's nothing very peculiar about my handwriting. It's regular and pretty clearly formed. No odd quirks about it. And I don't see why you couldn't imitate it perfectly!"

"Perhaps," I had to say. "Other people have been able to—forge."

"You give everything its ugliest name," he said with a scowl. "Don't you see that I'm the one who could be injured, and I'm the one who authorizes you?"

"Even to the signing of your checks?" I said suddenly.

He looked at me with a smile.

"Sam," said he, "don't you see that I trust your integrity a great deal more than I could ever trust my own?"

I thanked him, rather half-heartedly.

"Now what remains for you to stick at?" said he. "What is there that you could possibly bring up against me?"

"A rather big thing, after all. Every man has a speaking voice, and every one also has his own manners, his way of saying things, his habit of thought, and his trick of gesture. How about that?"

He chuckled.

"I've already arranged that," he said. "I saw that you could do most of these things, but that you could never be much of an actor, and so I arranged that I should do the acting for you!"

"What do you mean by that?"

"I mean that instead of making you act my part, I'm acting yours. My father has always been begging me to adopt better and graver and more formal manners. Well, old fellow, I've never known a more stiff-backed formalist —I beg your pardon—than you are. And, therefore, I've told father that I want to reform my ways of doing things. And I've gone about the house acting like a new man. It disgusts my sister. My mother is disturbed by it. But my father is hugely delighted. I call every one 'sir,' as you do. And I have developed a stiff, slow bow, like yours. Who taught you to act like that, old fellow?"

"My mother."

"Well, she must have been a wonderfully fine but very old-fashioned lady. Let that go. I've done the thing everywhere. I find it uncomfortable enough at the house, but away from the house, it's simply awful. Simply awful! The young fellows and the girls laugh in my face. I've told them that it's to please father and begged them to forgive me. But they make me lapse into my old self whenever they can, and it's a vast relief when I let them persuade me. You understand? Easier to be one's natural self! However, during the next month I'm going to work very hard on the new character—your character. And when you come into the house, you'll find everyone prepared for a grave, cold-hearted man—yourself! You don't mind my jokes, old boy?"

Well, he was cutting a bit deep, of course. But this was a hugely interesting affair, for I was beginning to have a chance to see myself as others saw me. And that's an opportunity that comes to few men.

And suddenly I couldn't help saying, "It can be done, and I'm going to do it!"

CHAPTER XV

Some Interesting Letters

It seemed to me that I should never be able to walk into Granville House and take the mother of another in my arms as if she were my own. And then, no matter how closely I memorized the part, might I not forget some vital portion of my rôle once I was in the house of Granville?

Well, I was already committed to the work, and now I could not turn back, so I set my teeth and faced forward. I knew perfectly well that the moment I glanced over my shoulder and began to feel regrets I would have little spirit for continuing, so I gave all my thought to the practical part of the work before me.

Among other things, that week Granville brought to me a closely worked map of the whole countryside around his house. And along with the map there was a well-drawn plan of Granville House with each apartment and its title indicated, which he had made himself.

The map and the sketch of the house I was to master as well as I could, and Granville left me for nine long days. They were crowded days, you may be sure. I began each morning by placing before me the specimens of his handwriting which he had given to me. For an hour and a half I worked conscientiously, first drawing out the characters slowly, taking pains to have every one perfect, and then trying to repeat them with more speed, so that the writing would flow naturally. He had a queer way of making his T's, for instance, and his signature was filled with loops and scrawls, very old fashioned in style.

I used to make the difficult letters very large to begin with, so that I could study their peculiarities, and then smaller and smaller, until they were of the natural size. Finally, I strove to write freely, and that was where the great difficulty came. However, every day I made some progress.

After the writing, I had a long session examining the photographs, and the notes which Granville had appended to them. The notes were done with a great deal of skill. For instance, one would tell that Dickon Chalmers was an old friend, but not a very good one, and that he had always treated Dickon a little more cordially than his feelings really warranted. And Rance Lacrosse was a rough and surly chap, but capable of being of real service. Rance aspired to be friendly with a few of the old families, and he was willing to pay for the friendship by losing a good deal of money at cards.

And so the list of names went on until I came to the girls. I thought that there would be no end to them! I had told him that I couldn't manage to have much to do with the women because, indeed, I had never known any women well. And here was a host of more than forty girls, to say nothing of older women!

Ah, well, my blood used to turn cold as I looked at their pretty, sophisticated faces. But I decided that I would make a vigorous protest the next time Granville came.

I did make the protest and, though he laughed at me, he finally agreed.

The chief danger is from the women," he admitted. "Men have no eyes, but women see things. They live in to-day. They haven't much thought of to-morrow. And the result is that there is never a film over their eyes. Now, how are we to keep the women away from you? I've been rather intimate with a lot of girls!"

"Rather!" said I, and I picked up the pile of photographs. I read off some of the notes:

"Isabell Craigie. She and I have become just good friends, after falling in and out of love several times. Be kind to Isabell. Because some day I may want to marry her, if she'll have me."

"She's a darling," said he, thoughtfully.

"Katherine Hotchkiss Akerville. An old sweetheart. We were in love for nearly a year. And she has never forgiven me. Don't let Katherine corner you or she may begin to reminisce. Louise Gloster. A relic of calf love. Louise and I used to sigh at one another every spring. But these affairs never lasted into the summer months. Louise is dangerous, because she knows too much about me and about everything."

"She does, too," broke in Mr. Granville. "A confounded girl. Has read everything and thought about everything. Even my father enjoys a chat with her. But she scares me, and she scares the other men, too."

"Olivia Guilbert de la Creillon. A former flame. Slightly cross-eyed, but very witty and modest and keen. Beware of Olivia! She is a good fellow, however."

"Look here, Charles," said I, "what about all these girls? You seem to have been in love with all of the women!"

He was a surprising man.

"Certainly I have been," said he. "A girl that you can't fall in love with at first is not going to be worth having as a friend later on."

"I've never heard of such an idea as that," said I.

"You never would, my learned Puritan," said Granville. "No, you never would, and I suppose that you see me hanged for my affairs."

He laughed at me; he often laughed and kept me from the necessity of making awkward answers.

"The fact is, Charles," said I, "that I never could treat those girls with the same air that you do. I never could do that!"

"True, true, true!" said he, with a pause and a sigh between each word. "You never would, and you never could! And now, what am I to do about that?"

"You see how many difficulties the whole scheme entails?" said I. "And, no matter how thoroughly we master some of the details, others will give us trouble and, in the end, betray us. Unless I am only to appear for a moment in the house of your father."

"The time. That's very important, but I can't exactly tell. It is my hope that you won't have to be there for more than a week. And yet it may be that you will have to stay for a fortnight."

"Impossible!" I cried.

"Because of the girls?"

"Partly that. Yes."

"Well, I'll make a tremendous concession about the girls. I'll gradually grow indifferent to them. I hate this like the devil, but I'll begin to have very little to do with them. I'll—I'll—be seen to yawn when I'm with them!"

"Thank Heaven!" said I.

He hardly seemed to hear me. He sat with his chin resting on his hand and stared blankly before him, as though this sacrifice would make him completely desolate.

"It means throwing away the labors of a lifetime," said he.

It was my turn to smile at him, now, and he didn't mind; in fact, it never hurt his feelings when one laughed at him, and that was a saving grace in a man who was, as I suppose you feel already, a good deal of a rascal. But a pleasant one, you know!

"But it must be done," said he. "It must be done! Isn't it a matter of life or death?"

He stood up and looked gravely at me. "I think I must tell you the exact reasons why I have called on you."

"I wish that you would."

"No, but I'll tell you the most important one. It's a story."

"Thank you."

"We'd been in the woods hunting deer, and when we returned to the lodge that we were using, I came in with cold, half-frozen feet, and stumbled against an old friend of mine, Eustace Baring. He was holding a cup of coffee, and some of the liquid spilled on his hands. He swore a bit and said that I might at least say that I was sorry. I told him not to be a bear, and sat down in front of the stove. 'Bad manners,' said he. 'Horrible manners, Charles.' 'Don't be an ass,' said I, 'I can't learn from you.'

"That irritated him. He said, 'You don't mean that.'

" 'But I do, though,' said I. 'Sit down and stop talking like an idiot, Eustace!' "

"He didn't sit down. He was tired, perhaps. I don't know what was the matter with him. I felt a cold shadow fall over me. I looked up, and there was Eustace, his face white.

" 'I won't have such talk,' said he quietly.

" 'Stuff!' said I, trying to bluff it through. 'You are really an ass, Eustace.'

" 'I won't ask you to explain that remark to me,' said he. 'But perhaps you will to a friend of mine.'

"And with that, he walked out of the lodge into the cold night. I looked around me. Everyone was serious. It worried me. Because a great many of us Southerners are such punctilious idiots, you know! I never have been. I've never gone in for that sort of thing. But most of the rest of the boys I know do. You can't push friendship past a certain point with them. You can't really know them unless your grandfather was chums with their grandfathers, and even then you have to be pretty polite or there'll be the devil to pay. But I'd grown up with Eustace Baring, and I really was staggered when Channing Lipton walked into the house the next day and made me a stiff bow.

" 'Hello, Chan,' said I. 'What's wrong? Are you on the stage?'

" 'I'm representing Mr. Eustace Grinnold Baring,' said he. He was speaking a set piece, you see. 'And I have come to ask you for an explanation of the words you spoke to him last night in the hunting lodge after—'

"Ah, the devil! You see what it was? A challenge to a duel! A duel with Eustace Baring! What a horrible idea! I couldn't do anything but accept, and three days before I was to die—"

"You were to die?" I interrupted.

"Yes, yes. Wouldn't have had a chance against him. Why, I've seen that fellow stand up and crack the stems of the two wine glasses with two shots at twenty paces! Quick shots, mind you! Well, as I was saying, just before I was to die he came down with a fever, had a slow recovery, and then had to go abroad for his health. But the devil of it is that he is coming back, and I have the following affectionate letter from him:

" 'DEAR CHARLES: I have begged your pardon before for my long delay. I am returning within six weeks. Then we can settle our little affair.'

" 'Little affair' to him, you see! But death to me. Am I to stand there and be shot at by an expert such as he is? Why, he has killed three men already! Tell me, old boy, did you ever really kill a man?"

CHAPTER XVI

I Change Color

IT seemed an odd question, popping out at me like that.

"Yes," I said at last.

"Really?" said he. "Then they haven't actually lied when they said that you were a great fighter! It was a fair fight, of course?"

"An Indian chief had taken a fancy to a pony I owned," I told Granville. "My mother had bought him to celebrate my fourteenth birthday, and the Comanche waylaid me. It was rather a close thing."

"The devil shot at you from the brush!"

"Yes."

"But he missed you?"

"No. His bullet knocked me off my horse."

"Hello! But you said you killed him!"

"He came to take my scalp, you see, but I got my senses back as he grabbed my hair. So I managed to stab him."

He leaned back and whistled. "How old were you?"

"Fourteen."

"My God!" said he. "Did you ever kill another?"

I sighed. "I don't like to talk about those things," said I.

"But they say that you are a great hand with weapons of all kinds. And you are, aren't you?"

"It gets away from your story," said I.

"No, no, it's the most essential part of it, as you'll understand in a few minutes. Look there—the frog on that branch that sticks out of the water—could you hit that?"

"I suppose so," said I, and I brought out a Colt from its holster beneath my arm and fired. The water was sliced across its surface, and the stain of the mangled body of the frog spread slowly.

Granville whistled again. And then he nodded. "That's just what I was led to expect," said he. "But how did you get that revolver into your hand?"

"By practicing two hours a day for ten years," I told him with a smile. "But I'd like to hear about your duel. I suppose that you'll be practicing for it?"

"Yes, of course, for everyone expects me to do so. I whang away at a target for a while every day, but my heart isn't in it. I never could be a good shot, and I'm not much interested in fighting. But of course you guess at my way out? When the day comes for the duel, you'll be the man who stands up to Eustace Baring!"

And he leaned back and laughed joyously. I was too stunned to make any answer.

He went on with a sort of childish pleasure, "I think that God put the great idea in my heart in the first place, that day on the boat, after I'd heard about your shooting skill. And here we are working out the great idea in detail! Like a fairy tale, I'd call it!"

Hot words came boiling up in my throat; then I remembered that I owed my life to this man, and was silent.

I allowed myself to say, after a pause, "Suppose that I kill Eustace Baring?"

"Of course you will!" said Granville. "And doesn't he deserve it for being so bull-headed about such a little thing?"

Well, I saw that there was no use arguing over such a matter. If God had not made him capable of seeing the shameful cowardice and treachery of his plan, it would be foolish for me to try to explain. Then I showed him the other side of the picture.

"Suppose that *I* am killed?"

His face wrinkled up.

"Of course," said he, "that's a bare possibility. But I hate to think of it. It would mean that I could never come back to my home. I'd have to be a beggar in the world! A beggar and a stranger!"

I thought that he might have something to say about me, but he didn't. The man was entirely wrapped in himself.

"But that will never happen!" said he, shaking his head with violence to reassure himself. "I know that it will never happen—it *couldn't* happen! And all will turn out

97

as it should! The moment I saw your face I knew that you were a man who couldn't be beaten!"

I was silent again.

And then he went on, "How beautifully it'll work out! You drop Baring, put him out of the way, and that same night I come back into the house!"

I couldn't talk. My heart was too filled with contempt and disgust at hearing him speak in this fashion.

And he bubbled straight on:

"After that, of course, it will be easy. I'll see that you're handsomely rewarded—"

I could stand it no longer. I thundered at him, "Don't mention money to me again, so long as I'm connected with you! Do you think that I can be bought to do a murder?"

He wasn't offended. No, he was an odd fellow. He simply stared at me for a moment, nodding.

"I understand," said he. "You're really a moral, fine fellow; whereas I'm a scamp, not very brave and not very good, though really better and braver than you suspect—but let that go! In the meantime, we're overlooking the facts of the case. I wanted to talk to you about the horses and the dogs on the place, to-day. That's important, too!"

And in an instant, he had plunged deep into a chat about the natures and the qualities of the horses in his father's stable, and about the dogs in his hunting pack.

You see, Granville was simply different from most men; there was little or no moral sense in him. And yet, I liked him a great deal. Perhaps you will, too, before the end.

We finished our interview that day and he left, saying that he would try to come to me at least once every two days, and so he did. I won't give any more details of the manner in which I worked. It meant slaving for twelve hours a day, and the only really amusing part, now, was to hear the reports of Granville when he came back and talked about the things he had done.

"By heavens, old boy!" he cried the next time he came back. "You've no idea what's happened! The girls haven't minded a bit my new ways! The more careless I am about them, the more interested they seem. And when they hear that I'm studying law, and haven't much spare time, they're still *more* interested!"

"You're studying law?" I asked him.

"Yes. I mean, I sit in the library with some of father's big books spread out before me. He almost fainted with joy when I told him that I intended to take up the work. Good old father! Not half the dragon that he seems. But I have to sit for three or four hours a day in my library, pretending to pore over those stupid tomes. What a dreadful bore the law is, though!"

"I'll have to carry that work on?"

"I suppose so. I pity you, old man. But I had to think of some way of explaining the change in me. The men think it very strange and they're inclined to laugh at me, but the sharp-eyed girls that I feared so much—why, confound it, with one exception, they like me better than ever!"

"And who is the one exception?"

"Of course, my sister. Nancy told me this morning that I was growing simply silly. Nothing can escape the eagle eye of that girl, once she's interested enough to give one a look!"

I nodded. I began to feel that I would have to be on my guard, concerning Nancy! Everything that I heard about her made her seem more dangerous.

But certainly I felt that Granville was setting the stage for me with a consummate skill, and as the days passed a greater and a greater confidence rose in me.

And then came the last visit.

Next day Granville was to start for New Orleans. The hospital was on the outskirts of the city. He detailed the situation to me carefully. He was to have a room in an outer wing. He would be there only three days, and he had insisted on making the trip alone!

So, the next morning, I washed the dye from my hair, left beard and mustache scraggly, and put on some sloppy, coarse clothes which he had brought for me. Then I rowed down the river to the steamboat landing beneath St. Pierre.

It was our hope that, with the black taken out of my hair, no one would ever notice a resemblance between me

99

and big Granville. But as I walked up the gangplank to the boat a man rushed up behind me and clapped me on the shoulder:

"Hello, Charlie! Going fishing?"

I turned around with a scowl, and the young fellow jumped back with an exclamation.

"Pardon!" said he. "Extraordinary resemblance!"

Of course, it had brought my heart into my throat; but at the same time I couldn't help being rather pleased, for if I could be taken for Granville with red hair and red beard, would not the resemblance be almost perfect?

There was little danger, therefore, that I would be identified as the ruffian who, those weeks before, had made so much trouble in Hardin; and, as a matter of fact, I had been so bleached by the steams of the marsh, and I was now so thoroughly in the character of Granville, that no one suspected me as I went down the river.

When we landed at New Orleans, I waited in the town until after dark; then I went out to the edge of the city and overlooked the situation of the little hospital.

Two days I waited. And on the third day I crept into the window of the wing which had been described to me, and found myself in a pleasant, moonlit room, standing beside the bed of Charles St. Maurice Granville.

He shook my hand with a feverishly strong grip.

"It's a success!" he said in a cautious voice. "I can speak and not recognize my own tones, though I don't let the doctor know that. I keep my voice under my hat. The throat is practically healed. Old man, are you willing to make the change now?"

I said that I was. I had dyed my hair and beard, of course, and in a brief half hour, the complete change had been made. I lay in the bed, and Charles Granville had gripped my hand in farewell, and climbed out the window in the loose, shaggy clothes which I had worn coming in. I carefully cleared away all signs of the footsteps going and coming. And then I lay down again in bed with a thundering heart, and hardly knowing whether or not my soul was actually my own or that of Charles St. Maurice Granville.

CHAPTER XVII

My First Test

AND yet I fell asleep!

I have wondered at that in all the years which followed. Surely my nerves did not exist in those days, and I was a man of iron. I presume that I had not lain stretched in that bed an hour, turning wild thoughts back and forth and half yielding to a frantic desire to flee, when my eyes closed, and I wakened only to find a broad shaft of sun striking across the room.

It was well on in the morning, and how long had it been since I wakened later than dawn? I got up, shaved, dressed, and ate two little tablets which young Granville had given to me. They had some astringent property which puckered the muscles of the throat and seemed to coarsen the tender membranes, so that I became decidedly hoarse. Perhaps I rather overdid the thing, for when some one knocked on the door I hardly had enough voice to bid him enter.

In came the doctor, beaming at me, and very well pleased with himself.

He bade me good morning. When I answered, he became grave and attentive.

"Well, well, Mr. Granville," said he, "I hoped to bring you a fuller voice, but I thought that yours was at least a half octave higher!"

I bit my lip and said nothing. He asked after the condition of my throat. I was afraid that he would want to examine it again, and of course that was a thing which I could not permit without betraying myself at once, but he was not in the least concerned with seeing it. When I said that I wished to go home at once, he quite agreed with me; declared that the operation had been an entire success, but that I should be careful to wash out the throat twice a day until all soreness left it. He told me that when-

101

ever I had a cold, for a year or two, I might be bothered with some hoarseness, but it would never again be as bad as it had been before.

I had breakfast at the hospital, thanked the doctor, and an hour later was on the way to the city. The doctor, however, would not take any money, and my only mistake had been in offering to pay my bill. For he received a fee once a year for caring for all the ailments of the family. I remembered then that, according to Charles Granville, everything worked upon a basis of credit throughout the South, but this little incident showed me how careful I would have to be to avoid error. No matter how fully I had been instructed by Granville, or how thoroughly I had studied my lesson, there would still be a great deal that I had not mastered.

When I got into the city, I could not make up my mind to take the river steamer straight for St. Pierre. Instead, I went to a hotel and got a room. And being now Charles St. Maurice Granville, my purse well filled with gold, of course I could not possibly go to any but the best hotel, and there I had to take the finest room. The manager showed me to a huge apartment, and I looked about and declared that the carpet looked badly frayed beneath the window.

As a matter of fact, it wasn't at all. But the manager agreed with me. He said that it was the fault of the service in the hotel, and that he could never get men to fulfill his orders efficiently. He begged me to let him know in what way he could serve me, and when I declared that I could think of nothing for the present, he bowed himself out of the room. He just paused at the door to say that he had often had the pleasure of entertaining my father and grandfather at the hotel and that he trusted he could make me as comfortable as he had seemed to make them.

He disappeared, and I sat by the window and looked down at the street, where a handsome carriage was passing, drawn by two dancing bays. While I watched, there was a tap at the door, and a Negro boy came in. He had been assigned to me by the manager. As far as I could make out, he was simply to stand about and wait on me, or run on any errands that I might require.

I could see that a Granville was a great man in New Orleans, and again I shrank from the thing before me. But I had hardly let that thought come gloomily over me when there was another tap at the door, and the little black boy went to answer it. He turned and announced that Mr. Raymond Ellison Whitmore was calling on me. And then a young fellow of twenty-four or five burst in and came toward me, waving his hand: "Dash it, Charlie," said he, "what a ghost you've turned into! I believe all the reports that we've been hearing about you lately!"

"What reports, Ray?" I asked him, fumbling desperately through my mental notes to locate his face history.

"Reports that you're turning into a sour person, studying for the ministry and—"

"Law," said I.

"Well, it's all one. One profession or another. What's the difference? And that you've sworn off drinking parties; and that you go to bed early and rise early; and that you turn your back on the pretty girls, and the prettier the face the quicker you turn your back! But I could believe everything except the last, you dog! But oh, man, where's your tongue? Why don't you tell me something?"

"I haven't had a chance," I answered truly enough.

"Zounds!" said he, blinking. "What's happened to your voice?"

"I've been in the hospital having that obstruction in my throat taken out," I told him.

"And the doctor cut the baritone out of your throat as well as the obstruction?" asked Raymond Ellison Whitmore.

"I suppose he did."

"Look here, Charlie, hang me if you're not drawing back into your shell exactly as they said you were doing these days! Are you going to turn me out in a minute, and say that you have some book work to do?"

I laughed, and he looked at me with greater wonder still.

"They've changed your laugh, too, Charlie," said he.

103

"And you never used to tilt your head back that way when you laughed."

"There used to be a hand gripping my throat on the inside," I told him, "and now the fingers of that hand have been taken away."

"Hum!" said he. "Poetically expressed. Hand gripping your throat—fingers relaxed— Hell! my dear boy, when did you begin to talk like this?"

I stared at him, and my heart was rapidly sinking.

"I suppose that you'll be sulking in another while," said Whitmore. "But before you get in the dumps, you'll offer me a drink, I suppose?"

I told the boy to bring him what he wanted. He asked for a mint julep, and the youngster turned to me.

"Hello, Charlie!" cried Whitmore. "You're not drinking with me, I suppose?"

"Whisky," said I, absently, for my mind was lost in many worries about the future.

If I had failed to impress this young chap as a faultless likeness of Charles Granville, and if he found my voice and my laughter and my manner strange, then what would the test result in when I came into Granville House, and was surrounded by people who had known Charles for all his days?

Then Whitmore leaned over from his chair and touched my shoulder.

"I know, old fellow," said he. "I know. Matter of fact, everyone knows! It's because that devil of a Baring comes back next Wednesday. We've all known that you were worried about it. And you wouldn't be human if you *weren't* worried!"

"Then why are all of you so hard on me?" I asked him.

"Shall I tell you, old fellow?"

"Yes, tell me frankly."

"Because you used to have plenty of bubble and froth. Do you remember when your father said that one good breath would blow all of you and me helter-skelter away?"

"I remember, of course," I lied.

"You were really the jolliest fellow in the world in those days, but how confoundedly you've changed within the last month. Changed in every way. Creep into New Orleans, and never send a word to an old comrade that you're here!"

"How else have I changed?" I asked him.

"Well, the bubble and froth have gone. Heavy handed, solemn faced—and how long have you had that crease between the eyes? But the men I've heard talk say that they think you're trying to—well, to make a good impression on the serious part of the world before Baring—well—"

"Before he kills me?"

"I hate to say that!"

"As a matter of fact, Ray," said I, "the prospect of that duel has made me think things over a bit. I started wondering what the devil I amounted to and why anybody should want to keep me alive on earth. I couldn't think of any reason."

"What? No reason? The finest old chap in the world—and couldn't think of any reason?"

"I hadn't done a thing worth mentioning, and it didn't seem that I ever *would* do a thing. You understand? I decided that I would start then and on the spot to get ready for work. And that's what I've been doing ever since. Practicing with a revolver every day, and drudging at the law, and trying to get my feet down in touch with a soberer earth. Isn't that worth while?"

He stared at me, shaking his head and sighing.

"It's all true!" said he. "By the way, do you know that the governor says that he'll prevent this duel from taking place if he has to call out every man in the militia of the State?"

"I hope he does!" I said with feeling.

"That's frank. By the way, how is your shooting? How is your hand? Steady?"

I couldn't resist a bit of a trick. I snapped out a revolver and held it straight at his head.

"Does the barrel tremble, Ray?" I asked him.

"By gad, by gad!" he breathed, blinking at me. "Steady as a rock. And you look grim as the devil. Why, I begin to think that Eustace Baring is to be pitied! Ah, here are the drinks!"

"Ray," said I, "come up the river and home with me, will you?"

"Hello!" he laughed. "That's more friendly. And what shall I do there?"

"Propose to Nancy, of course."

"Ah, that's more like your old self. And that's exactly what I should do before I'd been in the house a day. Suppose that I go?"

"Do," said I. "Because I may have a serious need of you!"

CHAPTER XVIII

Four-in-Hand

IN the manner which you have seen, I had become a criminal impersonator. I now went further and became a forger, for I wrote a letter from the hotel addressed to Colonel Peter St. Maurice Granville, at Granville House, St. Pierre, and in the letter I said:

DEAR FATHER: The operation has worked wonders. My voice has come back to me, and much deeper and stronger than I expected. It surprises me constantly. The doctor says that the removal of the obstacle in my throat would naturally lower the pitch of my tones. But still the change is so great that when I speak I hardly feel like myself.

I am coming back at once, very keen to get to work again, and also keen to do a bit of cross-country work. I hope that Palomides will be up to the mark.

Affectionately, your son,
CHARLES.

Palomides was the best horse in the string which Charles Granville habitually rode. I had learned all about his looks and his ways, and also that Charles Granville loved to ride cross country. I had been in an English saddle only a few times, but I trusted myself on the back of almost any horse with any saddle, or none at all. On the plains, one rode whatever came in one's way, of course. And after the pitching broncos that I had learned horsemanship on, I felt that I should be able to steer the stiffest of cross-country runners over hedge and ditch. But what was important in that letter was not what I said, but the signature at the bottom of the sheet. "Charles" was the important word, and I thought that I had it perfectly, the letters running downhill a bit and the final "s" tangled in a complicated scrawl.

I was glad of Whitmore's company on the way back. He had his baggage down at the boat just in time the next morning, and I think that he hardly stopped talking and bubbling all the way up the river, until the ship stopped at St. Pierre.

I shall never forget the emotion that swept over me as I stood on the deck and looked across at the sleepy old town of St. Pierre, with the mist tangling across the top of the big town hall, and all the life in the place flowing down toward the steamer landing. For every time a steamer landed, St. Pierre postponed all other functions and assembled en masse to watch the passengers flock down the gangplank.

I often think, now, that such things could hardly have taken place in this United States of ours, and that surely there was more sleep than life in the old South. For there was never any hurry, and though there might be a pinch in such matters as food, clothes, and lodging, there was always a vast superfluity of time. Yet things were done. Important things were done. And now though I admit that our hurry enables us to manufacture more automobiles and automobile roads, more clothes, more spades, more ships and railroads—yet I wonder if we have not paid for our advantages, and if the leisure of the old times did not give men a chance for thinking better and more important thoughts?

But there I was stepping down the gangplank of that ship and onto the shore; no, stepping out of an old life and into a new one! At least, I was glad that it was now the evening; and that it would be after sunset before we could really drive out to the house.

No!

For Whitmore exclaimed: "There they are! Hello, Nan!"

He began to stand on tiptoe and wave his hat frantically. And then I saw a slender girl standing in the crowd. No, not actually in it, for the others left her a little space to herself as if by divine right of youth and beauty, and she was waving and smiling back to me.

I lifted my hat.

"My God, man!" cried Whitmore. "No more than that for dear old Nan?"

I was confused and gritted my teeth. I had acted as though I were being shown to a stranger and giving a formal greeting! In fact, I had played the complete ass!

Then Whitmore burst on ahead of me, and the crowd surged past. I walked slowly through it, and came to the girl and Whitmore. One could see that he was mad about her. He fairly trembled with eagerness and delight when he so much as caught her eye, but she was cruelly indifferent to him.

As I came up, she hurried to meet me, smiling. I would only have shaken hands, I think, but she pressed in closer with her face raised.

"Charlie, dear, I'm so happy about it!"

I kissed her, and a fragrance mounted to my brain and left me giddy and uncertain.

"Thank you, Nancy," I managed to say.

And she shrank back instantly from me.

"Charles! Charlie Granville!" she gasped. "What a voice!"

Oh, triple idiot! I had failed to take one of those powerful, caustic tablets which disguised my tones with a little hoarseness, at least.

"Like the town bell, Nan, eh?" said Whitmore. "He isn't at all his true self now, though. Yesterday afternoon he was infernally hoarse, but when his voice really comes to him, I tell you what—everything will be said in low C!"

Well, I could have blessed him with a fervent prayer for that little speech, for it came at just the right time, with Nan Granville staring at me with wide-opened eyes and a streak of horror in them.

And then a husky old Negro was saying: "Ain't we lucky to have you back so soon, Mas' Charlie? Oh, but we is, honey!"

And there was a withered face—not exactly black, but

rather a deep and wrinkled gray—as though time had deposited on that skin a thin scattering of dust. He came to me with his hat in his hand, showing a polished ebony head, surrounded with a narrow fringe of dusty white curls. He was so old that when he smiled his face puckered quite out of the semblance of humanity, and his eyes became two thin beams of light.

I was amazed by the sight of him. And then I recalled him from the gallery of portraits with which my studies had crowded my memory.

"Hello, Uncle Rasmus. Is Palomides going to be ready for me?"

"Askin' foh you night an' day, suh," grinned Uncle Rasmus.

And while Whitmore and Nancy laughed at this, we started for the carriage.

It was such a carriage as I had never seen before. Four fine blood horses drew it. A coachman and old Rasmus sat on the driver's seat.

"But you drive, Charlie, and give us a jolly spin," said Nan.

What? Drive them out for a jolly spin?

That infernal fellow Granville had quite failed to tell me anything about his driving feats!

And I had never in my life had the reins on anything other than mule teams along the mountain trails in the summer months, when the hunting moons were bright golden over the Rockies! I hesitated just a moment.

Soon or later I would have to handle the reins on a team of horses, and I had a desperate desire to get the thing over with now. If they were going to discover me, let them discover at first and at once!

"*I* won't scream!" said Nan. "Not even if you gallop down Cherry Hill, the way Lorrie Wace did! Go ahead, Charlie!"

That determined me.

Old Rasmus climbed down and I sprang up to the driver's seat before a new and paralyzing thought came to me.

I had undertaken to drive these people home—and I didn't know the way!

Oh, yes, back in my mind there was printed a map of St. Pierre, and a list of the roads leading out from it; but my thoughts were whirling so wildly, by this time, that I knew it would be vain for me to attempt now to bring them into any order.

I gathered the reins, and the wild-eyed leaders snapped against their collars instantly. The carriage lurched—there was a shout from Whitmore, and a squeal from Nan.

"Charles, you're absolutely a devil!" cried Whitmore. "You nearly caught Nan under the wheel that time!"

It sent a shudder through me. The whole team at that moment got into action, however, and from then on I had my own present problem to think about and couldn't afford regret for follies of the past.

How would we get out of town? Well, suppose that the leaders, who seemed so full of the devil, were really only anxious to get home to the familiar rack of hay and the oat box in the corner of the manger?

There was nothing else that I could trust to. For my meeting with Nancy had so completely unnerved me that I knew I could never unravel the information which was somewhere at the back of my mind, like a name that had slipped from the tip of one's tongue.

The team went on. I kept on the leaders a check just tight enough to prevent them from passing out of a slow trot. And I did not try to overrule them when they swung off toward the right. Though my heart failed me, for they were heading down a narrow little dark lane, and I was sure that it could not be the broad highway that pointed on the map from St. Pierre to Granville House.

But there was no protesting word from any one in the carriage. It was a light coach, rather than a carriage, and it reminded me of the stage coaches which used to crash through the streets of Fort Bostwick now and then. After all, I had handled six wild mules as they galloped along a mountain road; and why should I not be able to handle four horses? Aye, but mules never had in them the fire that was lodged in the breasts of these fine animals!

They jogged out of St. Pierre. The better-built portion of the town lay behind us, and the constant hallooing of

111

the coachman on the box beside me cleared from before us the rabble of Negro children who were playing in the deep dust of the street.

"All right, Charlie. Nan wants speed!"

That from Whitmore behind me!

But I didn't care what Nan wanted. I was not going to create any crisis which would show my lack of skill with the reins. Yes, I could dimly remember, now that Granville had said something about four-in-hand driving.

So I let the team out at a trot as they came to a broad straight stretch of roadway.

"Oh, Charlie!" called out Whitmore, "this is too bad! We're being choked by our own dust!"

"Talking won't do any good," said Nan. "Charles is fond of yarning about daring things; he doesn't like to do 'em."

CHAPTER XIX

A Wild Ride

CHARLES had told me a good deal about the sharp tongue of Nancy; but this was my first taste of it, and it pricked me almost as deep as the heart, I can tell you. Yes, I had fallen into rather a sentimental trance about this young girl, and now I was roused suddenly out of it.

"Charlie likes to yarn about daring things, but he doesn't like to do 'em!"

And there was the coachman on the seat beside me swallowing a grin with difficulty! Nan's words painted a more complete portrait of Granville than any that I had been able to make before. Certainly a man who had another fight his duel for him was not a hero. But now I could see that the girl had merely been using a bit of unkind irony when she had asked me to drive out. Charles Granville's driving was evidently a joke across the countryside!

Well, I had taken his character, and it would be as well for me to stay inside of it.

The roadbed grew better and the dust less.

"They might canter a bit," called Nan, very cross. "The carriage can't very well topple over at a canter, you know!"

But I kept them to a trot, though a brisker one. And the grin of the Negro grew more hard to restrain. I wanted to take him by the neck and drop him in the road!

"Did Lorrie Wace really gallop down Cherry Hill?"

That from Whitmore, in the carriage behind me.

"Yes," said Nan. "Only last week."

"Gallop?"

"They say that he did!"

"But the corner?"

"Well, he managed it, somehow. He's a daredevil."

"He is, of course!"

113

"And that night in the club he offered two thousand to the next man who made the trip that way with a span."

"He only had a span, then?"

"Of course!"

"Still, it sounds a bit fishy."

"Oh, a hundred people saw him do it. Rod Stickney was with him, and so was Harry Leroy."

The leaders swung from the main highway and I let them go down another lane.

"Oh, bother, Charles! Are you *always* going to be afraid of Cherry Hill, even at a walk?"

I stopped the horses. I was blind with shame and rage. And turning in my seat I said: "I'm going to take you down Cherry Hill!"

I turned that team, and nearly dumped over the carriage doing it.

"Look out, Charlie!"

"He'll get over his huff before he comes to the hill!"

That from Nan. Oh, there was poison in her, I can tell you! I don't know whether the time was long or short before we came to the hill. No, it must have been only a few minutes, for I traveled the same road often enough afterward. But I was in a haze of fury, red, flecked with swirling spots of black.

Then the team topped a sudden rise and I looked down at a long, winding, criminally narrow street that twisted away to the left with a snaky suddenness at the bottom. That was Cherry Hill! And on either side of the way were houses, built right up to the edge of the road and seeming to crowd together at the bottom and limit it to the narrowness of a cow trail.

I motioned the Negro to throw on the brakes, and we screeched to a halt.

"I suppose we're going to have it at a walk," said Nancy sarcastically.

"Do you want to take it at a trot?" I asked her, keeping iron control over my voice.

"What a jolly old joker you are!" said Nan. "Five dollars that you don't trot it all the way!"

"And you, Ray?"

"Why, old boy, I'll go you fifty on that."

"And suppose I gallop it, Nan?"

"Oh, Charlie, what a silly thing to say!"

"Suppose that I gallop it, Ray?"

For I was utterly mad, you see, and ready to dash myself to a thousand bits in an effort to prove that I was not quite the same as this Lorrie Wace of whom they had spoken in such high praise.

"I'll tell you, old fellow. Five hundred if you gallop to the bottom," said Whitmore, with a decided sneer.

I turned my back on them. I was trembling with fury and it was a moment before I could say: "I'll take both those bets. Take off the brake!"

The coachman stared at me.

"Take off that brake!" I called.

He released it, with a scared look that gave me a sweet satisfaction. Oh, I was insane, I grant you freely, but if you had seen Nan Granville on that day and heard her talk as I heard her talk, you would understand me perfectly and not ask me to feel ashamed.

The brake went off, the wheels were released, and the carriage rolled up on the heels of the wheelers. I gave the leaders rein, and flicked the flank of the near one with the whip. I shall never forget the startled way in which that fine horse shrank from the touch and threw its head high and sidewise, with a red rolling of his eye, as though to ask me what sort of madness this could be.

So the carriage lurched forward for the descent of Cherry Hill on that momentous day, and in another moment the horses had passed from a trot to a canter.

"By heavens," cried Whitmore, "he's mad! He intends to do it! Stop, Charlie, you utter fool!"

I couldn't help turning my head and glancing back, and there was Nan sitting stiff and straight.

"Will you beg me to stop, Nan?" I asked her. "And pay your bet?"

"Charles," she said, "don't be contemptible. I'd rather be smashed to flinders than ask any one to take back a bet!"

Here there was a frightened screech from the coach-man. The brake had stuck, and he couldn't work it.

"Mas' Charles!" he screamed. "We gunna die—the brake—"

And the hysterical fellow leaped from the seat. Luckily he crashed into a bush at the side of the road, which was all that kept him from breaking every bone in his body.

Now that he was out of the way, I shifted over to the right of the seat and laid hold of the brake handle. It was lodged tight, but I loosed it with one jerk and thrust the handle forward.

I felt a jerk in response as the wheels locked and began to plow deep in the dust of the hill, gripping hungrily for the sounder earth beneath. They were like four blunt plowshares eating a scant distance into the ground, but even so they could not do more than slow the carriage to a trotting pace, for the descent was really at a fearful angle.

We came down to a trot, but only for an instant. I took the whip in one hand and the reins in the other, and I laid on the lash with a shout. It brought a yell of terror from Whitmore—but not a sound from the girl. Shame should have made me stop, after that, but there was no shame in me. The four horses, smarting under the whip, were galloping freely. The wheels, locked though they were, now bounced along, merely knocking up a cloud of dust, and twice the whole vehicle skidded terribly forth to one side and then to the other.

And then there was a babble of voices before us. I saw a woman dart from her house, scoop up a toddling young-ster, and leap back inside her doorway. With a great shout I gave warning to all that might be before us, and then we struck the deadly angle at the bottom of the hill.

I let the leaders gallop freely around it, for I thought I might need their speed beyond. The wheelers had the full force of my pull and it threw them back on their haunches. With planted feet they skidded through the dust, the pole of the carriage shooting far up and ahead

116

until the pull of the breechings steadied it. Then the wheelers lurched staggering to their feet.

We had turned the corner, but I felt sure that the next instant we would crash into the front of the house at our right.

Only speed that had brought us into this danger could snatch us out again.

Wheelers once more!

I gave the near one a powerful jerk to the left and a terrible slash of the whip. He leaped ahead, maddened with pain and fear, and the carriage swished past the face of the first house on two wheels—staggered for a fall— and then my reaching lash caught the leaders and sent them off racing. Their lurch caught the carriage in the nick of time. For fifty yards we balanced in a horrible suspense, and then the carriage came down with a crash, swayed far to the left, and settled again to the road while we shot out of the village of Cherry Hill onto the open and easy road beyond.

Let them all have the whip, now! It was pure joy and relief to let the horses race, and the carriage lurched and bounced like a bubble behind as they flew down the road. After all, this was like driving mules on a trail. Twice as fast, but not half so rough. I was beginning to feel every horse on the reins, and in another half mile I was perfectly at home.

"The gate!" screamed Whitmore, finding his voice again.

And to the left I saw a great iron gate, with a cloudy park of trees beyond it. I thrust on the brake and pulled in the wheelers, and by the grace of God we got through that gate—though heeling far over to the right as we did so.

Up the driveway we spun. The white face of a great, low-lying house grew out before us through the dusk. And so I drew rein, at last, before Granville House.

I climbed down and handed the reins to a groom who had come running at our approach.

I turned back to the carriage, from which Whitmore

117

was descending shakily. But his good humor was already back.

"You devil, Charlie," he laughed, "I never guessed that such stuff was in you. You've nicked me for five hundred. And you've scared me out of eight lives, too."

I looked to see Nan a white ghost of a woman.

No, she was covered with dust, but her head was high, and her cheeks and eyes were flaming. She threw herself out of the carriage and into my arms and kissed the dust on both my cheeks.

"Charlie, Charlie, Charlie!" she cried to me. "Oh, what a glorious day for us all!"

CHAPTER XX

At Granville House

I INTRODUCE you to Mr. and Mrs. Peter St. Maurice Granville as they stood at the door of their house and looked out from among the tall, slender, white pillars.

"Hello, Nan! What's this—a dust storm you've been through?"

And the tall old man with the white mustache, white Vandyke, and flowing long, white hair, brushes past Nan and takes my hand.

"How is it, my dear boy? Hello—husky still, aren't you? And that scoundrel of a doctor hasn't lived up to his promise!"

For I had put one of the valuable little tablets into my mouth and already I could feel it puckering my throat. And then the little woman who had once been so beautiful —yes, who was so beautiful still—came to me and I picked her up in my arms. I had thought it would be the hardest thing of all to do. No, it was the very easiest! The easiest thing that I have ever done in my life!

"Speak to me, Charlie dear!"

I spoke to her.

"Ah, ah!" said she. "What a voice. Peter, you are deaf not to hear the difference. And so much deeper! You promised us that it was. But such a difference! I'll have to get to know your voice all over again!"

We went on into the house.

"And, father—I want you to know—if you had only been there, father dear!"

This from Nancy.

"Well, Nan, what was it?"

"The grandest thing!"

"What was grand?"

"You'll be so proud when you know. You'll hardly believe it!"

"Believe what, Nan?"

"Ask Ray Whitmore, though! He'll tell you! I was frightened almost to death, myself. Weren't you, Ray?"

"I'll answer that I was. But you weren't. You loved it. You sat up and laughed at it all!"

"Caesar is left stuck in a bush in Cherry Hill village, father!"

"What under heaven is all this about?"

"Charlie!"

"Charlie's come home. But what are you talking about?"

"It was the grandest thing that I ever saw. It took the most perfect nerve. I wish I'd been sitting beside him. That's the only thing I wish!"

"Confound all women!" said the colonel suddenly. "My dear, find out what this silly child of yours is talking about?"

"He galloped us down Cherry Hill—the carriage and four! Think of it, Colonel Granville!"

"By gad!" said the colonel under his breath. "Do you mean that?"

"Ask Caesar if I mean it! He was so frightened that he leaped off the driver's seat and landed in a bush—"

"The scoundrel shall have the whip, for that. No—I'll sell him! Look at me, Charlie. Don't hang your head in a corner. Is this true? Did you gallop Cherry Hill, you unspeakable rascal? Did you risk the neck of my little girl for such a nonsensical thing as that?"

It was nonsensical, and thinking back to it, my courage melted and left me shaking. For suppose that I had hurt so much as a hair of her head—

Ah, but there she was, laughing and then smiling, and smiling and then laughing. She was a glorious thing to see at that moment.

And the colonel? As he looked at me, I thought that something like a film disappeared from his eyes, and he saw with a new vision.

"Come in here and sit down, all of you. You need a drink. That's the first thing. Then we'll let you go to your rooms. Are all the arrangements for Ray ready, my dear?"

"Everything," said Mrs. Granville. "But I'm going to have a last look."

"Not now, Mrs. Granville," he pleaded. "Please not now!"

"It's a rule that I've never broken in thirty years," said she. "Should I break it now and let you run a risk of being uncomfortable?"

Off she went, and a little battalion of Negresses formed behind her and went away down the hall. Nancy, who had been so shining and happy, disappeared with a like suddenness, and I found myself sitting in a great, dark library, with the newly lighted lamps beginning to cast glimmering highlights along the ranges of volumes. This was the room in which Charles Granville had carried on his farcical studies. Here I must sit also, above the big law books.

"Now I want the whole story," said the colonel.

"And I'll tell you," said Whitmore, "because it was the rarest thing that I ever—"

"I beg your pardon, Ray," said I. "I'll give it all the telling it needs. I was taunted a bit by Nan about the way Wace galloped Cherry Hill. We put a bet and a dare on it. And so I had to go through with it. That's all there is to it."

"Tush! Nonsense!" said Ray. "That's the ruin of the best story I know about. It was this way, colonel. As we got to the top of the hill—"

"I'll have to go up to my room," said I.

"Let it go," said Mr. Granville. "You mustn't drive him away, you know!"

"All right," said Ray Whitmore. "Brave and modest. Jack the giant killer! If I can't tell that story now, I'm going up to my room straight off. It's the same one I had last time?"

"My wife is there now, Ray: Run along, then."

Whitmore left us and, that instant, the colonel came over and took a chair close to mine. I could see that he was filled with a great and joyous emotion, but he could find no words for it.

121

"Charles," said he, "you've come back to us on the heels of unhappy news."

"What news, sir?"

"Eustace Grinnold Baring reached his home this afternoon!"

I nodded.

"Then he'll want to have me out at dawn, I suppose?"

"Yes."

"I'm sorry!"

"How sorry are you, Charles?" he asked me suddenly.

"As deeply sorry as a man can be."

"But—not nervous about it, my boy? Not after the trick that you turned this afternoon, I suppose!"

"That's not a duel. But I'm not nervous. No, yet I'd do anything in the world to call off this engagement."

"Everything except apologize, I hope?"

"Apologize? Gad, I would do it in a moment," I told him.

He stood up before me, tall and thin and straight, and a terrible anguish was on his face.

"Charles, do you mean what you are saying?"

"I could never apologize to him, because it would break your heart, and Nan would kill herself for shame."

"Ah, lad! And no shame on your own part?"

"None whatever. Baring is a good fellow."

"My dear Charles, certainly he is! Otherwise he would not be fit to fight a duel with a Granville!"

This viewpoint staggered me a little, and, since I had risen in turn, I rested my hand on the back of my chair and steadied myself while I studied the colonel. He was a rare old fellow. Like a sword blade. A little fine worn with age, but still possessed of a keen biting edge.

"But," said I, "the thing has gone on so long that I suppose there is no means of stopping the battle?"

"None, none! I shudder to hear you suggest such a thing!"

And he added: "It's a torture for me to hear you speak like this, Charles!"

"Ah, sir," said I, "you're not understanding. If I fight

with him in the morning, I'll kill him. And I don't want the blood of a decent man on my hands!"

"You're very sure, Charles!" said the colonel, peering at me.

"I am," said I.

"Sure and steady about it," he went on, nodding as he repeated the words. "Sure and steady! Well, well!"

He could not take his eyes from me.

"Charles," he said suddenly, "you're like a new man!" And he added: "Gloriously new!"

He took me by the arm and led me through the back of the house, taking a candle as he went. Out into the yard we went, and there he lighted the candle and wedged it in the top of a post twenty yards away.

"Could you hit that flame, Charles?" said he.

The faintly stirring wind fanned the candle flame short to one side, and almost put it out.

"If I do, sir," said I, "will you try to stop this wretched duel?"

"I? Yes, by heavens, I would!"

"Then mind you, sir—I'll put out the flame but not cut the candle!"

No hip shooting for that, of course. I took out the revolver and dropped it on the mark at the end of a stiff arm. The light glimmered up the barrel, caught in the sights—and I fired.

"Too low! Too low!" I called, as the light went out.

The colonel, with an exclamation, ran and brought the candle. Together we hurried into the house and there he stopped under the first light.

The top of the candle was deeply cut away where half the width of the bullet had gouged through the tallow. Colonel Granville stared at it for a long moment and then looked up to me.

"Charlie," said he, "I may be frightfully misunderstood if I do this thing—but to-night I'm going to call at the Barings' and give them warning of what they may expect. Only—forgive me, Charles—a lighted candle is not a man!"

I could not help smiling a little, for I thought of some

of the fighting men who had walked into the store at Fort Bostwick. The colonel did not ask for any other answer, but he hooked his arm through mine as we walked back into the library.

CHAPTER XXI

Unworthy of a Gentleman

I REMEMBER that that night during dinner there were pauses and stops in the conversation, and perhaps the meal would have been quite serious and dull if it had not been for Ray Whitmore, who was always ready to fill in every breach. But I knew what caused the silences. The family could not forget that by to-morrow, perhaps, I would lie dead on the field with a bullet from the pistol of Eustace Baring through my heart.

And I have always felt that that feeling must have smoothed over my first evening. For what there was strange about me they failed to observe very closely. Perhaps that foolish gallop down Cherry Hill may have made them a little sharper at watching me, but the sharpness was soon lost in a wave of tenderness and sorrow. And yet it seemed most wonderful to me that no one dreamed of suggesting that the duel be postponed, and that the only way in which I could get the colonel to interfere was by showing him that Baring would have very little chance against me.

In the middle of the evening there was a knock from the brazen rapper on the front door, and, a little later, a solemn-faced negro—the butler—came in to announce Mr. Channing Lipton.

I thought that I remembered the name as being that of the man who had carried the first challenge to Charles Granville.

"Mr. Channing Lipton begs to have a few moments of the time of Mr. Charles Granville."

Mrs. Granville jumped up and ran a few steps toward me. But the colonel called to her softly:

"You gave me your promise, my dear!"

"And I know—I know," said she. "I won't make it harder for any of you!"

She threw a look of agony toward me, and I went on past the colonel.

I went into the little study which was Charles Granville's own downstairs room, and there I received Channing Lipton. When he stood in the doorway, I thought him the finest specimen of young manhood that I had ever seen. He was not very tall, and not heavily made, but he was all wire, put together like a fine terrier, and graceful.

"Hello, Channing," said I, for I carefully remembered that this man was an old friend of Charles'.

"Pardon me, sir," said he, "but I believe that you are Charles St. Maurice Granville?"

"I am," said I, frowning a little at this unnecessary formality.

"I am Channing Lipton," said he, "and I am calling not on my own behalf, but on behalf of Mr. Eustace Grinnold Baring, of Baring Manor, Baringdale. I am instructed to deliver a message to you, sir."

I nodded, and offered him a chair, but he remained as stiff as could be and did not seem to understand my gesture which invited him to be seated.

He said: "Mr. Baring wishes me to convey to you again his profound apology for his late treatment of you, and particularly for the manner in which he broke your last engagement. He begs you to believe that it was through no fault of his that the engagement did not take place, and he has sent me to arrange with you whatever formalities may be necessary to resume the course of affairs which was at that time under way. Mr. Baring wishes me to tell Mr. Charles Granville that to-morrow morning, at dawn, he will be waiting at the place which was formerly appointed—that is to say—at the corner of Jefferson Park nearest to the river. Mr. Baring begs to know if the time and the place of the meeting are agreeable to Mr. Charles Granville."

I said stiffly: "Tell Mr. Eustace Baring from Mr. Charles Granville that Mr. Charles Granville will be only too happy to meet Mr. Eustace Baring at the time and the place Mr. Eustace Baring has appointed, and that Mr.

Charles Granville presumes that the weapons to be used at this friendly encounter will be revolvers of the Colt pattern."

"The fashion of weapon is left to Mr. Granville's choice," said the emissary, "but Mr. Eustace Baring had expected that the meeting would take place with dueling pistols, single or double barreled!"

"Mr. Eustace Baring does not object to a Colt for Mr. Granville, if Mr. Granville permits a dueling pistol for Mr. Baring?"

"That, sir, is of course your privilege."

"I have nothing further to say, then."

"Well, that's over, God be praised!" said Lipton, smiling and coming toward me. "And how are you, Charlie, old fellow?"

He shook hands with me, and went on: "You look bigger to me, or is it your bigger voice? I'm tremendously glad that the operation was such a success. And—confound it, Charlie, how happy we'll all be when this wretched affair is over!"

"Yes," said I, a good deal surprised by his change in manner as soon as his message was delivered. "I'd like to have it ended. I'd like it better than anything in the world. What slaves we are to public opinion, eh?"

"Exactly! Exactly!" said he. "You've hit it off to a T. Slaves to it! And I know that Baring is sick of the affair. Though of course he has to go through with it!"

"Chan," said I suddenly, "tell me seriously if you think that the affair could be turned off harmlessly?"

He looked a bit askance at me and said rather coldly: "I don't exactly see what you mean."

I wasn't to be shamed out of saying what I meant, for the solemn and wise face of Marshall O'Rourke remained clearly in my mind's eye, and I had not forgotten his good advice.

"I'll tell you what I mean, in brief. We could fire at one another once or even twice, and after that perhaps Baring would be willing to declare that his honor had been satisfied. We would fire blank cartridges, of course!"

127

A sick look came on the face of Channing Lipton, and he stared uneasily at the floor for a moment.

"I believe," said he stiffly, "that such a thing has never been heard of before, between gentlemen."

"You ass," I cried at him, "do you think that I am afraid of Baring?"

"Very odd language, Granville! Very odd language, sir," said Lipton, getting colder and more edgy than a steel-sword blade.

"Is it odd?" said I. "I have language still more odd at my command. And I could ask you why something new might not be done on the field of 'honor,' as you people call it!"

"And since when, may I ask, have you ceased to be one of these 'people?'" said he.

"The moment that you take to ridiculous customs!" I replied.

"I heard," said he, biting his lip, "that you had galloped a four-in-hand down Cherry Hill to-day. I was hardly prepared to hear such language as this from you this evening, Granville."

I stared at him, growing hotter and hotter.

"You think that I'm in a blue funk about meeting your man Baring," I told him, "but you're wrong. I simply don't want to murder him."

"When men have equal chances," said he, "I believe that their encounter is referred to as an affair of honor, and not murder."

"Equal chances?" said I. "Unless Baring is very different from what I think he is, he has no more chance with me than the man in the moon. He's a dead man if he faces me, Lipton!"

"Of course," said he after an icy pause, "you don't expect me to take these—disheartening messages to my principal?"

"Lipton, you talk like a perfect fool!" I cried.

He answered me like a young tiger showing its teeth: "I've taken one disagreeable speech from you this evening, sir. I shall not swallow the second one!"

I cannot defend the passion into which I flew. But in an

How do your cigarette's tar and nicotine numbers compare with True?

20 CLASS A CIGARETTES

TRUE

MENTHOL FILTER

LATEST U.S. GOVERNMENT TESTS:
13 MGS. TAR, 0.7 MGS. NICOTINE

Place your pack here.

Compare
your cigarette's
tar and nicotine
numbers
with True.

20 CLASS A CIGARETTES

TRUE

FILTER CIGARETTES

LATEST U.S. GOVERNMENT TESTS:
12 MGS. TAR, 0.6 MGS. NICOTINE

No numbers on the front of your pack? True puts its numbers right out front. Because True, regular and menthol, is lower in both tar and nicotine than 99% of all other cigarettes sold. Think about it.

Warning: The Surgeon General Has Determined That Cigarette Smoking Is Dangerous to Your Health.

LATEST U.S. GOVERNMENT TESTS:
12 MGS. TAR, 0.6 MGS. NICOTINE

© Lorillard 1971

Regular or menthol.
Doesn't it all add up to True?

Regular: 12 mg. "tar", 0.6 mg. nicotine,
Menthol: 13 mg. "tar", 0.7 mg. nicotine, av. per cigarette, FTC Report, Aug. '71.

instant all the good teachings of O'Rourke, all of my good resolutions in the meanwhile, seemed to disappear; and suddenly it was as though I was standing behind the counter of the store in Bostwick once more with the chance for a battle opening before me.

"Are you armed?" I asked him.

"I am, sir," said he.

"Then draw your gun," said I. "If it's murder that you people want, I'll start by showing some excellent examples of killing. Draw your gun, Lipton, or I'll make the first move for mine!"

He stared at me, rather pale, his eyes wide with amazement.

"Do you suggest a shooting match in your own house, man?" asked he.

"Is that more absurd than for you to suggest that I would insult you under my own roof?"

"Your language was very free, sir."

"Not as free and strong as I'd like to have it, however. And, as a matter of fact, I don't know that I could find just the breed of word that's needed for this murdering imbecility! I have to kill a man or else he will kill me—for what? For the sake of public opinion! I won't do it! That's flat and final. Baring may be damned with his appointment at dawn, but I'll never go to meet him on such a fool's errand!"

"Man, man," said Lipton, "I want to believe that you mean this honorably!"

"You mean that you want to believe that I'm not afraid?"

"You put it bluntly."

"Then I'll tell you, sir, that I really am not afraid. As for fighting, I've always liked it too well—"

A faint smile flickered across his face, and I saw what it meant. The record of young Granville had decidedly not, it appeared, been one of a fighting man, and now Lipton hardly could control his contempt.

"I understand what that smile means, Lipton," said I. "God give me a steady temper! Now you'd better leave me before I forget myself again with you."

"I think, sir," said he, "that you are commissioning me to return to Eustace Baring and tell him that you will not meet him."

"You are to carry him that message."

"Sir, this will make a tremendous sensation, and I don't need to tell you that it will be a tragedy in the house of your father."

"You don't need to tell me a thing about it. I understand what I am doing."

A silence that grew more terrible each moment fell between us. At length he backed toward the door, passed through it, closed it softly behind him, and without a word disappeared.

I understood. I was now a dog unworthy of a gentleman's speech!

CHAPTER XXII

In Disgrace

WELL, it was a painful trial for me, because at that time I don't think that there was a man in the world with an uglier temper than mine. But, as best I could, I kept in mind the grim face of O'Rourke as it had looked when I last talked with him—as another, more religious, man might have kept through a season of temptation the image of a patron saint.

St. O'Rourke!

Well, I could not smile at the idea just then. I was too sick of the work that lay before me. And that work, I felt sure, must end in a murder, with or without my will. Stand up against these polite sons of polite families? I who had been bred in that terrible school of the great West, hardened by battles with ruffians of every hue, and seasoned on many a war trail? No, I couldn't do it!

And if O'Rourke had been right in feeling that I had taken a vicious advantage of my natural skill with weapons in that land of fighters, how should it be here, where guns were a mere matter of amusement, and not at all of necessity? I felt that I should stick to my point, even though it meant breaking the word that I had plighted to Charlie Granville.

But that did not rest heavily on my conscience. I was here to take all the obloquy that should be heaped on my head. Charles would have to taste the infamy, and before he returned, I hoped to have put him right before the eyes of every man.

Yes, it was a hard thing to do, but it was the right thing to do. I had no doubt about that. It sickened me to think of passing through the ordeal that lay ahead of me, but at the same time I knew that I would have to do it.

I went out of the little study and walked into the living

room, where the family were still sitting. Their grave, stricken faces turned toward me.

"Father," said I, "and the rest of you—I'm not meeting Baring. He invited me for the morning, and I have refused!"

Aye, well! Let me get over it quickly, for it turns my blood cold to remember the horror and the disgust with which Nancy looked at me, for she was a true child of that society. The colonel started up and tried to speak, but the words failed him, and he turned with a groan to his wife, and she to him.

That instant I knew that I was shut out from the family circle.

I withdrew and went up the stairs to Charles Granville's room. I knew it perfectly. He had described everything in it so many times, down to the foolish little secret passage that opened from beside the fireplace, that it was almost like stepping into an old, familiar scene.

I sat down miserably by the window and tried to draw some comfort out of watching the stars, and all at once I wished with all my heart that I had never seen Marshal O'Rourke, for so I should have escaped this crowning misery—and the scorn in the eyes of Nancy Granville!

There was a tap on the door, and when I called out to enter, Nan came in and whipped the door shut behind her.

She said sternly to me: "Do you mean what you've said to us all?"

"Yes," said I.

"Will you tell me your reasons?"

"There's one short one. Young Baring couldn't stand against me. I don't want to commit a murder and call it a duel!"

How her lip curled!

"Young Baring," she said slowly, "breaks the stems of wine glasses at thirty yards!"

"It used to be twenty yards," said I. "But let that go. I've given you my answer. I shall not meet him."

"I understand the gallop down Cherry Hill, now," said she bitterly. "You knew what you intended to do about Baring. And you thought that with one daredevil exploit you'd be able to silence the world. But you won't! You won't! Courage with horses is one thing; courage to face a gun is quite another. Oh, Charlie!"

That heartbreak in her voice almost melted me. I leaped from my chair—and then I slowly sat down again.

"I can't do it," said I, turning sullen.

"Have you a right to break mother's heart and kill our father with shame?"

I hadn't thought of it as strongly as that. It made me wince. After all, it *was* a dreadful shame that I was bringing into the family. And against my oath to Charles Granville.

But I felt that I had one duty more sacred than that oath!

"If this breaks their hearts—their hearts will have to be broken," said I.

"Ah, you coward! You coward!" cried Nan.

I got up and stood towering over her.

"Listen to me," said I, lessoning her with a lifted forefinger. "I understand what you think of me. But I'll tell you that I'm not what you think. You don't know me. They'll scorn me and laugh at me now, but the time will come when they'll have to change their minds. I'm afraid of many things, but not of men or guns. As for the other things that you want to say to me, I don't care to hear them. This is a business which you can't understand. You're blind with pride. Now leave me alone, and never speak of this to me again!"

I expected a flare from that little spitfire, but she merely opened her eyes at me and shrank back out of the room, leaving me to the bitterness of that silent place.

Oh, the night that I spent there!

But the worst time of all was later. I had gone to bed, and five minutes after the light was out, there was a soft stir down the hall, and Mrs. Granville came into the room and leaned over my bed.

"Darling Charlie," she sobbed over me, "try to find courage for the sake of your father. Nothing matters except that. The rest of us don't count. But he's lying on his

133

bed, now, crying like a child! His life is ruined. Oh, Charlie, pray for courage!"

And I said: "I shall pray. I shall pray!"

She left me, and pray I did—stuttering out some sort of an appeal to whatever powers there may be that I might have the courage to stand the strain that was put on me now.

But stand up to poor Baring?

I knew how it would be. Walk, back to back, ten paces from a point of meeting, and at a word of command turn and fire—But how could he bring his gun into position and fire as fast as I could swing about and snap a bullet at him from the hip? And how could I possibly miss a man's heart at twenty paces?

I set my teeth—and presently I was asleep!

When I wakened, the world had turned into a hell for me.

The colonel met me when I came downstairs, and I've never seen a man so changed by such a few brief hours. He said simply: "I've thought it over from the first to last, and I think that you must take a trip abroad—and settle down in another country. With a change of name— who can tell? You may still find a life to live!"

"Well, sir," said I, "the fact is that I've determined to live this thing out right in this community. I understand how you feel. But you're wrong. You think that the trick of shooting out the candle was merely to persuade you to go to Baring and frighten him out of the duel. But that's not the case, and I'll stay here until I've proved it."

He gave me no answer, but turned away with a drooping head. The spirit seemed to have slipped from the body of the old man, and I suddenly remembered what Nan had said. Yes, it would be quite possible for this proud fellow to die of a broken heart. He was more than halfway to the grave even now!

That day brought me one of the cruelest minutes of my life. I had gone out to the stables, and there I found the Negroes with drawn faces. Not one of them would meet my eye, and when I asked for Palomides, they brought him without a word of cheerful answer.

In a way, it was better. I could grow accustomed to their faces in this manner. And when they felt like chattering after a time—as I hoped the time would come—I would have them more familiarly in mind.

But what I hoped most of all was that Charles Granville would return and demand furiously that I relinquish my place to the rightful owner of it! How cheerfully, then, would I pass away from Granville House and forget it all —except Nan. Her I could never forget!

I rode straight down to St. Pierre. It was the last place where I wanted to appear, but I would not spare myself. And as I rode into the town, my punishment for all my sins of the past began. I think that Oliver Randolph was the first of Charles' acquaintances whom I met. I waved my riding whip to him, but he deliberately turned his head away from me, and walked on down the street with a stiff back of conscious pride.

Then I turned into the square and came fairly upon a carriage filled with friends of Charles. I raised my hat to them—and they drove past me with averted faces and not a sign of acknowledgment.

That was enough. I turned the head of big Palomides homeward. The cut had stabbed me to the soul. Certainly this society knew how to rise in defense of its institutions!

To-morrow, I would try again. And again, and again, until I could endure the horrible pain of it. They should not outface me!

When I reached Granville House, there was a letter waiting for me. My name was printed neatly on the outside, and inside the message was printed, also, and unsigned:

You infernal scoundrel, you gave me your sacred word of honor!

That was all, and that was enough, for of course it came from Charles Granville.

Ah, well, I thank God that the hours I spent brooding over that note are far, far behind me! That night I went down to the dinner table, and found that the colonel and

135

Mrs. Granville were not there. Both were "confined to their room with a headache."

There was only Nan sitting opposite me, silent, white, and sad; and the still more silent servants, moving softly around the great room, past the portraits of all the brave Granvilles of old who had fought for joy or honor in all the quarters of the globe.

Now the name for the first time was made dishonored!

Well, I cannot dwell any longer on those dark days. It was nearly a week—a week of torture—after I arrived at Granville House that something happened which was important enough to take the attention of men from my shame. Word came around to us that little Hugh Darnell, a boy of thirteen, had been found strangled at the edge of the marsh, and Vincent Ogden's big Negro, Luke, had disappeared.

I joined the hunt.

CHAPTER XXIII

A Rare Lad

I DON'T know why I was so keen to enter that hunt which was beating the marshes, but somehow I felt that I must have action, of any kind whatever, to free me from the deathlike gloom at Granville House. And besides, I had a vague idea that public service might reinstate the name of Charles Granville.

At any rate, I rode out by myself, armed with a description of the missing Negro. He was owned by Ogden, the cotton planter, a brutal man who employed a brutal set of slaves, and this fellow was one of the ugliest of the lot. He had been six months on the place, and already he had been flogged twice for resisting the overseer—once flogged almost to death!

The case was clear enough. So before I mounted, I looked to the condition of the rifle I carried, and saw to a pair of Colts; but I spent my half day of search in vain, until turning back toward home, I came across a number of searchers luckier than I had been.

There were half a dozen riders crossing a field before me, and one of them led behind him like a beast a Negro with a rope tied around his neck, and his hands fastened behind his back.

It was Ogden's Luke, of course.

I jumped Palomides across the next fence and came up with them at once, and there was young Channing Lipton at the head of the riders. The others were five of his Negroes, all armed to the teeth. Behind the last of them stumbled Luke, at the end of the rope, a dreadful picture of a man.

He was a huge-thewed giant, and had evidently passed through hell. The mud of the marshes was plastered over him and matted in his hair, and his clothes were torn to ribbons. And as he walked along I could not help feeling that tragedy ennobles those who suffer by it, for from his raised, set face not a murmur of complaint or appeal came.

I raised my hat to Channing Lipton. He looked me fairly in the face and passed on, with his Negroes sneering openly at me. For when none of the rulers of the land fell, he was lower than the lowest of the blacks. I felt that—I had been made to feel it before by the subdued hate and disgust in the faces of the slaves on the colonel's place. But I had endured so many rebuffs of this sort in the past week that I could endure this new one without changing countenance.

And then, just as they were passing, Luke stumbled, pitched on his face, and was dragged a few yards by the neck.

"Stop!" I thundered.

By heavens! they made no attempt to pause, and the brute who had the rope noosed over the horn of his saddle merely turned and grinned at the captive.

I leaped from Palomides' back and reached big Luke in an instant. A slash of my bowie knife cut the rope, and in another moment I had loosened the noose around his throat. He struggled, gasping, to his knees, his face convulsed by strangulation, his tongue thrusting out, and covered horribly with dust.

I had a flask of brandy in my pocket and gave him a swallow of it that brought him back to life. That same instant the horse of Channing Lipton thrust in between us; the shoulder of the animal struck my breast and sent me staggering away, and I heard Lipton saying:

"This is the third impertinence I've endured from you, Granville. And I give you warning that if you interfere again, though you won't fight like a man, you will be pistoled like a dog!"

He was very hot and contemptuous, and the Negroes, as they got another rope ready for the prisoner, scowled at me. And suddenly, as I looked at the men before me, a burst of joy came flooding through my heart and brain. There were six of them. And though five were Negroes and perhaps not experts with weapons, yet all were armed, and not even Marshal O'Rourke could ever accuse me of fighting with the odds on my side.

I simply said to Lipton: "Once before I told you to go for your gun if you dared. I tell you now again!"

"Why, by the eternal!" cried he in scorn and disgust. "I think you feel you can bluff me down—a notorious hound such as you are, Granville!"

"This is not a duel," I told him, and I couldn't help smiling as I spoke. "You remember I told you that I wouldn't fight Baring because he wouldn't have a chance against me. But there are six of you here. And now I *can* fight. I tell you, Lipton, that you'll apologize for the language you've just used."

"Apologize? And what if I don't?" he said, white with rage and disgust at me.

"I'll take you from your horse," said I, "and thrash you like a rebellious dog!"

And I moved a step forward, with my left hand outstretched. I suppose that, low as they thought me, to have been touched by my hand would have been like being crawled over by a snake.

He had a pair of revolvers in his saddle holsters, and now he snatched for them with an oath; certainly he had plenty of start to get them out, and certainly it was proved then that these people were capable of standing up to me. I had so much time on my hands that I didn't have to shoot to kill. I simply picked his right shoulder and shot him through it.

He whirled in his saddle with a gasp and a groan, the guns which he had drawn falling from his hands; and his Negroes were so wonderfully slow that before a single rifle could be fired *I* had put in two more bullets. No, not bullets aimed to kill. There was no need. The first shot had thrown them all into whirling confusion. So, with a gun in either hand, I braced my feet and simply had a bit of target practice.

But ah, it was sweet to hear the guns speaking once more, and to feel their honest kicking against the palms of my hands! I put my second shot through the head of a scraggly pony and down went horse and rider, the man with a dreadful screech as though the bullet had torn through his vitals. And the second bullet I sent through the thigh of a leg that was thrusting far out in the stirrup as a horse turned toward me.

One, or perhaps two, rifles exploded then. But that was all. Two men lay on the ground, and one was fleeing on foot across the field. The other three couldn't stand the pressure of such danger as this, and they bolted as fast as they could flog their horses over the ground.

I looked to big Luke first, and then I realized that he had not attempted to flee.

"Man," said I to him, "are you guilty, or innocent?"

"Innocent, sir," said he. "So help me God, I never touched the little boy!"

I believed him instantly.

"Don't try to bolt, Luke," said I.

"Mr. Granville, sir," said he, "I'll never leave you!"

At that, I cut the rope that tied his hands.

"Take care of that nigger. Tell him that he's not going to die, unless he keeps up that screeching."

He went to the second wounded man. And I went to Channing Lipton.

Well, that was a rare lad, if ever there was one. He had propped himself up against a bush and was making a vague effort to stop the flow of blood. And as I came up, he said quietly: "By heavens, Charlie, you were right all the while, and we were wrong! You ought to put another bullet through my head, now. I don't deserve anything else at your hands."

"Stuff!" said I.

But ah, I was happy to hear that speech! For I foresaw that there would be an end to my miseries before long.

After all, it mercifully turned out to be a simple wound, for the bullet had clipped cleanly through the fleshy part of the shoulder and had not broken a single bone. I bandaged the hurt and then tied his arm stiff against his side.

"You can ride now, I think," I told him after that.

He was white with pain, but he could smile at me. He was a fellow of iron nerve, I can tell you. The true fighting strain.

"Charlie," said he, "even now, I can hardly believe it —that a fighting man like you could have endured the hell we've put you through without striking back!"

"Tush!" said I. "Tush! Here come some friends of yours!"

Twenty of them, I think! They came like a cavalry charge across the fields, four or five white men in front, and Negroes to the rear, jumping the fences as if they were after a fox. At his own request, I helped Lipton to his feet and he waved his sound arm toward them. They came to a halt, spilling out in a circle around us, and among them I recognized Andrew Parkinson and Lewis Kirkpatrick.

Said Channing Lipton: "Hello, boys! You're just in time to hear that I've had an argument with Charles Granville about an affair that all of us know of. He proved to me that I've been wrong. I've been glad to apologize, and I think that perhaps you fellows will see fit to apologize before long also."

They stared at me as if I were the man from the moon, but apologies come slowly from men of their breed, with pride enough in each one of them to furnish a regiment of old Roman soldiers.

I ignored their confusion, and together we got Channing Lipton back on his horse. But before the work was over, every one of those young gentlemen found an opportunity to touch my arm and say: "I hope you understand we're sorry, Charlie? We've been fools. Confounded fools! Forgive me?"

Of course I forgave them. Courage was simply the one essential of their lives. Rob their society of that, and on what base would it stand? Certainly not on the base of productive industry!

But what about Luke? The newcomers were amazed to see that he did not attempt to bolt after his hands had been freed, and he was put on a horse, too, and allowed to ride close behind me toward the town.

Half a dozen miles before we came to St. Pierre we learned the truth. A rider stopped to tell us that the murderer of poor little Hugh Darnell had turned up in the

141

person of a half-witted white man who had killed the boy for the sake of the fine small-bore rifle which he was carrying.

And Luke? He was simply a runaway Negro!

CHAPTER XXIV

Happy Home-Coming

PERHAPS I shouldn't say "simply a runaway Negro" for, after all, a Negro who ran away was placing himself in a desperate predicament; and I had an apt illustration of it a moment later as we rode on toward St. Pierre. A wagon had come for poor young Channing Lipton, and he had been driven away, smiling very cheerfully and waving his unwounded arm. What a rare fellow he was, really! And, after that, a big man on a great black horse came thundering toward us.

"Mistah Vincent Ogden!" one of the Negroes exclaimed, and I looked sharply at Luke. He simply threw his head back a little, and there was a hard glitter in his eyes; but he showed no fear and winced not a whit.

Mr. Vincent Ogden, his square-trimmed beard divided by the wind caused by the speed of his horse, rode up and made straight for Luke.

He had only a light riding whip, but he laid it half a dozen times with all his might across the shoulders of Luke, and I saw a sick look spread on the faces of the young gentlemen who were with me. A great deal of nonsense has been written about brutality on the slave plantations, but I never saw a slave flogged at Granville House, and I don't think I heard of it on any of the adjoining places. A few masters here and there were cruel fellows, but the majority wanted to treat their black boys humanely. Vincent Ogden was an out-and-out brute, and famous for that quality.

I wanted to knock him down on the spot, but a young fellow with a face pale with disgust and anger rode up and almost pushed between him and Luke.

"Confound you, sir," said Ogden, "keep from between us! This whip has no manners."

The youngster kept his temper, though his eyes were

143

shining, and said: "Look here, Mr. Ogden. If you take that fellow home with you, he'll have a knife in you, some fine dark night!"

Luke hadn't stirred under the punishment, but kept his eyes steadfastly fixed upon the face of Ogden while the blows were falling. And now, as Ogden stared at him, the eyes of the Negro never wavered. There was a devil in him, beyond any doubt, to match the devil in his master.

And Ogden saw it and understood.

"I'll have the pleasure of seeing the dog flogged to death," said he.

And he quivered with rage.

"That's an expensive amusement, sir," said the young fellow who had interrupted the flogging.

"Not so expensive either!" said Mr. Ogden. "He's a known rogue and for all his size I couldn't get eight hundred dollars for him at a sale! I've tried it!"

That was my opportunity and I couldn't help taking it.

"I'll be glad to give you a thousand dollars for that fellow, Mr. Ogden."

"Ah, ah?" said he, turning and glaring at me. "You think that you could use him, eh? You know better how to handle the black devils than I do?"

He was as offensive as could be. But I kept my temper. I wanted to get this black man from him. What would come of it, I couldn't tell. Luke might be a plain villain for all I knew, and the colonel might refuse to pay money for or have such a creature on his place. However, I wanted more than anything in the world just then to see that black man safe.

"I don't pretend to know much about it, sir," said I, "but I'd like to try my hand with Luke, if you don't object. I've made my offer. A thousand dollars for him, Mr. Ogden."

He thrust out an arm at me.

"I've got witnesses, here. I'll take that offer, young man!"

"Very well," said I.

"Pay me the money, then."

"I'll have to give you my note."

"Your signature is enough. I suppose that the colonel won't let it be dishonored, eh?"

I scratched off an I O U on the back of an envelope and gave it to him, and he read it over and pocketed it with every sign of satisfaction.

Then he grinned offensively at me.

"You'll wake up one night with a razor passing over your throat, Charlie Granville!" said he.

"No, sir," said I. "I think that I can show you the difference between a Negro treated as a beast and a Negro treated as a man."

"What? What?" thundered Ogden, glowering at me, and whirling his horse suddenly toward me.

I laughed in his face.

"I have what I want out of you now, Mr. Ogden," said I. "And now I want to tell you what most people guess already—that if it hadn't been for the unspeakable brutality with which you treat your servants, Luke would never have left you!"

"You lie, Granville!" he shouted, black with rage.

But he seemed to remember himself at once. "That's a little broader than I intended to put it," he added quickly. "But I tell you, Granville, that you can't come in here with your gun tricks and your cleverness without reaping a hard reward for it one of these days. Remember me, sir! Because I intend to remember you!"

"I let you go to-day," I told him, "because I think that you're a little mad with anger. But if I hear a word from you hereafter, I'll go find you and horsewhip you, Mr. Vincent Ogden, wherever you may be!"

He gave me one more devilish look, and then wheeled his horse about and galloped away.

"Whew!" whistled Andrew Parkinson. "That fiend of a man wants to have your heart's blood, Charlie. And one of these days, he's going to try to get it!"

"Aye," broke in young Kirkpatrick. "I should never want to have him whole-heartedly against me, as he is against you at the present moment. He's all black inside! Black as a hell-hound! I fear him as I do a plague!"

145

I feared him too, for that matter. He seemed to me the sort of a fellow who would mail you poison or hire an assassin to cut your throat at night. However, there were many things lying ahead of me, just then, and I couldn't pause to think over my folly in antagonizing such a person as Vincent Ogden.

I say that there was a great deal happening now, because I had spent a good deal of time with Lipton after the shooting and before his friends came up to his help. And during this time, the news of what had happened had been carried far and wide over the countryside, as fast as fine horses could gallop. By the time we got into St. Pierre—

Well, I should cover up that scene, I suppose, but I won't. I glory in it, as I think that you would have gloried if you had been through such an experience. The people of St. Pierre had been detesting me with their entire heart and soul, but now they changed with a marvelous suddenness. There was nothing that they could do for me that was enough.

When we came into the central square, we stumbled on fifteen or twenty young people whom I was supposed to know, and they all swarmed around me in a trice, with dancing eyes and happy voices, hailing me back to them. And then, in front of them all, Eustace Grinnold Baring rode straight up to me.

The people who were with me parted to right and left and an open space remained for our meeting, a sort of triangle hedged in with watching and listening faces.

I hardly knew what to do. I could see that there was a set and desperate purpose in the face of Baring, and I half suspected that he intended to call on me to defend myself and then try to shoot me down in the broad highway.

He did nothing of the kind. He rode straight up to me and raised his hat.

"Charlie," said he, "I've been half scoundrel and half fool, and God forgive me for the shame that I've brought on you lately! Will you pardon me?"

God bless me! I was never so happy as when I took his hand. We smiled straight into the eyes of one another, and

146

I knew that I had a comrade at arms in young Baring from that moment forward.

Ah, those were days, and those were men! Terrible as lions and sensitive as children. There was a veritable cheer from the watchers. And the Baring-Granville feud died that moment, choked down by a flood of joyous congratulations.

"And let me ride home with you and get down on my knees before the colonel and your dear old mother," said Eustace Baring.

I could not have asked for a more exquisite pleasure, and that was exactly what happened!

I skip the ride out, and bring you to the veranda of Granville House, where there is unusual stir and excitement. The news of strange things, you see, has preceded us, and now every Negro in and out of the house is chattering. I shall never forget the butler's smile as he opened the door to us, or the amazement with which he gaped upon handsome young Baring a moment later.

But in we went, and found the colonel and his wife coming down the stairs in haste. By the first glance at their faces I knew that they had heard, and the eyes of the colonel were shining, and the eyes of Mrs. Granville were reddened from weeping for joy.

And as they came down the stairs, young Baring dropped on one knee before them.

"I've apologized to Charlie before the whole world," said he, "and now I've come to apologize to you, Mrs. Granville, and to Colonel Granville. Tell me if you can possibly forgive me for placing Charlie in such a light?"

They raised him up between them, and Mrs. Granville walked into the living room with her arms around Baring's waist, and his arm around hers.

"Where's Nan?" asked Baring. "I want to see her, too! Ah, ah, I thought that I'd never see this beautiful old room again, Colonel Granville!"

"Dear lad," said the colonel, "no one will ever be more welcome in it! Why is there nothing to drink? One would think that this is some common day!"

The oldest wines were brought forth and such a mellow

147

good cheer spread through the house that I ventured to mention the subject of Luke to the colonel.

He made a wry face. "The price is nothing. No, no, not a thing! But do you know that that ugly fellow has the making of a first-rate murderer in him, one of these days? But to-day I can refuse you nothing!"

CHAPTER XXV

Luke Becomes My Servant

So BIG Luke was given to me.

I went to the overseer at once. He was an educated half-breed with a nobly modeled head—a man of fifty-five, I presume—who was called Oscar Cherrill. Of course the last name was derived closely from "Cherry Hill!"

I went to Oscar, therefore, and I asked him what could be done with Luke. Cherrill seemed greatly worried. He stood behind his desk, out of respect for me, biting his lip. He said that he had followed the record of Luke carefully and that he had seen the Negro after he arrived on the place.

Luke, he said, was a most dangerous type. He was a Negro from Kentucky, educated like the son of a white man, and then by a bit of bad luck sold far south into the hands of a cruel master who had completely brutalized the fellow. The reputation of Luke on the place of Vincent Ogden had been a terrible one. Not only his master but his fellow-slaves hated him. In the first place, he feared nothing—not even the whip. Death had no terrors for him, and he was willing to risk death by torture in order that he might wreak some small private revenge.

I remembered the large apelike nostrils of Luke, flaring wide when he was in a passion; the high cheek bones; the powerful jaw, broad and blunt; the thick lips which writhed back from his teeth. I remembered this ugly picture and felt inclined to agree at once with Cherrill. But still I could never forget the fine, upflung head of the big Negro when his furious master rode down upon him. Out West, this Luke would be rated neither red nor white nor black, but simply a man. I could not help giving him the same consideration now, because I was so recently from the great plains.

I had him sent to my room, and he came in, ragged,

dirty, and as ugly and grim a specimen of manhood, I suppose, as has ever been seen outside the pages of a caricaturist.

He stood before me with his great muscular arms half exposed by the rents in his shirt.

"Luke," I said suddenly, "they tell me that you're a bad one."

"Yes, sir," said he, with no more change of expression than if he had been speaking from behind a mask.

"They tell me that you're an educated killer and rascal."

"Yes, sir," said he.

"They tell me that you killed a man up north."

"Yes, sir," said he.

"And that was why you were sold down the river."

"Yes, sir," said he.

"They tell me that a thousand dollars was twice your real value," said I.

"Yes, sir," said he.

"And that I'll never have any good out of you until I sell you again."

"Yes, sir," said he.

"Now, Luke," said I, "these are the things that I've heard about you. I think that in a way they are entirely true and that in a way they are entirely wrong. No matter what other men have found in you, I've found something that I like and something that I'm willing to trust."

"Yes, sir," said this great baboon of a man.

"Who owned you in Kentucky?"

"General Thompson Rigby, sir."

"What work did you do for him?"

"Secretary and valet, sir."

"You had to have a bit of education for that?"

"Yes, sir."

"Where did you get it?"

"From the tutor that taught General Rigby's son, sir."

"And then you murdered a man?"

"Yes, sir."

"That's very black against you, after the advantages that you've had."

"Yes, sir."

"Now tell me, Luke, if you're willing to be trusted by me?"

He was silent for the first time, frowning at me.

"I mean, Luke, that I take you to be a man with a sense of honor. Are you willing to be put on your sense of honor?"

"Sir?" said he.

"If you are not," said I, "I'll sell you again. Not to a cotton planter, but up the river once more—back to Kentucky, if you prefer. Otherwise, you'll give me your promise to treat me honorably and honestly!"

He stood silent and staring.

"Answer me, Luke. Or do you want to think it over? Then sit here. I shall be back after a time."

I went to the stables to see a young filly that had been bought by the colonel only a few days before, and it was rare to see the change that had come over the grooms. They had hardly more than touched their caps to me since I arrived at the place, but now they flocked around, wreathed with smiles. Every boy in the stables was about me, and it required a round half dozen to bring me the filly, a sleek, strong-boned one with all the lines of speed and yet plenty across the loins and in the quarters.

"She'll go," I suggested.

"And come back, suh!" said one of them. "Even under your weight, Mas' Charlie!"

"An' she ain' gun shy!" said another.

And all of the rascals laughed loudly and joyously. The shadow had been lifted from the name of Granville, and they could afford to laugh and be gay.

I spent an hour looking over the straps and saddles and what not, and at some of the other horses. And then I went back to the house. I met Oscar on the way.

"Luke, sir?" said he.

"Waiting for me in my room."

"In your room, sir!" cried poor Oscar, covered with fear and surprise.

"Why not?"

151

"There are guns there, sir. And money, too! Guns and knives—and he knows how to use both!"

"I don't suppose that he's allowed to have weapons?"

"Luke? That would surely be fatal."

I went back to my room. Luke was standing by the window, where I had left him.

"Now, Luke," said I.

"I'm ready to give you my word of honor, sir," said he.

"I'm glad of that," said I. "Now for your duties."

I went over and unlocked the gun closet, where all of Charles Granville's collection of shotguns and rifles and pistols and revolvers and knives was kept.

"You take care of these," I told the Negro. "I expect every one of them to be in perfect order at all times. I want them kept as clean as the guns of a soldier ready for inspection. Do you understand what that means?"

"Yes, sir."

"You can look over the lot, and pick out a rifle and a revolver and a knife or two for your own use. You should have plenty of spare time while you're working for me, and I won't object if you want to take a walk across the woods and do a little shooting for your own amusement. Do you shoot straight?"

"I'm a fair shot, sir. But—"

He paused.

"But what?"

"I don't shoot the way you do, sir."

"I'll teach you how to fan a revolver, if that's what you mean. I want you to learn to be an expert, Luke."

I had reasons. When young Charles Granville returned, it might be that I could persuade Luke to go to the West with me, and there he could make a new name and fame for himself as a man among men!

For the first time he seemed to be really interested, and a flame came up in his eye.

"I should be happy to learn, sir."

"Very well. We'll manage that. In the next place, you're to take charge of these clothes."

I took him into the dressing room. Charles Granville

was a little fond of dress, and that room was full of clothes of all kinds. In those years, Southerners dressed in earnest!

"These clothes and boots you'll look after, also. You understand that work, I suppose. And when you look over these clothes, pick out something to fit you. Let me see your foot."

He thrust it forward. It was much smaller than those of most of his race, and I thought that he could wear a boot that fitted Granville or myself.

"Help yourself to boots, also. And hats as well. Those gloves will hardly do for you, however. So I want you to go to St. Pierre to-morrow and have yourself fitted. There are shirts. Take what you need. A valet has to be as well dressed as his master, Luke. Now come on with me."

I led him past the dressing room to a little chamber which opened on the west, with the afternoon sun accordingly shining through the windows. A small balcony ran under the tall windows, and over the railing of the balcony climbing rose vines swarmed, all bright with blossoms. It was a gay room, with a good bed in a corner of it, and a comfortable chair cut on large and easy lines.

"Here you are, Luke," said I. "I rather envy you this balcony, though! But this is your room. Take care of it well, because it seems to be worth care. The rest of your work to-day will be get yourself outfitted and look over the stock of clothes and guns. Do you understand?"

There was no answer, and when I looked askance at him, I saw that his head was turned sharply away. But, even so, I could tell that his face was working.

I left him abruptly, and went back to my own room. I was still rather afraid of what might come of this experiment, but I hoped for the best. For there hasn't been a time in my life when I haven't believed that a little kindness will do wonders with any man.

I went back to my room, as I have said, and sat down to think a little about the events of this great day which had reinstated Charles Granville, discharged my obligation to him, and placed me in firm situation in Granville House. It looked as if my dangerous game might possibly be played to a successful conclusion.

CHAPTER XXVI

Discovered?

I HAVEN'T said anything about Whitmore for some time, and the reason was that there was nothing much to say. He kept himself strictly out of my way during the days of trial; nevertheless, I and every one else in the house greatly appreciated his staying on. For he gave us a sort of moral support at the time when the House of Granville most severely needed it. I had no doubt that he really remained not so much because he was a friend of Charles Granville as because he was so desperately in love with Nancy. However, there he was in the house during all of the days when the rest of the countryside had set its face against us.

That afternoon he got me as soon as I had finished with Luke, and I think that no man on earth was ever merrier or more amusing than he. It was a time for laughter, you may be sure, and that whole evening was a festivity, for all the friends of the house who had been kept away by a sense of shame during the days when the social code was broken by my refusal to meet Baring, now dropped in one after the other, apparently for a casual call, but in reality to renew old pledges of a friendship which had survived without a strain for generations and generations.

There was only one fly in the ointment, as the saying goes, and that was the conduct of Nancy. I wanted her approval more than I wanted the approval of any one, but she had not spoken a word to me since I came in from the encounter with Channing Lipton.

And speaking of the Liptons, both Mr. and Mrs. Lipton came to see the Granvilles that night, and they proved to be people just as charming and as open-hearted as their son. They came up and shook hands with me.

"Chan tells us that you could have sent that bullet through his heart," said the father, "and that you deliberately picked a spot that would cripple him, but leave him life and limb. I believe it, Charlie, and we appreciate your conduct in the whole affair. It was a strain at first; no one could understand how Charlie Granville had so suddenly risen to a moral plane above that on which the rest of us live. But we understand and believe it now. I'm glad you sent that bit of lead through Chan. It may let some of the hot blood out of him and keep him a more temperate fellow for the rest of his days!"

What a speech to be made by the father of a man who lay on his back with a bullet wound that might have cost his life! But that was the South of the old days. Under the formal exterior there was always a heart of gold.

However, not even the coming of the Liptons had any effect upon Nancy, so far as I was concerned, and when I caught her eyes, she turned her glance away from me.

I couldn't stand it any longer, and when I saw an opportunity, I trailed her out to the veranda, and cornered her.

"Look here, Nan," said I, "what's up? What's wrong between us?"

"Nothing," said she, very short.

"I can't believe that!"

"And why not, if you please?"

"You've been studiously avoiding me."

"For how long?"

"Since I came home to-day."

She raised her head a little and looked me more fully in the eyes.

"I've meant to keep my reason quiet," said she, "but I suppose that I'll have to talk it out to you."

I felt a sudden start of fear, with those grave, steady eyes upon me.

"What is it then, Nan?"

"Have you the right to call me Nan?" she asked.

It was very queer. I don't think that even the leveling of a pistol at my head could have had such an effect upon me. No, I am sure that it could not. Why should I have been so suddenly and so dreadfully afraid?

I mastered myself as well as I could.

"You should ask me what I mean," said Nancy.

156

I was silent, watching her.

"You should say that I have some foolish, silly idea."

Still I said nothing. And that seemed to frighten her a little bit in turn, for she moved away from me, her breast rising and falling rapidly.

"But I know," said she, "that the man who galloped down Cherry Hill and fought six armed men is not Charles Granville!"

There it was, out and at me! And she stood with her hands clenched at her sides, staring back at me, as I stared at her.

"How am I to prove it? How am I to prove it?" she asked. "When the face is just the same? And the hair and the eyes the same color—and when you seem to know everything—about the family—I don't know! I *couldn't* prove it—but just the same, I know that you're not Charles Granville. For one thing, he never could have your voice!"

I made myself smile at her, thanking Heaven for the dimness of the light on that veranda.

"This is very odd talk, Nan," said I to her.

"Very odd, isn't it?" She nodded at me. "And I'm a great fool for forewarning you. I should have worked privately and secretly. I should have wormed out the truth. And perhaps detectives would have found somewhere the dead body of the man whose part you are playing—you murderer!"

Murderer! Aye, and it was well indeed that there was no light by which she might study my face when she said that.

I managed to say: "This is a pleasant ending for a pleasant day, Nancy. I've always known that you've hated me. And now this is a fine proof of it."

"That's like the Charles Granville that I knew," said she, critically. "That's more like him than the other things that you say every day."

"Tell me, Nan," said I, "what are the reasons that you feel I'm not—myself?"

"Charlie used to pretend to be grave and silent. You are so by nature. Charlie used to try to be grave and dignified.

You are so by nature. And no doctor in the world could change his voice into yours."

"Is that all?"

"Why should I tell you all the evidence against you?"

"Because you yourself know that you're talking rather foolishly, Nan."

"Don't call me by that name—you haven't a right to do that!"

"By gad!" said I, "I'll have to tell the colonel about this. You're pushing me rather too far, my dear!"

"That's the sort of thing that Charlie would say, again," she nodded at me.

"You're going to cling to your illusion, Nan?"

She shook her head vigorously.

"You can't fool me," she said. "I would stand on the housetop and shout my conviction for the world to hear, except that, down in my heart, I don't think that you really could have murdered Charlie—but rather it's a game that you've made up between you. He's given you the information. And God gave you the face and form for it. But God gave you different hearts, and in reading the heart you find the difference!"

"What difference, if you please?"

"Oh," said she, "whatever your real name may be, it never could be Charlie Granville. I've seen Charlie grow up. And I've known for years that he has no more strength of mind than most. But you have. And strength of hand, too! I saw you move with one hand a brake that was lodged so tight that that frightened black man couldn't budge it with both of his."

"Of course not," said I, "because he was tied up with terror. That was what made him weak, as any one could understand!"

"That's a neat explanation," said she. "But—I watched you from the window the other day, and saw you catch the bay filly in the pasture. And I saw you hold her by the mane! Charlie could never have done that!"

"I don't think that a law court would hold up that point," said I, with a smile.

"Perhaps not. I don't suppose that the strength of

158

Charlie was ever tested by the weight that he could lift. But the difference is there, and I can see it. But tell me—if you really know Charlie—do you think that he could even have dreamed of standing up to that young firebrand, Chan Lipton, and the five armed Negroes behind him?"

"Five Negroes! Five ciphers! They amount to nothing in a fight!"

"You know that you don't think that!"

"Ah, but I do!"

"And I'll tell you a last and more convincing proof than any of the others."

"Please do."

"If you really were Charlie and I dared to talk to you as I've done this evening—why, I would have been soundly insulted by this time, I can tell you! He never devoted much courtesy or attention to me, and I laugh at the thought of Charlie deigning to come after me—worried because I paid no attention to him!"

I bit my lip. Certainly I had made a wrong move in that.

"It appears that I am not myself, then," I smiled at her.

"Ah, but you're yourself," said she. "And such a self as Charlie never could be. You have courage and strength. I think that you're kind and simple, too. So I'm going to wait, and do nothing rash. But I want to warn you that I'm in the lists against you, and that I'm a detective. Father and mother may not see through the sham so clearly as I do. No, they don't see through it at all. And to-day has hypnotized them completely. But I'm still watching and waiting for the truth to pop out!"

She was so entirely frank about it that I was on the verge of committing the whole story to her, telling her exactly what I was and why I was there, but something held me back irresistibly, and that was my oath to Charles Granville.

"Nan," I said finally to her, "if I talk to you more seriously than I used to, it's because the coming of that duel and the hell that I've gone through has made me a more serious man. I'm not a boy any longer. I never will be again, I hope. I really don't wonder that you think I'm

159

changed. Not a bit! I feel changed myself. Very greatly changed, in fact!"

"Then we'll rest it there?"

"If you wish, Nan," said I.

"Good!" said she, and walked past me into the house.

CHAPTER XXVII

In the Moonlight

I STAYED behind Nan on the veranda for a time. In part, I was bewildered because she had been able to see through me; in part I was amazed that she should have told me about her suspicion. Apparently I had not made any great blunders, but I had simply been unable to pull a sufficient veil between her eyes and the truth. As for her talking about her suspicions, it was exactly what no man, for instance, would have done; but that girl was so entirely frank and honest that I suppose it was impossible for her to keep her secret to herself for a moment. She had to face me with the worst thing that she knew about me.

I saw that that interview was the beginning of the end, and if I tell you that I was sorry, perhaps you won't believe me. For I had grown fond of the colonel and his wife; I suppose that I was in love with Nan; and the old house itself, and the Negroes, and the gay, inconsequential life that everyone in the place led appealed to me for the very reason that I had never known anything like it before.

But now I knew that it was verging toward an end, and that this conversation with the girl was a warning to me to be ready to leave at once.

How could I leave, however, so long as Charles Granville chose to have me here in his place?

Well, I put what face I could on the situation, and yet I was a miserable man during the rest of the evening, in spite of the kindness and the consideration which every one had for me. They were doing all they could to prove that they thought I was a true Granville and a worthy member of the community. And yet that could not save me from my own thoughts. And the watchful, critical eye of Nan, when the evening ended, made it hard for me to kiss Mrs. Granville goodnight.

"You're really a good actor, I think," said she to me.

And so I left them and went up to my room.

On the way, I met Oscar Cherrill. He was waiting for me and full of anxiety.

"Luke is making trouble already," said he. "He won't let the other servants come into your room to open your bed for the night. I don't know what is to be done, sir. But I thought that you would rather have me talk to you than directly to Mrs. Granville."

"Exactly right," said I. "I'll see what's wrong."

And I hurried up to my room with a beating heart. After all, that fellow had a bad enough name, and I might find almost anything when I opened the door. What I *really* expected was that the stock of guns would have been plundered of its finest specimens; that Granville's private stock of jewels and of money would have disappeared, and Luke along with these articles.

I was wrong! I opened the door on a chamber as sweet and pleasant as care and thought could make it. Yonder stood a vase filled with young roses—the moonlight shining through the window upon it. And the covers of the bed had been carefully turned back, and my night clothes laid out to warm below a low fire. Just enough of a blaze to give an air of cheerfulness to the chamber, without adding to the warmth, for there was no need of that.

No Luke, however!

I pulled the cord which connected with the bell in his room, and he appeared suddenly and softly, not making a sound as he came.

He startled me. Frankly, I was not prepared for the complete change which he had effected in his appearance. He had taken the oldest suit that he could find, but it was of good stuff, and it fitted him without a wrinkle, as though he had been gloved into it.

He wore a high stock; his hair was neatly dressed; and altogether he looked like some dignified and well-mannered gentleman, turned out in the very latest mode. A rather ugly gentleman, to be sure, but if his skin had not been black, I could have said that I had seen many worse looking.

162

"Has there been any trouble with the servants who tried to come into this room, Luke?" I asked him, but without the slightest touch of anger.

"Certainly not, sir," said Luke. "Except that when they came I told them that they were not concerned with the care of this room any longer."

"Ah," said I. "I neglected to tell Cherrill about that. But I don't expect you to act as a chambermaid here, Luke."

He hesitated a minute.

Then: "I prefer to do everything—if I can satisfy you, sir!"

I understood. His ugly face remained expressionless, but I understood at once that Luke was prepared to serve me in all the ways that the invention of man could suggest. He felt that he owed something to me. Well, perhaps he did.

I sat before the fire that evening for a considerable time, and Luke brought me, unasked, an apple and a glass of sherry. Existence with such a man to serve one was as smooth as a happy dream, and the shudders no longer went down my back whenever he passed behind me. For I felt that I had invested a great trust in this fellow, and that I would be repaid by him to the end of time.

And I should have to give up Luke with the rest? No, perhaps I could manage to take Luke with me, when Charles Granville came to resume his place in the household. And when would that time be?

I went to sleep that night with melancholy in my heart, and I dreamed of the end of the world, and Nan Granville appearing to me in a cloud of fire to announce that the whole universe understood the sham which was being practiced in Granville House!

I was wakened by a sudden scuffle and a choking sound. I leaped from bed, and by the moonlight saw two men struggling on the floor. I leaped at them, and saw Luke holding Charlie Granville down by the throat.

One word from me stopped the fight—or killing, rather. For in the mighty hands of Luke, Charles Granville was as helpless as a lap dog in the teeth of a bull terrier. I carried Granville to the bed, and as the moon shone on his face, I heard a wondering exclamation from Luke. For he had seen the face of Granville for the first time!

An instant later, Granville's wits came back, and he sat up on the bed gasping, his eyes rolling.

"Good Lord, Sam," said he. "I surely thought that was the end of me!"

He fixed his stare on Luke.

"That black devil! How do you happen to have him with you here? He came at me like a tiger!"

"What happened, Luke?" I asked.

"I heard a small noise, sir. I took the liberty last night of leaving my door and your door a little ajar. Mr. Vincent Ogden, sir, had made a threat against you. And when I heard the small noise, I came to find it."

"And nearly killed it," said Charles Granville, fumbling at his throat.

He added: "You—there—get over in that corner of the room."

He drew a revolver and leveled it at Luke to reënforce his threat.

"Don't be afraid, Luke," said I.

"I am not, sir," said he.

Granville kept his glance fixed firmly on the big Negro, but his rapidly muttered words were for me.

"I've come back, old fellow. What a magnificent job you've done of it! No man will ever dare to challenge me to a duel again, if I live to be five hundred! And the gallop down Cherry Hill—but we'll talk about that after we've disposed of this fellow. Why, he's Vincent Ogden's Luke, isn't he?"

"Yes."

"He has a reputation that ought to frighten even a man-eater like you, Sam, my lad. What are we to do with him? I mean, where can we put the body?"

"You expect to murder him, Charlie?" I asked.

"Why, man, what else can we do? You don't refer to the shooting of a nigger as murder, though, I hope!"

"I do."

"Hello! What a devilish bright conscience you have!

164

Then tell me what's to be done. Tie and gag him and sneak him out to the marsh and let him die there?"

"Why that?"

"Why, man, he's seen us face to face, hasn't he?"

"I suppose he has."

"Then our secret is known to him, isn't it?"

"Yes, I suppose it is."

"You suppose? Unless the fellow's a fool, of course it's known."

I said: "Look here, Charlie. Why couldn't we trust one more person with this secret?"

"One more? Three is as bad as three million, for the keeping of a secret."

"I don't agree with you."

"Would you actually tell him that?"

"I actually would let him know everything."

Charles Granville whistled, and he stared at me with amazement.

"We'll have to do this my way!" he said finally.

"Charlie," said I, "you can't have your way with this."

"I think that I have an oath from you, Sam," said he.

"An oath is a great thing," I admitted. "But not when it leads to murder!"

"Morals, morals again!" said he. "Damn your morals, man! Show me another way out of this mess?"

"A very simple way. You don't want him here?"

"Certainly not!"

"Then wait till I've gone into the West. I'll send back for Luke and will pay for his passage up the river and out. Then he can come to me. I think that he'd want to."

"And in the meantime, I keep him here, to tell every one what he's heard and seen to-night? Am I mad?"

"There's no other way," I said firmly.

"Besides," Charles added suddenly, "you're not to go West. You're to stay for a while within just a few miles of Granville House. I have need of you!"

And he gave me a single guilty look.

CHAPTER XXVIII

Things Look Black Indeed

THE folly that he had been guilty of was, of course, beyond my imagining. But I guessed that it was bad enough, and that I should be involved in some more ugly work. I drew a long breath, and yet I hardly knew whether to be glad or sorry. I was to remain a little longer near Granville House. Perhaps I should see Nan and the rest again—

I didn't dare to round out that hope any more fully.

"But the nigger spoils everything! Do you think that he would stay here with me, after I've tried to murder him, and he's tried to murder me?"

"Let me ask him," said I.

"Very well. Though what good questions will do, I can't tell!"

"Luke!" said I.

"Yes, sir."

"Suppose that this is seven in the morning."

"Yes, sir."

"Tell me what has happened to-night."

"You came upstairs at fourteen minutes past eleven, sir, and you went to bed at a minute or two after twelve. I was asleep by half past twelve. I woke up at six, and got up and dressed. Mr. Granville rang for me at seven. That is all, sir."

"Nothing happened during the night?"

"No, sir."

"No noise, say?"

"I don't know what you mean, sir."

"Well?" said I to Granville.

He grinned broadly. "The fellow has a head on his shoulders. But do you really think that any Negro could keep a secret like this?"

"I feel a little more confident of him than of any man I've ever known," said I. "If it weren't for me, he would

166

be in hell just now—sent there by a lynching. And he knows it. Now I'll tell you what, Charlie: Trust that man, and he'll be worthy of his trust. Distrust him, and he'll probably cut your throat!"

Granville shuddered. "You leave me a pretty alternative!" said he. "But, by gad, I think that you know him better than any other person has ever known him! We've heard plenty of ugly tales about him, but I'll take your word for it that they're all wrong."

"Yes, take my word and let the matter drop. Luke'll stay here and take care of your room, and turn you out perfectly every day. He understands that sort of work, has had experience in it. He sleeps in the little room beyond the wardrobe. And you'll never need a watchdog while he's there. You've had a taste of him as a watchdog already."

Granville beckoned, and the big Negro approached.

"Luke," said he, "you nearly choked me to death, tonight. Do you know that?"

"Yes, sir."

"Besides that, you're dangerous to me. You know that there are two of me, and the rest of the world doesn't know. You understand?"

"Yes, sir."

"Do you know which is the true one?"

"You are, sir."

"How can you tell?"

"By your voice, sir."

"How could you explain that away?"

"Very simply. I left a blanket off your bed and you caught cold again last night."

Granville grinned more broadly than ever, for he was increasingly pleased. And so he might well be, for there was something manly and absolute about this Negro, and one could not help trusting him.

"I think that we can keep him on," said he. "Are you willing to stay here with me, Luke?"

Luke turned a steady glance on me.

"I stay wherever the other Mr. Granville tells me to stay, sir."

167

"Yes, but suppose that I buy you from him. I become your master, don't I?"

"Yes, sir."

"What price would you put on yourself, Luke?" went on Granville, more and more pleased with this dialogue.

"Danger of death, and your life risked for my life," said Luke, "and kindness, and trust."

"Hello!" cried Charles.

"That is the price that the other Mr. Granville paid for me," said Luke, without a smile.

"That's an odd fellow," said Charles to me. "Luke, I think that I'm willing to keep you here. And, you understand, my own personal preference might have been to make you safe—with a bullet through the head."

"Yes, sir," said Luke, "I understand perfectly."

"Then go to your room, and remember that you have slept straight through the night."

Luke backed to the door and paused there.

"Yes?" said Charles.

"Do I see the other Mr. Granville again?"

"I am going to send for you, Luke. Would you come West to me?"

"Yes, sir," said he.

"Good night, Luke."

"Good night, sir."

And he disappeared through the doorway.

"Why," said Charles Granville, "you've taught that nigger to love you, I think!"

"I hope so," said I.

"And you're rather fond of him yourself?"

"Yes."

"Queer devil you are, old fellow, and lucky in your way of forming friendships. And now, tell me what's happened since I last saw you. Not about the fight with Channing, and the refusal to fight Baring, and that part. I've heard that *ad nauseam*. The whole countryside is worshiping a new hero. Wonderful things you've done—though you're leaving me a coat that's a great deal too big for my shoulders, you know! But what I want to know about is the

168

affair as it runs in the house. What's happening here? And how do you get on with everyone?"

"With everyone all right, except with Nan!"

"Ah, you've had a quarrel with Nan? She couldn't get on with any human being that bore my name. It isn't in her to get on with any one called Charles Granville."

"No, we haven't exactly quarreled. But to-night she told me she knew that I was not her brother."

"Ten thousand devils fly away with her! What had you done?"

"Nothing important, as far as I could see. But I suppose that it was simply a stroke of feminine instinct. I think that there really is such a thing."

"Instinct for making trouble. That's what she has plenty of! And she's started it with you, eh?"

"Not making trouble. Not threatening anything. Only waiting, and vowing that she would not speak again, until she'd had a chance to prove that her suspicion was right, and I know that she'll do as she says."

"That she'll prove her suspicion?"

"That she would have, if you had stayed away."

"I haven't stayed away, though. I've come back. And by gad! it will be a great satisfaction to have her say that I'm not the real Charles Granville."

"You think that she'll not know you? But she will, at once!"

"Let her go! Let her go!" said he impatiently. "The fact is, that we can't waste any more time on her. But now if that settles what you've been doing here, I've got to tell you what you're to do next. For I have a whole year of your time, Sam!"

"Yes," said I. "I don't deny that!"

"You go back to the marsh and the house there. You'll find the skiff hidden under the willows down at the mill, as usual. Go up to the shack, and there you'll find everything that you can need. I've been living there since you came here."

"Very well," said I.

"About dusk to-morrow, you row down the creek to the mill and there you will find three men waiting."

"Yes," said I.

He hesitated and cleared his throat several times.

"As a matter of fact, Sam, I have to take you further into my confidence. I've had a bad habit of getting in too deep at cards. You understand I've lost a great deal of money. And on one occasion, I dropped eight thousand in a single night. The colonel had warned me that my gambling losses were not to exceed a few hundreds at a sitting, and I was afraid to face him with this sum gone. I couldn't go home. I went to another home instead, where I knew of a fine bit of jewelry."

"You stole it?" I asked him, writing him down "scoundrel!" in blacker ink than I had used about him in my thoughts before this time.

"I had to," said he, weakly. "But the real devil of it was that the lady was giving a houseparty, and some of the guests saw me slipping away. Three young bucks set after me, and ran me down when I wrenched my ankle. They caught me, but when they found out who I was, and when they saw what I'd done, they agreed that it would be a terrible thing to inform on me. It happened that all three of them were rather poverty-stricken. That string of pearls was worth nearly twenty-five thousand dollars. And, to cut a long story short, the four of us agreed to sell the stuff and split the profits. You understand?"

"Perfectly," said I.

"You're despising me, of course? Well, I suppose that I deserve it," he went on, growing a deep red. "But the fact is, I was ruined unless I did what they wanted me to do. I swore to myself that I would never get into such trouble again, but —confound the cards! And then one of the three came to me one day and said that the rest of them needed money again, and that they had a scheme for raising it. Well, I had to go with them. They had me under their thumbs. And since then—well, we've been a regular company. Not often, you understand. And more for sport than anything else—but—they expect me tonight, and if I don't show up, they'll arrange to ruin me! You understand? You have to be there to take my place!"

CHAPTER XXIX

Birds of a Feather

It's a foolish man who wastes time cursing, but I have to confess that while I listened to Granville some of the mule-drivers' vocabulary crowded up in my throat and I had to fight it back. And now I was committed to the part of a common housebreaker by this precious black sheep of a good old family.

I merely said: "Who are they?"

"You've seen them all before this," he explained to me. "They all have complained that I've been slighting them lately. Lorrie Wace is one, and Dick Ransome is another, and Will Locke is the last of the three. They're all rare good fellows, Sam. You don't need to doubt that. Full of grit. And there's not one of them that wouldn't stand by you to the last ditch and, if you needed it, give you the shirt off his back!"

"No doubt!" said I.

"I've gone down to zero in your estimation," he went on, still an uncomfortable color. "But ours are only young frolics, and one of these days I'll have no more to do with these fellows. I've told them that to-night is the very last time that I go off with them. And I mean it. They know that I do!"

I smiled, and said nothing. I knew the three that he talked about. They were all birds of a feather—hunting, shooting, hard-riding sons of fairly good family, all poor as could be, and all given to spending ten times as much money as they ought. They had won rather a black name due to their gambling propensities, and some people called them card sharps, while others declared that they were simply foolish. They were still received in most houses of the countryside, but they were gradually slipping from grace, and were barely tolerated on account of the good repute of their families.

171

And now I was to make them midnight cronies and break houses in their company!

I spent another couple of hours relating everything that had happened in the house in his absence, and telling him the minutest details of all I had done, down to my instructions to the grooms about the horses. In the end, I felt that I had covered the ground thoroughly. I did not reproach young Granville, for I knew it was useless.

He wasn't exactly what you would call a villain. He was simply weak, and he always took the unmanly way out of every difficulty. Otherwise, he would never have conceived the complicated and dangerous scheme of getting another man to take his place against young Baring when the duel had to be fought. I wondered, many a time, how there could be two such different members of a single family as Charles and Nan. There was enough spirit in her to serve not alone for one woman but for one man, also. And a big and brave man, at that! However, it was foolish to think about her any longer.

I simply said: "After to-night, do I finish my contract soon, Charles? It's going to be dangerous keeping me in make-up, and so comparatively close to you!"

"Aye, and I know that," he said sullenly. "I've got myself in a fine kettle of fish."

"You risk a good deal sending me out with that trio. They all know you well. Won't they wonder to find your voice changed so much?"

"Tush! They think that I grow hoarse every evening, as it happens. They'll suspect nothing, and you'll have nothing to fear. But go with them to-night. It will be nothing to you. But I simply haven't the nerve. The fools! They're going to try to rob General Mcgruder's house!"

"Mcgruder!" I gasped.

"Aye, it makes even you blanch a little! Well, imagine what it does to me! Horribly folly! But I couldn't hold them back. They want the Mcgruder diamonds!"

"Very well," said I. "I suppose that I'll have to go. Good night."

"Good night," he said. "And if I need you again—I'll come out to the shack in the marsh, and find you there!"

172

I opened the door to the secret passage, and climbed down the old stone steps, slippery with moisture and overgrown with strange pale moss. It led into the cellar, and from the cellar I worked my way to the outside of the house. I had almost reached the hedge at the left of the house when a voice called out behind me. I recognized Mark, the Negro, one of the two night watchmen, and I jumped behind a tree without answering.

The next instant, his rifle rang, and the bullet hummed past me. That was more than I wanted, and I lit out at full speed. Mark followed with his gun, but no man with a gun could have kept up with the pace that I was setting.

When I felt that I was deep enough in the woods to escape quick pursuit, I turned back toward the river, found the skiff beneath the willows at the mill, as Charlie had said I would, rowed up the winding creek, and eventually turned into the marsh.

There I found that the shack was well supplied with provisions, particulary with whisky, and a number of empty bottles gave eloquent proof of the manner in which Granville had been spending his time there.

It was dawn before I had made the place fairly clean. Then I turned in under the mosquito netting, for which I thanked the Lord, and fell soundly asleep.

I did not wake until afternoon. Then I got up, ate a bite of cold cornbread, took a taste of whisky, and prepared myself to wait for the evening.

Now that I have come to this moment, I should like to invite you to consider my state of mind.

I don't think that any one could have persuaded me of my own free will to enter into a plan for robbery, but now that Charles Granville, by means of the oath I had given to him, had dragged me into the affair, I couldn't help reveling in the excitement of the game, for the game's sake.

I had met General Mcgruder and I couldn't say that I liked him at all, or anything that he stood for. He was a crotchety old chap who had got the title of general because he happened to command the State militia for a single summer. He had married an elderly widow for her money. And altogether, I don't think that there was a member of the community who was held in less esteem than General Mcgruder.

It was said that he had broken the heart of the rich widow after he married her. The diamonds were part of the heritage which she left to him. He kept them in a safe in the house, partly because he wouldn't trust such valuable things to any bank, and partly because he loved to show the jewels to his guests. As for their value, I had often heard it placed at a sum not lower than fifty thousand dollars, and there were estimates ranging from that figure up to two hundred thousand.

At any rate, it was a rich prize, and well worth a great gamble. And certainly the three young robbers were gambling desperately when they attempted to enter the house of the general.

To be sure, he was not much of a general, but he was at least enough of one to understand the value of men who can shoot straight and who obey orders. He had in his house a dozen Negroes or half-breeds who were well practiced with their guns, and it was the boast of Mcgruder that a company of regular infantry would have their hands full if they attempted to attack his house.

Moreover, there were always half a dozen dogs of a ferocious breed hanging about the premises. And how were the thieves to get past that outer barrier without arousing the garrison of the old house itself? And, once roused, the defenders would be sure to head straight for the treasure safe.

I spent the afternoon pondering over these points and coming not a whit nearer to their solution. I was glad when evening arrived, and as soon as it was fairly dusk, the prow of my boat was pushing down the marsh runlets as fast as my arms and oars could drive it.

When I got to the mill, however, all was quiet. I remembered, now, that on another day I had heard two men talking in a strange manner in that place—two of them had been called Lorrie and Dick, and they had been waiting for a third whom they called Will. Why, the case was perfectly plain. Lorimer Wace, and Dick Ransome, and

174

William Locke were the three, and that evening so long ago they had been planning one of their bits of deviltry around the countryside.

Why, that was clear enough! I laughed as I walked up and down in the shadow of the trees, waiting. Three precious rascals—and yet how happy I was to be going out on this lark with them!

Well, no doubt I was just as guilty as they could be, because I was certainly a consenting party to the crime.

Presently, I heard the soft sound of footfalls, and down the road came three men. They whistled as they drew nearer, and I stepped out into the light of the stars.

"Hello, Charlie!"

"I'm here!" said I.

"Then we're off, old fellow."

There they came, all three of them, striding along in great style, Lorrie, Dick, and Will, as fine a trio of robbers as the world ever saw. I relished them in my heart of hearts more than I can tell you.

We cut straight across country by the shortest route. "You have fixed the dogs, Will?" asked Wace.

"Yes. I gave the man five pounds of chopped meat with the stuff in it. He promised that every one of the brutes would have its share of the meat before night, and if that's the case they'll not bother us."

"I'd rather have men against us than such dogs. Regular man-eaters."

"Aye, and I know that! But there's no worry about the dogs!"

"You're sure of this fellow?"

"I gave him fifty dollars. He's never seen so much money before, and he'll never see so much again. His eyes started out of his head, and I knew that I was buying his whole soul. And here we are at the house!"

CHAPTER XXX

Fire!

THERE it stood in the night, tall and white as a cliff of chalk, and I could not help feeling a new tremor of dread at the sight of the house.

The four of us crouched beneath a hedge and peered through. There was not a sound. All in the great house slept, and the black windows yawned like the mouths of so many waiting cannons above us.

"Well, Lorrie, you have the lead here."

"Yes, and I'm ready for it. I'll do as well as Charlie did the last time, I hope."

And he chuckled softly. It was plain that Charlie had not done so very well on the last occasion that these reprobates went plundering.

At length Wace told us what we were to do. We were to crawl toward the house and try the windows one after the other until one of us found an opening. After that, we were to pass inside and meet again in the great hall of the house.

I stalked the house softly and swiftly, thinking of a day when Uncle Steve and I, with a dozen others, stalked a camp of sleeping Apaches in just this manner. And I cannot tell you what an odd thrill of joy I had, when I had to leave cover at last and glide a few steps across an opening.

If any eyes were watching, I would surely be seen.

But what of the others? Well, it made me nervous to listen to them, for I assure you that they moved like a troop of horses. Or so it seemed to ears which scouting on the plains had made hypersharp on such occasions.

Let each man take care of himself. Still, it seemed to me a clumsy arrangement—each of us to make his own way in, and then to meet in the great entrance hall. I strongly suspected that my companions were amateur burglars, to say the least.

I found a side window which stuck at first, but which I forced softly with my hands until the catch gave with a small squeak. Then I raised it and climbed in, and Will Locke climbed in behind me.

Crouching on the inside he said: "You have never seemed so much at ease on one of these trips as you are to-night, old fellow. And how did you learn to walk over dead leaves without making a sound?"

I tapped him sharply on the arm, hoping he would take the hint that words were not wanted at a time like this. And then we started for the hall. It was a big living room which we had entered. It gave straight on the entrance hall, and as we entered it, we heard a soft scuffling sound from beyond and the other two of our party came in.

They were whispering together, and I could distinctly hear them thirty feet away.

"For God's sake be quiet, will you!" I warned them as we met.

"Steady, old heart," said Dick Ransome, not even whispering. "There isn't a chance that any one is in the house. They've all gone out. We're as safe in cracking this nut as though we were sitting out at the mill in the room that we know about!"

"Where's the lantern?" asked Wace.

"Here," said Ransome.

It was unhooded, and we went forward, with Wace leading. I could see the faces of the others from time to time by glints and reflections of the lantern, and they looked perfectly calm and at ease.

It was not so with me. I had thought that I liked danger as well as any man, but the danger on the trail or even in the store at Fort Bostwick was nothing compared with the danger in the house of General Mcgruder. I expected people to rush out at us from every door we passed, and I thought a dozen times that I heard whispers running up and down behind and around us.

When we came to the stairs leading to the cellar, I broke into a perspiration. Once down there, we would be well in a trap, and how simple it would be to cut off our retreat!

"You're not funking it again, Charlie?" asked Dick Ransome, looking back to me. "Not after the grand things you've been doing lately, fighting six men, and galloping down Cherry Hill?"

How close I was to giving up the game I'm ashamed to confess. I didn't like it a bit! But down I went behind the others, and followed them to a narrow hall, the walls of which sweated an underground dankness.

They marched on to the end of it. At that end a small door confronted us.

"Hold on, boys!" I called out softly. "There's something stirring above our heads!"

"Nonsense," said Dick Wace, speaking out loud with the greatest boldness. "There's nothing there. What could there be?"

And at that instant we heard a faint creaking above us!

My heart stood still. But when I looked back at the other three, I saw that they were smiling at one another, and at me.

"Your nerves are certainly spotty, Charlie, old boy," chuckled Will Locke. "But then, they always have been. What of that noise? Why, every one of these old houses is filled with creaks and sounds every time the wind hits it!"

I was about to say that it had seemed a very quiet, windless night when we entered the house, but I was thoroughly ashamed by this time. I didn't think that these fellows would be any steadier than I under most circumstances, but they had done this sort of thing before, and every man is, as they had said, bound to have his weak spots.

I heard Locke say that the safe which held the famous jewels was in a room beyond the end door of the passage, and Wace now inserted a key in the lock, worked it for a moment, and pushed open the door.

Its rusted hinges screeched under the strain of that movement, and I looked behind me in sudden terror.

178

There, filling the hall through which we had just come, stood half a dozen armed men, faint, shadowy figures, the dim light glimmering on the weapons in their hands! And did I not see still others on the stairway above them?

I gasped: "My God, we're lost!"

"Funking again, Charlie?" said Wace out loud, then he turned, and saw likewise.

That fellow was wonderfully cool, I must admit. I leaned against the wall, weak and sick. But Wace said, rapidly and quietly: "Boys, they've cut us off from behind. We've got to charge straight back through them, because this is a blind alley. Some of us are going to hell tonight."

What a trio they were! They whirled about with guns in each hand, and at that moment the light of two strong bull's-eye lanterns streamed down the hallway, made powerful by reflectors within. The lanterns had been placed on the floor, so they gave a perfect light for the marksmen at the end of the hall.

Wace sprang forward, shouting: "Go through them like steel through water, lads! They can't stand against us."

He fired at the group down the hall. And then, as he and his two friends charged, a volley came in answer.

Those men at the end of the passageway seemed to have held their fire until they drew ours, or else there was among them one shrewd old fighter who understood the value of volley firing. In the narrow hall, I thought that the roar of the guns was like the thundering of cannon.

Then I saw that Wace and Locke lay sprawling on the floor, but Dick Ransome was gallantly rushing ahead.

And I came to my wits. Partly because of the bravery of these three, and partly that after the first noise of the guns I felt more at ease and at home, I started in my own turn to break from that death trap, before the riflemen could reload, but as I ran, I was shooting from either hand.

I didn't make the men my target. I could hardly kill them all. But if I could shoot the lights out the slaughter would be a blinder affair.

The very first bullet smashed one lantern to smithereens. The third shot crashed against the other, knocked it open, and suddenly the floor of the hallway was alive with rapidly crawling, fuming, flaring, burning oil.

The first flash of it made the blaze seem much worse than it really was. There was a scream of fear from the posse; and I saw General Mcgruder vainly beating at his companions and bidding them to stand their ground and make sure of the remaining pair of robbers.

However, he himself was swept along on the wave of confusion. Other voices were shouting upstairs. The whole house suddenly rolled and rocked with the effect of the panic.

I got to Dick Ransome, who was standing dazed at the bottom of the stairs.

"Out at their heels, Dick!" I breathed at his ear. "Come with me, lad!"

And I plunged up the stairs and into the midst of the fire fugitives. We mixed with them, Dick and I, and swept with them into the hallway beyond.

I think that there were thirty men in that hallway. My broad-brimmed hat was drawn low across my eyes, and yet I feared that I might be recognized as Charles Granville. Through that crowd I rushed at the top of my speed shouting "Fire! Fire!"

And up the cellar stairs came a burst of foul oil smoke and a glimmer of flames to verify my cry, though I knew that the oil could not really ignite anything in the lower hall. The mere idea of fire is a great maker of panic. The whole mass of men rolled out of the house behind Dick and me.

I now saw a group of horses held by a few men near some trees not far from the entrance to the Mcgruder grounds. That explained everything. The scoundrel of a slave who had sold his master to the three robbers had sold them in turn to his master, and Mcgruder, like a wise warrior, had planned a little surprise offensive. He had brought up his forces for a rear attack, and only the accident of the oil fire had kept him from laying four dead bodies in the hallway of his cellar.

But in the meantime, those horses offered us our one hope of escape.

I called to Ransome to follow, and sprinted for the group by the trees; behind us I heard the high, nasal voice of the General calling: "There they run! You good-for-nothing scoundrels, are you going to let them go?"

Then a broken groan; I looked back over my shoulder and saw Dick Ransome stumbling and reeling drunkenly. He had been hit!

CHAPTER XXXI

Flight

I SPRANG back and swung him up over my shoulder. Never did I give such thanks to God for my strength as I did at that moment.

With Ransome over my back, I still had a hand free for a revolver, and I fired several shots at the feet of the men who were holding the horses.

They fled at once with loud yells that told me the General had made one mistake, at least, that of securing his base with such undependable fellows as these. Then I went on. I had no chance, unfortunately, to pick out the best of the mounts. I merely caught the first pair that I could, fairly hurled poor Ransome on one, and leaped into the saddle of another.

I got under way with difficulty. I had to hold Dick steady on his horse with one hand, and with the other control the reins of both horses. But I kept them straight down the roadway, driving them like a pair hitched to a wagon.

Behind us was a continual rattle of musketry; and now the roar of hoofs. For the entire rout had mounted, and they rushed along behind us as fast as they could goad their horses.

There was starlight, or they could have riddled us with bullets. And yet even by the starlight I could tell at once that they were going to outdistance us. Some of those horses were much faster than the one I was riding, and doubtless had lighter burdens to carry.

I was beginning to despair, when Ransome came to himself with a gasp and a groan and cried out: "Where am I? Lord, but I thought I was gone! Good old Charlie! I never thought that you'd be the gamest of the whole lot!"

"Can you handle your horse?" I called to him.

"Yes, yes."

I threw him the reins of his own mount.

"Look here, Dick, where are you hurt?"

"I don't know. Oh, damnation, here in the head! But it's no more than a glance. They nicked me and knocked the wits out of me, but that's all. It's stopped bleeding already!"

It was the best news I had ever heard, coming as it did just when I thought that we both would have to be captured for the sake of one.

"Can you keep the saddle well enough?"

"Better than ever," he sang out cheerfully.

"Then cut to the right into those trees. That may divide them!"

"Ah, the devils, how they are raging for us! But we'll make fools of them, still. Charlie, you turn into the woods, and I'll keep in the open way."

"Do as I command you!" I roared at him. "Is this any time for argument?"

"Then I'll look for you at the mill again, Charlie. Good-by, and God bless you, old fellow!"

He jerked his horse aside and rushed straight into the trees, and, looking back, I could see the foremost pursuers turn sharply and follow at full speed the course which Ransome had taken.

I suppose I should have been sorry to see the fastest riders after him, but I confess that at the time I simply heaved a sigh of relief.

My relief didn't last long. The remaining riders held after me, and by the rate at which some of them rode I began to suspect that they were by no means mounted on the slowest horses, but just simply had had the slowest start.

They gained on me, rapidly and steadily. My mount was a rascal, tall, and good-looking in outline, but with nothing at heart. He wilted under the work and my weight, combined with the pace at which we were traveling. The scoundrel began to let his head bob up and down, and when I beat him with my heels, he simply staggered. Oh, for one of those thick-legged, hump-backed mustangs of

183

the Western plains! Not half so showy but ten times as useful as most of those spindle-legged blooded horses!

I was dismayed at the thought that the crowd behind might ride me down; and I knew enough about such affairs to guess that they might give me, if they caught me, the same medicine they had been promising to Luke when I had interfered.

In the meantime, I used Indian methods of torture to get every ounce of strength out of my half-hearted mount. I got him up the last hill before the valley in which Granville Hall lay, its windows glowing brightly in the distance. And as I dipped over the hilltop, I sprang to the ground and gave the gelding a blow on the flank that sent him galloping down the hills through the trees.

I myself took another and straighter way toward Granville House, and felt a wave of hot joy when I heard the pursuit smash through the underbrush in the direction of my horse. They were following that clew!

I cut across the hill, aslant, hoping that I should be able eventually to turn off toward the creek, in the tangled willows of which I should be comparatively safe until I could get back to the marsh, and thence to the little secure shack of which Charles and I knew.

An explosion of guns and a distant shouting led me to think that the pursuit might have come up with the riderless horse, and I hoped that they would begin to comb the brush around the nag in the expectation of finding me lurking near.

So I steadied down to a long, striding gait, such as the Indians use for a five-league race. I came in a few minutes to a break in the woods, but I did not hesitate to leave the covert and take to the open, for I felt that the hunt must be far behind me. Over my shoulder, to the right, I saw a thin edge of the moon push up above the eastern horizon, bright gold.

I was nearly across the clearing when I heard a shout; then a full chorus of voices behind, and, upon turning, I saw about a dozen riders streaming after me!

The devil was in my luck that night, or else the devil was inspiring those hunters! I got to the next woods in a leap, and turned sharply to the right. It was a long time since I had done much running, and I was fast losing my wind. I had no doubt now that I could never stand the pace unless I got to covert quickly.

And what covert was there before me except Granville House? I turned desperately toward it.

I heard the riders enter the woods and ride straight on after me; perhaps they would keep to that false scent long enough for me to reach the shelter of the house. And now before me the windows of the old mansion glimmered through the trees!

I gave my last strength to the work and sped out of the woods and straight toward Granville House—and then I heard the cursed halloo behind me! There they were, streaming out of the forest almost at my heels!

I gave them a snapshot without ceasing to run, and the bullet checked them an instant. Then I plunged under the hedge at the rear of Granville House and entered the cellar through the side trapdoor.

I was blind and half sick from the run. My breath came so loud and hoarse that it covered the noise of the pursuers as they swept up to Granville House. But I fumbled through the darkness to find the secret cellar door to the passage which led up to Charles' room. I found it, by the grace of good fortune, opened it, and as it closed a ray of light entered the passage with me. The hunters were already in the cellar and an unhooded lantern had sent that ray!

Had I been seen taking refuge here?

I hurried fast up the narrow flight of steps, and stepping quickly into Granville's room, found Luke before me, a leveled shotgun in his hands!

He recognized me with a widening of his eyes and a gasp.

I closed the door and leaned my back against it.

"Luke," said I, "I've been hunted here. A whole mob! They'll murder me if they catch me. Where's Charles Granville? And—"

At that instant, I heard the noise of feet climbing the secret stairs in haste. Then a hand stirred the bolt. Luke, stepping quietly and swiftly past me, laid his hand on the door and held it fast.

"Who's there?" he asked.

"Archibald Crosswick and John Marston. We've got you, my lad. Open the door, or we'll fire through it!"

"Fire through this door," said Luke, "and I'll fire back —and God help you! Mr. Crosswick, if you want to enter this room, you've got to have the permission of Mr. Charles Granville. I'm his man, Luke."

"I'll make it all right with Mr. Granville. Luke, who came out of this door just now?"

"I don't know, sir. I heard something, but when I came here I just found the door open—and the door into the other hall. Perhaps whoever it was ran straight across the room and out."

"Open this door, then! It's most likely! The scoundrel has fled straight on into the house, and we'll soon have him."

"I can't open the door, gentlemen. I'm sorry, but I have my master's orders and I daren't disobey them!"

"Luke, you talk like a fool! It's a robber that we're after! Open this door!"

God bless that big, steady Negro! He turned his head toward me. I shook mine, and he replied gravely: "I'm sorry, sir. You can go round the other way."

"And have him duck back down these stairs? No, confound you! But we'll make you pay for this foolishness, Negro!"

"I've got to do my duty, gentlemen. I'm mighty sorry. But Mr. Charles Granville gave me his orders that he don't want these rooms entered by nobody."

It seemed a very thin excuse to me. And there was a good deal of cursing from beyond the door, then: "Go on down and around, Archie. I'll stay here and guard this door with my shotgun. God help whoever tries to get out this way! Go around and have the room entered from the other side. Find Granville. That's the only thing we can do."

Crosswick apparently left. We could hear his retreating footfalls. For my part, I went into the wardrobe and lay down on the floor on my back, utterly spent.

I don't think I had lain there more than five minutes, but I was much more myself when I heard voices at the other door of the bedroom.

"Open this door, Luke!"

"Yes, sir. When I have my orders from Mr. Granville, sir!"

"Confound you, Luke!" gasped Charles Granville, apparently coming up on the run. "What do you mean by making this trouble? Open that door at once!"

I got up on one knee at that, and took a Colt in either hand. They would never take me without a struggle. So much I was determined on!

CHAPTER XXXII

New Dangers Ahead

"Very well, sir," said Luke.

A long, stealthy step brought him back to the door of the wardrobe.

"Will you have this shotgun, sir?" said he. "And you and I can fight them off together!"

I tell you, his ugly face was full of the devil as he looked down at me.

"Luke! Luke!" Charles Granville was shouting from the hall. "What the devil is the matter with you?"

"Go open the door and trust to young Granville!" I whispered to Luke.

He turned without question and did as I bade him. I heard him say at the door:

"The latch seems to have stuck a bit, sir. There it is! I'll have to oil that lock, sir."

"You'll have to oil your wits, you fool!" cried Charles, entering. "Now what the devil is up here? Who's in this room?"

"Who's here? Why, sir, nobody but me!"

"Nonsense, Charlie," said a panting man in whose voice I thought I recognized Crosswick. "We followed right at the heels of the robber. He must have entered here. Probably bribed your Negro to hide him. Let's have a look about!"

"As you please, boys," said Charles Granville. "Luke, if you've done this trick, there'll be a flogging in it for you!"

"Yes, sir," said the big fellow, as steady as stone. And I felt my heart go out to him. His color might be black, but he was all man.

In the meantime, I had taken the best covert I could find by stepping into one of the big closets of the wardrobe and, cowering behind the mass of hanging clothes, I pulled the door shut behind me. It was a cramped, uncomfortable position.

A moment later, a number of voices entered the room, and I heard some one saying: "Let's have these closets opened, old fellow!"

"All right," said Charles Granville. "Wait a moment. You go on to the other room, and I'll go through these places myself. You'll excuse me if I don't want my clothes to be messed about any more than is necessary!"

"Very well. Let's look in here. What's there?"

"Luke's room."

"Then I'll bet that the black rascal has hid away the robber here. Keep your guns ready!"

At the same instant the doors of my wardrobe yawned wide, the clothes were brushed away from before me, and I found myself looking into the eyes of Charles Granville.

Had Luke managed to give him a warning? At any rate, I shall never forget the sudden pallor that swept across his face. He slammed the doors shut upon me and went on, I presume, to open others.

Long seconds passed, and I heard exclamations of disgust.

"Let's put the screws on Luke, and have out of him what he knows!"

I trembled at that, and then breathed again. No, the slave would never betray me!

"You fellows use a bit more common sense, will you?" Charles was saying. "I think that you've made enough confusion here for one night!"

"Nevertheless, Charlie, this is no small thing. We've hunted that devil across the whole countryside. We lost him twice and got his trail twice, and this is the third time. Now, look here. Those wardrobes could contain twenty men. Just let us have a look inside of all of them, will you?"

And, as the voice spoke, the doors before me swept wide again. I gripped my guns and waited, my teeth set. I determined that when I was seen I would leap out, firing from each hand, make for the window, and dive through it. There was a chance that I would land in the shrubbery underneath the window, and in that case I might fall without a broken bone.

But Charles Granville cried out: "Crosswick!"

"Well, Charlie, what's the matter?"

"I've looked through that wardrobe myself."

"What of that? The best of us overlook important things!"

And the hand of the searcher rapidly rustled the clothes aside, coming up the length of the rack toward the ones which screened me.

"Crosswick!" called Granville more sternly.

"Aye, aye, Charlie."

"Do you think that I've hidden the man here?"

"Why, no, but——"

"Then leave that wardrobe!"

I heard a step taken away from me. Then: "You speak very sharply, Mr. Granville."

"Confound you, Crosswick, I'll not have my place turned topsy-turvy like this. I've had enough of it!"

"Mr. Granville," said Crosswick, his voice becoming high and squeaky, "do I understand you?"

"You understand me any way you wish! I've stated the facts about what I'll stand and what I'll not stand!"

"Very well. You haven't heard the last of this! You may be a very devil with a revolver, Mr. Granville, but that will never give you the right to bully a Crosswick! Never in a thousand years!"

"Don't be a fool, man!"

"That's what I desire to escape being called—a fool, or a coward. But I'd rather be a dead fool than a living coward! Granville, I'll have a friend call on you!"

"Nonsense!" broke in several voices. "You're pushing this too far, Crosswick. Charlie was simply nervous about having his clothes messed up any longer. And you have to admit that it's pretty silly to think that the robber is really in one of those wardrobes, listening to what we have to say!"

"Is it silly?" asked Crosswick. "A man owes a duty to his own dignity. I've taken more than I can bear from

190

you, Granville, and I'll have an apology from you on the spot, if you please!"

"Bah!" cried Charles Granville, his own voice high and nervous. "Why—I can't do that—I—"

His voice trailed away. The huskiness had choked it off completely, as it often did. And I could see that the operation of the expensive doctor in New Orleans had done his throat no good whatever.

The men evidently passed on into the other room, as their voices became less audible. And it seemed that the robber was quite forgotten.

For my part, I was furious to know whether or not Archie Crosswick would really push this matter to a fight. That Southern blood was hotter than one could believe!

It was about fifteen minutes before Luke opened the door and told me that it was safe for me to come out of the closet.

I came out and stood stretching and straining, trying to get the cramp out of my limbs. Luke fell to rubbing me with the skill of a real trained masseur.

A little of this, and I was quite myself again, my fatigue gone, and my spirits recovered; though I still failed to see in what manner I could get away from the house—and every moment that I remained in it made it vastly dangerous for both Charles Granville and me.

Granville himself now came hurrying in. He was in a terrible state of excitement.

"Have you heard anything?" I asked.

"Everything!" he said, with a terribly black look at me.

"They've caught Dick Ransome!" said I.

"Shut up, man," he snapped. "Isn't the Negro still here?"

It angered me to hear him speak in this fashion of Luke. I couldn't help saying: "You can trust Luke as far as you can trust me, Charlie."

"And how far can I trust you?" he stormed. "Just far enough to get me into a horrible mess—worse than anything that I've ever been in before!"

"What mess, if you please? You mean my being here?"

"That's only part of it! They're watching the house!
191

They suspect something. Young Marston as good as told me that they think I'm—Luke, go to your own room."

"Yes, sir."

And, as Luke left—"As good as told me that they think I'm in some way connected with this affair! And the General has been here telling my father that if I kill young Crosswick in a duel, I'll be run out of the country like a red-handed murderer! He swears that I picked the quarrel—God, you heard it, Sam!"

I nodded.

"And did I pick it? No—but my heart was standing still —I thought that he'd actually put a hand on you—and then a raging devil wearing my face would burst out into the room and murder them all—and—oh, Lord, what's going to become of it—and me!"

He was completely out of hand. He walked up and down the room, wringing his hands, begging me to do something or say something, and interrupting me the moment that I began to speak. So I kept silent and let him talk himself out. At last he fell into a chair and dropped his head in his hands.

I felt some pity for him, and a good deal of contempt. And every time I saw him give way to such hysteria as this, I recalled more vividly than ever the brave, happy face of Nan Granville.

She should have been the man in that family!

"Are you afraid to stand up to Crosswick?" I asked Granville suddenly. "Are you afraid to meet him in a duel?"

"Crosswick? Crosswick?" he repeated nervously. "All the Crosswicks are fire eaters. Revolution—War of 1812 —Mexican War—they love battles. Archie's father has killed six men in duels. Archie's the very same stuff."

"You can take the ground that I took before," said I, "that you won't fight a duel because you're not going to take advantage of your superior skill."

He closed his eyes with a groan.

"Do you know what Crosswick will do?"

"Well?"

"Slap my face in public!"

"Then knock him down."

"Knock him down? He's as big as I am, and a trained boxer. He looks the part of a paid pugilist!"

"Well?" said I.

"Sam, you've got to come back in my place again!"

CHAPTER XXXIII

Twenty-four Ways Out

I TO come back in his place!

"Charlie," said I, "it would never work. Your people have had you back among them. They've been wondering at the difference in you already, I've no doubt. And especially Nan."

"Ha, Nan!" he said, forgetting his seriousness and beginning to laugh again very gaily. "I wish that you could have seen her this morning! She came up to me and said that my pretended sore throat and choked voice didn't deceive her a bit, and that she was surer than ever that I was not really her brother. I wanted to box her ears. But instead, I remembered that some day I might have a need of you. And I kept inside the rôle as you had created it. I wasn't sharp with her. I turned her away with a soft answer. Then this afternoon she sat down and began to talk with me. She wondered what part of the country I came from, and how long I had studied to learn my part so well. And I simply laughed at her and let her talk. It staggered her a good deal. Suddenly she jumped up and cried out: 'Oh, my head really begins to spin! You *are* Charlie, after all!'

"Do you actually admit that I'm myself?" I asked her.

"She was so bewildered that she backed away from me, staring! You see how the thing is going, old fellow. She's completely confused. She'll never guess if I disappear tonight."

"How will you disappear?" I asked him. "Particularly now that the house is being watched?"

"I'll simply go out for a walk. And in the morning, *you* will come downstairs. You see? If they wonder how I managed to get back unobserved, you can simply let them wonder. Then get this horrible mess with Archie Crosswick straightened out, and I tell you what I'll do, old fellow: I'll make it the last time that you have to step into my boots and play my part!"

"It will be the end of the game, Granville?" I asked him.

"Yes," said he, "on my honor it will!"

"And I shall have to stand up to Crosswick and kill him?"

"You worked another dodge before," he said weakly.

"I can't do the same thing twice," I answered.

"Well, confound Crosswick!" said he. "He brought this on himself. I never did like the fellow. Always proposing a boxing match or wrestling. Never satisfied unless he's rolling some one on the ground. Same way in school. Never changed. And now he deserves what's coming to him! I'm not sorry for him! By the way," he added suddenly, "mother has been after me to use an old cough remedy for my throat. I'll go get some now, and promise her to use it before I go to bed. When you go down in the morning, you will simply be the proof that the mixture worked a miracle."

And he broke out laughing again. For he was a careless chap, and never let troubles weigh on his mind very long. He left the room at once, and came back presently carrying a bottle of the precious mixture.

"General Mcgruder is down there having a talk with father," said Charlie. "He swears he knows that the fugitive came into this house, and that he could not have left. He's going to guard the house all night, and in the daylight they'll all have a complete search. I tried to protest, but father is in the finest fury at the idea that so-called young gentlemen have been going about the countryside burglarizing houses. He's very hot. You can hardly blame him in a way!"

"Hardly," I admitted.

"So they're drumming up more men. There'll be fifty or sixty camped around the house the entire night, making a complete net. Well, that's the beauty of it! I'll walk through that net, and you'll be here in the morning. What a circus there'll be at the expense of the General and his fine idea of a blockade!"

"Hold on!" said I. "You've got to remember that, after all, a man hardly *could* get through that line."

"Nonsense!" said he. "Everybody will accuse everybody else of having gone to sleep. And there you are!"

It was useless to argue with him, and after all my task was to obey. Then I asked Granville what further word had come about the robbery.

Mind you, he had not asked me a single thing about the tragedy; and now he said in the calmest way possible that he had heard that Wace and Will Locke lay dead in Mcgruder's house and that Ransome and the fourth man had escaped!

"The fourth man is described as being almost a giant," said Charlie, laughing heartily again. "And, by the way, what in the world have you done to that fellow Luke?"

"Nothing," said I. "I've treated him like a human being, and he seems to have repaid the treatment. Have you noticed anything wrong about him?"

"I intended to sell him up the river," said Charlie blandly, "because I didn't want to have him around as a witness. But, after an hour or so of him in the morning, I decided that he knew his business here so well, and had so much sense, that it would be folly for him to talk out of school. I would trust that Negro, Sam!"

"I think you're wise," said I.

"And it's worked wonders with the rest of the boys," went on Charlie. "Poor Cherrill is perfectly bewildered. He tells me that I have done more for Luke than any other person in the world could have done. And all the rest of the servants—why, they follow me around and try to wait on me! They seem to think that I'm the one man in the world who actually understands Negro ways."

He laughed again.

"And where'll I find Dick Ransome?" he asked suddenly.

"You'll find him at the mill."

"Aye, I want to find Dick. How did you leave him?"

I told him, briefly, about the way the attempted robbery had gone, and how Dick and I had escaped. He listened attentively, and finally said: "Well, that fellow Dick

196

should feel under an obligation to me as long as he lives."

This was his one reflection! No gratitude that I had not been snared. No relief that his old companion Dick Ransome had also escaped; nothing but a selfish hope that some gratitude would be felt toward him—a gratitude which he had not earned and which he should have been ashamed to expect or to accept!

I think it was then that my opinion of Charlie Granville ebbed to the lowest point. It could not have fallen much lower!

I said to him finally: "Then won't you please tell me just what I'm to expect?"

"Only this. You arrange the Crosswick affair. And after that's handled, you may expect to see me very soon. That's all. Then I'll take my old place, and you may go."

"I have your promise that I may go, then?"

"Wait a moment," said he. "Don't be too insistent on that. After all, it's a great thing to be able to duck out of this house and have a lark on the side. A great thing, by the Lord! Makes a fellow free as a confounded angel, Sam, my boy!"

I couldn't answer him. I was too hot and too disgusted with him and his ideas. When he had finished outlining his plans, he wanted to be gone at once. He was not in the least concerned that I might have to fight another duel on his behalf. He simply suggested as he left: "And I say, Sam, be a little kinder to the girls, will you? There's Elizabeth Holcombe, for instance. I'm going to marry that girl one of these days. And she told me that I had been neglecting her dreadfully. Be a bit kinder to Betty, will you?"

I told him that I would, and then I asked him if there was any way of disposing of the old clothes which I had worn into the house. He advised me to give them to Luke to keep until I should need them again. Then he waved to me, and walked off down the hall, whistling as he went.

I turned back to Luke's room. He stood up when I entered. I searched that black mask of a face, but could not read a thing from his expression.

"Luke," said I, "tell me frankly: Am I a scoundrel?"

"No, sir," said he. "When a man has been sold, the man

that bought him is responsible for the crimes that he has to commit."

It startled me a little, that speech. But, after all, there was a shred of truth in what he said. Really, I was no better than a slave for this year of my life.

Then, out of the distance, we heard Charlie Granville whistling as he went down the drive, and I looked solemnly at Luke, and he at me.

"However," said I, "I really should rather break my oath to him than do the things that he expects of me!"

"Aye," said Luke, "that might be expected of an angel, sir, but not of a man!"

He had an odd, straightforward, convinced way of saying a thing that gave his words a great deal of weight.

"Luke," said I, "I have in mind the very place where you and I will do well together."

"Yes, sir?"

"West, Luke. I drove myself out of that country by picking up a habit of manslaughter. I love a fight, Luke."

"Yes, sir," said he, and ran the tip of his tongue over his lips. The eyes of the rascal shone.

"But if I had you out there with me—"

"I could take all of that off your hands, sir," he suggested, rolling down his eyes very meekly.

"H-m-m!" said I. "You're going to be a problem to me, Luke."

"Yes, sir," said he.

And we laughed contentedly at one another. I understood him thoroughly, and he understood me.

"In the meantime," I said to him at last, more gravely, "there is apt to be some hot work here."

"Yes, sir," said he.

"I'm called back to Granville House. I have to step into the rôle of Charles Granville once more. By the way, my real name is Samuel Cross."

"Yes, Mr. Cross."

"And if any of these people have the slightest idea that I am Samuel Cross, they will take me out and hang me up by the neck, Luke!"

"Yes, sir," said he.

198

"Unless something unusual happens," I went on. "And I can't keep up this imposture very long. Sooner or later, I'll be found out."

"Yes, sir," said the black scamp, "but I think that you have twenty-four ways out of most troubles."

"Twenty-four ways?" I repeated.

"You carry two six-shooters, sir, and so do I!"

I smiled, but I felt very serious about it. Because I knew that he wasn't giving me mere lip service.

CHAPTER XXXIV

No Thoroughfare

A LITTLE after dawn, I wakened and called Luke. He was instantly with me.

"Now," I told him, "I'm supposed to have come into this house during the night. I'm supposed to have returned from a walk. How have I come? By the secret stairs from the cellar?"

He shook his head.

"I went around late last night, and again only half an hour ago, sir," said he. "They have a strict watch kept on the cellar private stairs."

"They're not very secret, those stairs," I reflected gloomily.

"No, sir. Almost the first thing I heard about when I was sold down the river to Mr. Vincent Ogden was the secret stairs that ran from Mr. Charles Granville's room down to the cellar of Granville House. They simply gave him a separate back door as you might say!"

I bit my lip. This matter of how I had returned to the house seemed more and more difficult.

"How do you suggest that I could have come in, Luke?" I asked him. "Look yonder! They've been actually awake and stirring all night, I suppose!"

Sitting up in bed, I could look out of the window and see two small camp fires burning, and around them in the early morning light several figures were moving.

"They've walked the rounds every few minutes," said the Negro.

"All night?"

"Yes, sir."

"Did you stay awake to watch them?"

"Yes, sir."

I was silent for a moment, thinking the thing over. I wanted to praise and thank him for his steady devotion, but somehow it seemed to me that praise and thanks were rather futile for such a man as Luke. He served me with deeds; and I would have to show him my appreciation with deeds.

"It looks as though we are caught, Luke," said I. "I can't imagine how a man could have passed that guard during the night."

"Straight up to the front door, sir," said Luke, "runs the winding driveway. There was no guard over that, because I suppose they didn't think that the man they hunted would dare to leave that way—so openly, I mean. Suppose that you were to walk out that way, now? You might go straight through them; and that would be a proof that you could have come in by the same way."

I saw the point. I dressed as fast as I could, and the sun was not yet up when I stepped out of the front door. I had taken the precaution of putting one of the caustic tablets in my mouth. For certainly, since the real Charles had been back, I would need as much of a disguise for my natural voice as I could get.

I had opened the door softly, but I did not hesitate or walk too stealthily. I simply kept close to the columns as I went down the steps, and walked on the side of the path where the grass fringed the gravel and where my footfalls would not make any noise. Right and left of me, through the thin morning mist, I saw camp fires, and figures around them. But there was no great danger, apparently, that I should be seen. I went forward briskly, very glad of Luke's advice, and had turned the first bend of the driveway, when a voice roared at me: "Stand, there! Stand, or I'll fire, by heaven!"

I saw a short, fat fellow rush toward me out of the mist. It was General Mcgruder himself, calling out over his shoulder as he came: "I've got him, boys! Close in behind! By heavens, I think that I have him at last! Stir a foot, and I'll blow your head off, my man!"

He had a sawed-off shotgun in his hands to make good his words, and I was afraid of the old fool's unsteady trigger finger, I can promise you. However, in another moment he had a clearer view of me, and he cried: "Damnation! Charles Granville!"

"Charles Granville, but not damned, I hope," said I.

He then came up closer and peered at me.

"Well, Charles," said he, "you're coming back from your night walk in a strange direction! How can you be coming out of the house, having already left it and not returned?"

"Very simply," said I. "I came down this same driveway earlier in the night. And not a soul saw me. I have the laugh over you, General Mcgruder. You posted your guards very well, but not at this spot!"

He glowered at me, his eyes fairly bursting from his head.

"Rankin! Gloster!" he shouted suddenly.

Two men came running up. Others had surrounded me, and a chuckle was going about on account of the "capture" which the General had made.

"Rankin," asked Mcgruder, "where did I stand guard last night?"

"By the driveway, sir."

My heart sank. I felt entirely confounded.

"How many were with me?" went on the General.

"Five or six, all the time, sir."

"Did we go to sleep standing up?"

"No, sir, at least three of us were stirring about at your orders all the time."

Mcgruder turned back to me: "Look here, Charles, you've heard what those fellows say. Now change your story about how you returned to the house. You certainly didn't walk down that driveway."

I would gladly have changed it. I thought like lightning of half a dozen possibilities. I might say that I had crept through the hedges, and if that seemed improbable, I could have said that I did it as a sporting proposition, to see if I could slip through the lines of the watchers. But when I specified a particular place by which I had come, I would probably find that that point had been heavily and thoroughly guarded. On the spur of the moment, I could not think of another subterfuge. I decided that it would be best to stick to my first statement.

"I'm sorry, General," I said, mustering a slight laugh. "But down this driveway I certainly have come in the night!"

Mcgruder pushed a hand across his forehead. And then he scowled at me.

"No, by heaven!" cried he. "I certainly haven't made a mistake. You could not have broken through!"

He added: "Tell me that you came in by some other way!"

"Not at all," said I. I pretended to grow angry. "You're really pushing this point too far, General Mcgruder!"

I turned my back on him, with a good deal of dignity, I felt; but he instantly caught my arm, crying out: "Wait a moment, Charles!"

I struck his hand away.

"Don't touch me, General," said I. "You're still young enough to be called to account for bad manners, you know!"

"Hey, and ho!" he shouted, flaring up with rage. "Bad manners? I'll have your—"

He paused suddenly: "By heaven, where did you get such an arm as you have beneath that coat, Charles Granville? Hold on—I grow dizzy—what a wild thought is this that comes over me!"

"You can sit down and get your wits back, sir," said I. "They seem more than a little addled at the present moment. Excuse me if I go back to the house. I'll send out a hot glass of punch for you, if you wish!"

I would have stepped away past his men. But he called sharply: "Stop that man!"

I don't think that any other fellows in the neighborhood would have obeyed him, but these were his own men, his petty tenants, who held his land on subleases and farmed it for him. Men said that he made very little money out of the arrangement, but it pleased him to have a small cohort of dependents at his bidding. He treated them as a troop of feudal retainers, and saw that all of them were well armed, and had horses to ride at his command.

How well those men could ride and how well they were mounted, I could attest after the chase of the night before!

They obeyed the General implicitly now, closing before me in a solid mass. It made me very hot, and I gripped my fists. But after all, I saw that fighting was not my rôle here. I was the gentleman of the manor, and could not afford to lose my temper or my dignity.

"What do you mean, sir?" I asked, whirling back on Mcgruder.

He still was staring at me, half frightened and half dazed by his thought. He came nearer to me and pointed a finger in my face: "You may think me mad," he said. "And every one else may think me mad—but you're going to march into that house under guard, until I've had a chance to talk to the colonel!"

I was too stunned to protest, and I let myself be marched as he commanded straight into the house under guard. Mcgruder sent for Colonel Granville. As I looked around me at the circle of watchful, keen, resolute faces of those rough men, I knew that if I attempted to break through them, there would be trouble indeed.

I assumed a manner of contemptuous indifference, and smoked a pipe while I waited for Colonel Granville to appear. General Mcgruder, without saying another word to me, paced hurriedly up and down the room, pausing sharply now and then as though a sudden thought came to him and shocked him to a halt.

Glancing out of the window, I saw Luke bring up Palomides and Hear Say and tether them in front of the house. I wondered what had made him saddle the horses at this unearthly hour of the morning, when there was no hunt on that I knew of; certainly he had no orders from me.

A little later, he appeared in the door of the library, where I was sitting.

"Any orders, sir?" he asked. "You wanted the horses, sir?"

I understood him, suddenly. He had seen me brought in by Mcgruder, and he had worked out the solution instantly. What a brain he had in that curly head of his!

If the worst came to the worst, and there was a need to use violence and break away, his guns and mine might shatter the circle of these watchful bulldogs; and, once out of the house, there were the two fastest horses from the stables to carry the pair of us.

I gave him a single keen glance to let him know that I appreciated what he had done.

"I'm delayed for a moment," said I. "I have changed my mind about a ride, Luke. Perhaps later on."

And at that moment, the Colonel, and Nan—of all persons!—came hurriedly into the room. General Mcgruder leaped up to meet them.

"Colonel Granville!" he cried, "I am about to give you the greatest shock of your life!"

And suddenly I knew definitely what was coming; I had only guessed at it before!

CHAPTER XXXV

In Suspense

COLONEL GRANVILLE stared at the General, and then turned a baffled eye toward me, for it was at me that Mcgruder was pointing with a stiff arm.

The Mcgruder henchmen fell back.

"Guard the doors and the windows," said Mcgruder to them. "And if this fellow attempts to break away—shoot —and shoot straight. And mind that big Negro, there. I have my doubts of him, too!"

"I don't understand you, sir," said the Colonel gravely, but very sternly. "You seem to have brought your armed men right into my house, General Mcgruder?"

"In the name of God, Colonel Granville," said the General, "will you kindly pay attention to what I am going to say without bursting into a rage at me? I'm not the politest or the smoothest man in the world, but now I'm fighting your battle, sir!"

Colonel Granville sighed, and nodded.

"I intend to be perfectly patient, sir," said he. "Perhaps you can tell me what's up, Charles?"

"A bit of the absurdest nonsense I have ever heard of," said I.

"Hello!" said the Colonel. "That cough mixture has worked wonders already, hasn't it?"

"A miracle, sir," said I. And I added "Good morning, Nan!"

Her keen, grave eyes fixed steadily on me.

"Good morning," said she, and since she didn't speak my name, I knew that she had instantly felt the change between me and the true son of the family. I wanted a great deal to have her out of the room. I feared her sharp wit more than I feared all of the blundering General's ideas.

"He calls it nonsense," said the General. "He has to call

it that. But I want to insist that you have a little patience, Colonel Granville, and hear me from the first."

"Very well," said the Colonel shortly.

"You know that I kept a guard around your house last night?"

"Yes," said the Colonel. "Two of the camp fires were shining through my window all night long."

"The fires were never out," said the General, "and the men never rested. Those fires were so close together that the light from one always blended with the light from the fires on either side; and my men in relays walked up and down, armed to the teeth, keeping a careful guard."

"Well?" asked the Colonel.

"You know something of hunting, sir?"

"Yes."

"And so do I. And we both know that when a bear is treed all he can do is to climb."

"Yes."

"And eventually he will have to come down."

"Certainly."

"Now, the robber that we chased last night was driven into this house."

"Yes."

"And he took refuge in the room of your son."

"You mean that he passed through that room."

"So the big Negro said. Very odd, though, that the fugitive should have known about that secret stairway—"

"By heavens, General Mcgruder, what are you driving at? Do you suspect that Charles, who was with the family all evening—"

"No, no, no! Not what you think, sir! I'm not heading in the direction that you suspect."

"I'm glad of that," said the Colonel coldly, his thin nostrils quivering with anger and excitement.

"I want simply to point out that it was strange that Luke should have guarded the door and threatened to shoot if any one tried to break in!"

"Well?"

"That was odd conduct, sir!"

"Luke is an odd servant," said the Colonel. "And he is

207

wonderfully devoted to my son. For that matter, he has reason for his devotion, as every one knows!"

"No doubt, no doubt," said the General, frowning as he met with this opposition. "But let's keep our minds open and go back to the point that we had established. I say: We drove this fugitive of whom we were speaking into Granville House, and the guard that I established made it impossible for the robber to escape."

"I think that's clear," said the Colonel making every admission with an obvious ill will.

"Then before I go any further, I am going to ask two concessions from you!"

"Very well."

"Even if they sound odd, I beg you to grant them."

"Certainly, if possible," said the Colonel, impressed in spite of himself by the sincerity of the General. For the latter was trembling with excitement, and his eyes shone.

"Then," said Mcgruder, "let us order every man we can dispose of to search this house from top to bottom and visit every nook and cranny where so much as a dog could be secreted! And while most of the men are doing that, let four or five of my fellows who I can trust remain here to guard—this man."

As he spoke, he pointed his stiff arm at me. Colonel Granville turned pale, and stared at me earnestly.

"Charles!" he exclaimed.

"Sir," said I, as calmly as I could, "I suggest that you do as General Mcgruder wishes. He has an idea—I don't know about what. But I'm sure that he means us no harm."

"I think so, too," said the Colonel. "By all means do as you say. I'll lead the search, because I know every inch of the place!"

In five minutes that search began, and for a whole hour it continued; and during all that time I sat smoking in the library, biting the stem of my pipe with nervousness, while General Mcgruder and seven of his henchmen kept armed guard over me. Twice Luke passed the door to the hall slowly. And twice I shook my head slightly at him. I would not abandon the post to which Charles had committed me until the battle was definitely fought and lost.

At the end of the hour, the Colonel returned. He was thoroughly grave and perturbed by this time.

"A very odd thing!" he said. "A most extraordinarily odd thing! The man's not to be found anywhere! By heavens, Mcgruder, I tell you that he's melted away!"

"Are you sure of that?"

"Absolutely."

"But Colonel, you're wrong. The man is in this house!"

"Come, come, General Mcgruder. Don't pretend to know Granville House better than I do!"

"Sir," cried Mcgruder, his voice shrill as the bark of a fox, "there is the man!"

"By the eternal heavens!" breathed Colonel Granville, and, starting back a little, he stared at the General.

"No, no!" cried the General. "I understand your thought, but I'm not mad. Not a whit! I'm in the purest earnest. I say: there sits the robber that we chased last night!"

"My son—my son Charles—"

"Who was with you last evening? No, not your son Charles."

"Mcgruder, I think that you mean honestly enough, but at the same time you are making my head swim. I don't want to be hasty, but I'm sadly tempted to say: Stuff and nonsense!"

"I thank God you have too much patience to dismiss this idea without discussion," said the General. "Let me tell you again what I work on. The man who committed the robbery entered this house; he has not left it; therefore he must be here. That's logic. Yet he cannot be found even by you and your searchers. Now go a little further with me. Charles Granville left the house last night for a walk. I spoke with him as he left. He was very hoarse, I remember; I could barely hear him. He went for a walk—and he did not return!"

The Colonel started and looked at me with a frightened light in his eyes.

"I was watching," insisted the pompous General, "and

209

so were all my men. No human being could have entered this house without our knowledge!"

He said it with such tremendous conviction that even I was startled.

"This morning, just after dawn, this man walked out of the house. Seen through the mist, he was the exact shape and height of the robber. I stopped him. Coming closer, I saw that his was the face of Charles Granville. I arrested him for a moment of talk. I asked him how he could be coming out of the house—when he had already left it! He answered that he had walked down the driveway during the night; but his voice was not the voice of the Charles Granville with whom I had talked during the evening!"

"Well, General Mcgruder," said the Colonel, breathing a sigh of relief: "I can explain the mystery for you. Ever since the operation on his throat, my boy's voice has been wonderfully altered, and it was quite clear until yesterday. Then it became hoarse and stifled as before. A hundred people could have told you that."

"Oh, I'd heard about the change in his voice. That startled me—but did not convince me. I happened to remember that I myself had been guarding that driveway all the night. I knew that I had not closed my eyes; and there was never a time when at least four or five of my best men were not on watch with me at that spot. I knew that Charles Granville had not come down that driveway during the night!"

The Colonel was silent; frowning, turning his intense and baffled gaze from me to Mcgruder, and back again.

The General continued:

"I was so excited that when he turned angrily from me I put my hand on his arm to stop him. He struck that hand away. But not in time! I've known Charles for long. I've seen him stripped for swimming and boxing. And I knew that the arm which I felt was not the arm of Charles Granville. Charles is stout enough. But the arm beneath that coat, sir, is the arm of a young Hercules!"

He again pointed at me his stiff arm.

"You know the body of your own boy, sir," said he.

"Then let him strip to the waist before you, and have the testimony of your own eyes!"

I had forgotten that possibility. Certainly the idle life of Charles Granville had not given him the set of muscles that hardy campaigning through the Rockies had given me. I felt that the time for escape had come and, looking toward the doorway I saw that trusty Luke was there, constantly waiting.

And we still had twenty-four arguments to use, between us!

CHAPTER XXXVI

Reprieve

THE General should die first for his infernal foxlike sagacity. And afterward, the big red-bearded fellow by the doorway. Through that door into the hall I would break—

"General Mcgruder," said Colonel Granville, "this is like a weird ghost story. Listening to you, I've begun to doubt the evidence of my own senses, which tell me that that is my son, sitting there; that that boy was with us at the time your house was robbed and the robbers were killed or hunted across the fields. I admit that what you say is very logical. But there are two loopholes. In the first place, a desperate man—hunted and in danger of his life if he's caught—will accomplish wonderful things; and immediately after he entered my house, the robber may have fled from it again, slipped through your lines, and hurried across country—"

"He was spent and staggering with exhaustion when he entered," said the General. "What does an exhausted fox do when it's run to cover? Lie still and pants until it has its wind back!"

"Very true," said the Colonel, frowning thoughtfully again. "But, according to your idea, the robber took refuge in my son's room. There Luke guarded him. There my son found him. They made an arrangement together. My son walked away. And since it happened that the fugitive was exactly the height and build of my son and could wear his clothes without a wrinkle—"

"I admit that it's an amazing likeness," sighed the General, biting his lip.

"Most amazing," said the Colonel coldly; and I began to breathe a little more easily.

"My son having connived at a robber's escape," began the Colonel.

"Any young man of spirit," interrupted the General, "would be apt to help a hunted rascal to escape."

"This fugitive, it seems, had also a beard and mustache exactly like my son's—"

"Why, a beard and a mustache can be trimmed down to any fashion, Colonel."

"And hair and eyes of the same color—"

"Beard and hair can be dyed, sir!"

I was hot with anxiety again. The devil seemed to have filled Mcgruder with the shrewdest suspicions.

"Beside," said the General, "I don't think that the likeness can be as great as you imagine, and that—"

He stepped up to me as he spoke, and with a swift gesture snatched at my beard. He plucked it sharply, and sprang back with an exclamation of disappointment.

"I expected that beard to come off, sir!" he cried.

"General Mcgruder," said the Colonel sharply, "you are going very far in this!"

"By heavens!" I cried, angry in real earnest. "You are young enough to be called out, General Mcgruder, and out you shall come for this infernal insult!"

"I'll abide by my actions," answered the General. "I'm too old a man to fear death from a pistol ball. Colonel Granville, I ask you once more—will you make the simple test of having this fellow take off his coat and shirt?"

There was so much dignity and courage about this last speech that the Colonel regarded Mcgruder very seriously; for, as I think I have said before, Mcgruder did not have a very high reputation for bravery. We were all surprised by his bearing. But, as a matter of fact, he was so keen in this matter and so excited that he was raised far above himself.

"It's a simple thing, after all," said Colonel Granville. "I don't know that I could refuse you that request—if Charles is willing?"

It was a stickler to me. I knew that the instant my clothes were off, the jutting muscles at the points of my shoulders, and the long cords that twisted down the length of my arms would surely betray me. And the arch of my chest, which made the clothes of Charles fit me so snugly,

213

would certainly be another thing to distinguish me from him if I were seen stripped to the waist. I knew that I could not submit, and I took refuge, like many another hounded man, in a pretense of injured dignity.

I said: "This is very odd, sir. You wish me to prove that I am your son, and to prove it before the eyes of a boor and his crowd of yokels?"

"Let him insult me as much as he pleases," said the General. "I endure the insults. But I wish to serve you in this matter, Granville. What have I to gain by it, personally?"

"Only the reputation of a fool," said I hotly.

"Be quiet, Charles," said Colonel Granville gravely. "You let your tongue run away with you—and in my presence! Take off your coat and shirt, sir. It's a small thing to do. And I see no reason why we should not do that much to convince my honest neighbor and friend, General Mcgruder."

"Thank you, Colonel," said the General, white with eagerness. "And then look at his arm when you can. When I fingered it, it was like digging one's hand into the hard shoulder of a horse!"

I turned slowly toward the door. I took the top button of my coat and unbuttoned it.

"You insist on shaming me, sir?" said I.

"No shame, Charles. No shame, lad! It really is only right. The General is doing this for my sake. He has a right to be satisfied that I have done all I could to assist him in his search—and to protect myself!"

I unbuttoned the second button.

"Very well, sir," said I. "I do as you say."

And at that instant Luke stepped into the doorway, his face set and his eyes blazing.

"Close the door. You had better leave the room, Nan," said the Colonel.

She had been standing silent during all this conversation, but now she stepped suddenly in front of me and faced her father with her little hands gripped at her sides.

"Father," she said, "it's a wicked and shameful thing to force Charles to do this! You make a public mock of him!"

"Nancy!" he said sternly. "Have you forgotten yourself completely?"

But he was more bewildered and amazed than angry. I suppose it was the first time in her life that she had ever raised her voice against him.

She cried again: "I haven't forgotten myself. I remember myself; and I know that I'm your daughter, and that this is my brother—I won't have him made ridiculous in this way—and in his own house—by his own father! It's shameful and horrid!"

And I had thought that she doubted me! Well, I blessed her now, I can assure you!

And the muscles began to relax in my eyes, and the ache went out of my compressed jaws. But in another half second I had intended to leap for that door with a revolver in either hand—and God help those who strove to block my way!

The Colonel stepped back a little, frowning.

"Leave the room, Nan!" he commanded sharply.

She gave him one look and then hurriedly left.

When she was gone, my heart hardly beat.

The door had closed behind her. My retreat that way was shut off. For the delay in pausing to open the door again would probably be fatal. There remained either of two tall windows. But I would have to smash through the glass—

"I see that Nan is right," said the Colonel. "I was carried away by your enthusiasm, General Mcgruder, and nearly permitted myself to doubt my own son. But my dear girl had the wit to speak at the right moment, and she has cleared my senses!"

He stepped forward and laid a hand on my shoulder.

"It won't do, Mcgruder. You ought to see that for yourself. I have sympathy for your keenness. But it won't do!"

Mcgruder remained for a moment staring fixedly at me.

"No," he said, with a sigh. "I suppose that I've been semihysterical. Confound it, now that I see you beside him, I can trace the family likeness. Same color of eyes—why, confound it, eyes can't be dyed! I think—I think my logic

215

has made a fool of me this time. Charles, may I ask your pardon now?"

His strength of conviction had given way, now that the Colonel had definitely committed himself.

He stepped forward, hand outstretched. But I drew back from him at once. I decided that dignity, but not anger, would be about the right attitude.

So I said: "I cannot take your hand, sir."

"Do so, Charles," said the Colonel. "After all it was for our own good that General Mcgruder was working."

"Yes, sir," said I, "that may be. But I've been treated very oddly, and guarded here. Remember, I am my father's son, and I have a right to consult my sense of honor before I know how I am to act toward you after this affair, General Mcgruder."

"Well," sighed the General, "the longer I look at you and listen to you, the more I see that I have made a fool of myself. I suppose the whole countryside will hear about this and begin to laugh at me at once! Well, let them laugh! For a while I thought I was on the brink of the most amazing bit of detective work that any man has heard of! Let it go! Let it go! Those bright eyes of Nancy's certainly could never be mistaken in her own brother!"

It was Nan, then, who had turned the trick with him as well as with her father.

I blessed that girl again. I had thought that I valued her before this as highly as any man could value a woman. But now I saw that her real merits were only beginning to be revealed. Aye, and she was a woman who would be at home on the great plains. That was the place for her. Away from this sleepy, old-world atmosphere of sun and idleness—

Oh, how fast and far a man can dream!

The Colonel went out to see the General away. And everyone that I saw was wearing the broadest of smiles when I met them. The story had gone the rounds already.

For my part, I went up to Charles' room and threw myself on my bed, thoroughly fagged and done up. Luke brought me a glass of brandy and I took it at a swig and

216

hardly felt the burn of it, I was in such a great need of a stimulus.

"Luke," said I, "I've come almost to the end of the tether."

"Yes, sir," said he. "In a few days, they'll see the truth. The General has started them thinking."

It was true. He had launched the general doubt, and from this time on I would be sharply watched.

CHAPTER XXXVII

Silhouettes

I HAD no time to spend worrying about my situation, however. Before the day was two hours older, John Marston called on me and told me point-blank that Archibald Crosswick considered himself insulted by my words to him at the time of the search, and desired reparation. I began to tell Marston that I would not fight with a man who probably didn't have a chance against me, but he interrupted me at once. He said that Crosswick had half expected that would be my attitude, but he hoped to show me that a fight with him would be quite another matter from such a battle as I had had with a confused mob of Negroes led by an inexperienced white man. Marston was so blunt that my temper flamed. I finally told him that I should be ready whenever Crosswick desired. It seemed that Crosswick was a hot-head. He wanted to have the matter over at once, and asked me to meet him at noon on the bank of the river just outside town. I agreed. And I think my chief reason for doing so was that I felt such a fight would serve to establish me beyond question as the real Charles Granville.

As soon as Marston had left to carry his message of acceptance to Crosswick, I sent Luke to find Whitmore. For Ray Whitmore had been visiting for several days at the Cranston house. I wanted him as a second in this affair, and I told Luke to ask Whitmore to meet me at the appointed place on the river bank. In the meantime I went downstairs to walk in the garden and think matters over. I still had the greater part of an hour before it was time to start.

I met Colonel Granville when I got to the ground floor. He came hurrying to me and laid his hand on my shoulder.

"My dear boy," said he, "you have no hard feelings against me because of the trouble this morning?"

"Not at all," said I. "Mcgruder was so convinced himself that he would have shaken any one's faith."

He nodded.

"And now tell me what sad business brought young Marston here," said the colonel.

"He came over to talk up a horse trade," said I.

"Nan!" called the colonel.

She came at once.

"Nan," said he, "I'm afraid that Charlie is deceiving me. He tells me that Jack Marston came here to work up a horse trade. Did Jack's face wear a very satisfied expression when he left?"

"He looked very pale and set," said Nan, smiling a little. "What horse did he want to trade, Charlie?"

"His White Heather for Palomides," said I.

"Hello!" cried Nan. "That *would* be a trade—for Jack!"

I saw that I had made an error.

"With something to boot, of course," I corrected myself.

"Ah?" said Nan. "How much?"

"Two hundred dollars," I said offhand.

"And he stuck at that?" asked the colonel.

"He did."

"Extraordinary! He was at the sale when I bought Palomides. He knows that the horse cost me twelve hundred more than he paid for White Heather."

"As a matter of fact," said I, "it was a foolish offer. That was why Marston may have looked black when he left."

They were both silent, watching me.

"That's the truth," said I.

"On your honor?" asked the colonel.

I could hardly answer that, and the colonel went on:

"It had nothing to do with the challenge that Crosswick was talking about, of course?"

I managed to murmur something, I can't remember what, but Nan said: "He won't talk, father. I can see silence in his eye!"

The colonel sighed and shook his head.

"I'm not worried," said he. "I'm only sorry for Archie Crosswick. He's such a fine, spirited lad!"

And then he added quietly: "It won't be to-day, Charlie?"

"Trouble with Crosswick? I hope not," I replied.

I hurried out into the garden, glad to be clear of them, but I was not clear yet. For Nan followed closely after me.

I stopped to let her catch up, and all my doubts and troubles vanished like a mist before the sun as I watched her cheerful smile. It was a glorious day, cooled by a steady wind that kept the tops of the trees nodding; and the flowers glowed and flashed in the garden as the wind touched them.

"I have to thank you, Nan," said I, "for telling father this morning that I was myself, and not somebody else."

"Do you think it was for your sake I spoke?" she asked me, canting her head a little to one side.

It was delightful to have her smile at me; but it was not so delightful to have her smile in just that quizzical way.

"I don't know what else could have made you step into the breach, Nan."

"I'll tell you, then," said she. "It was because I took pity on the general and some of his men."

"What! Pity on the general?"

"Well," she explained, "they tell me that the new Charles Granville can use two revolvers at once in amazing fashion, and that he can fairly mow men down. The *old* Charles could never do that! But it occurred to me that in another moment a storm of lead and fire might blast away every one who stood between you and the doorway. And —I didn't want that to happen, as you may imagine!"

I could only stare at her, half frightened, and half admiring.

"You are the strangest girl in the world, Nan."

"Not a bit!" said she. "Just a normal, natural girl. And —I suppose that I didn't want our Charlie to get into trouble because of things that you might do!"

"I'm *not* myself, then?"

"You are most decidedly yourself," said Nan. "That's why I followed you out into the garden this morning. To

220

tell you that you're so decidedly yourself that there's no mistaking you for Charlie."

She went on, since I didn't answer her: "Now you're going to fight Charlie's battle against Archie Crosswick. And I've got to give you a warning about that, too!"

"Yes?" My voice was cold.

"Yes. If you kill Archibald Crosswick, I'll see that you are brought to justice!"

"That would be a novelty," said I. "For a man's own sister to inform against him. Do you think I'll take advantage of Crosswick?"

"You will," said she. "You take advantage of any of these boys when you fight with them."

"Are they so much younger, then?"

"No, but they haven't been trained in the same school that you've passed through."

"What sort of school was that, Nan?"

"I don't know. I've been trying to think. But some place where danger comes every day, and grows so familiar that you're almost lonely without its presence. That's the sort of school that you've been through, I'm sure."

"Good," said I. "If you would only name it."

I knew that she was right, however. It was the disciplining that Uncle Steve had given me, in addition to the long days of peril in the trader's store. Certainly I had never realized what I was going through in that place until the marshal himself informed me. But it had been just such a school as Nan now spoke of. She was right. She was entirely right. And I was more amazed than ever by her penetration.

"Fighting is glory around here and all through the South," continued Nan. "But where you've been, fighting is just fun. Isn't that true?"

I couldn't answer.

"And as for my Charlie," said Nan, with a rather twisted smile, "the fact is, and you ought to know it, that his nerves are not of the best. In fact, he's a little less brave than most."

"Suppose I were to say that a man has a right to change?" I asked her. "And I had never been put to the

221

test, really, until that trouble with Baring came to a head. I myself didn't know what I should do!"

"Don't you think," she asked, "that you could risk the truth to me?"

"What truth, Nan?"

"The truth about yourself."

"That I am Charles Granville, living at Granville—"

"Ah, well," said she. "I was foolish to think that you would really be frank with me."

She turned away with her head down, and there was something about the bending of that head, and the grace of her body as she stepped against the wind, that overcame me. I followed her with a long stride and touched her arm.

"There's one thing that might make me speak to you, Nan," said I, "even though I break an oath by doing so!"

She whirled about, on fire with eagerness at once.

"I've been right, then! Yes, yes, but I've never had any doubts about that. You're not the man who sat opposite me last night at the table! But I want to know—all—about yourself!"

She stammered in her haste.

"You've got to know first," said I, "what makes me talk."

"Well?"

"It's because I'm so tremendously fond of you, Nan."

"Hello!" cried Nan, turning pink. "This is news!"

"Very well," said I. "We won't dwell on that."

"Why not?" she demanded shamelessly, and threw up her head. "Why not dwell on it?"

"Because you'll pay no attention, not to me!"

"Do you think that I'm running away from what you have to say?" asked Nan. "No—I want to hear it all. And —if I've made you talk—"

"Because I really care a lot for you. So much, that I want you to know the facts about me."

"Then begin at the beginning."

"I love you, Nan."

She flinched a bit. "That's not the beginning," said she.

"Yes, and the ending. What do you say to that?"

222

"If I don't answer," said she, "I suppose that I'll hear no more?"

"No, I'll tell you everything, however you answer."

"Then I'm not bribed?"

"Not a bit."

"Why—whatever your name may be—why, then, I'm so much interested in you, that other men seem like paper silhouettes to me—and not real flesh and blood at all!"

CHAPTER XXXVIII

Nancy and I

WHAT? Was that all she said?

Although that sentence has been sounding in my ears for so many years, it still rings in my imagination like the chiming of many bells, and comes to me like music on the wind. And yet when I write the words down, they are unimportant enough. It was all so matter of fact, that conversation, and my declaration of love to her was such an everyday statement, so stumbling and blundering, that when I look at this record in black and white it seems as though nothing of importance had occurred. But the actuality was very different. And, you see, so much is left out when tones and faces are not heard and seen, and when the drifting of the clouds across the sky, even, does not appear, that all is altered from the truth, and the very heart of it seems transformed.

It was a mighty moment for me.

"Now look here, Nan," said I. "This is growing serious! I know that you're not saying this simply to lead me on and hear me rave!"

"Not one whit," she answered.

"Very well, then. It seems that you *could* care a bit for me."

"Yes, and I do, even if you *are* a night robber," said Nan; and she was serious, indeed.

"And do you care enough to let yourself be whisked away from this house—this whole existence, I may say—and planted in another?"

"Well?" she queried, frowning with earnestness.

"Whirled away into a hard-working life."

"Oh, oh!" cried Nan. "I hate work. And I love comforts, yes, comforts."

"Stuff and nonsense!" I exclaimed.

She broke into a joyous laugh.

"Yes," she said, "it *is* stuff and nonsense. Well—tell me, where would that place be?"

"West—West!" said I. "Out on the plains or in the mountains—where I'd be hunting, fighting Indians, or living with them, or herding cattle—"

"You wouldn't have a penny to put into the business, I suppose?"

"No, hardly a cent."

"I'd like that," she said slowly, half closing her eyes. "I mean, I'd like the fight upward. Instead of just being somebody's daughter and marrying somebody's son—why, it would be glorious to work up from the beginning, and watch something grow—a vegetable garden or a herd of cows—I don't care what! And to have a rifle in the house instead of a padlock on the door!"

She began to laugh again—laugh with me, you understand—her eyes shining.

"My God, Nan!" I cried. "I think that you are actually accepting me as a husband!"

"Am I?" said she. "Well, I really think that I am!"

She added: "Without even knowing your name!"

"My name is Samuel Cross."

"That's different from Granville, or Crosswick, or Grinnold-Baring, or Ellison-Whitmore, or all the other names one finds down here. Just Sam Cross. *Mrs*. Sam Cross. The girl with the freckled nose. I would get freckles, if I lived out of doors, Sam."

"God bless you!" said I. "How wonderfully sweet and delightful and, and—"

"Ridiculous!" she suggested.

"Yes," I agreed, "and ridiculous, and beautiful you are."

"I don't want to hear about myself," said she. "That wasn't the bargain. I'm to marry you if you'll tell me about yourself."

"I can, in three words almost."

"I doubt that."

"I was born. I asked you to marry me. You said that you would."

"Stuff!" cried Nan.

"My father died when I was little," said I. "My mother raised me at Fort Bostwick and taught me to speak English without much slang."

"I'm sorry for that," said Nan. "Perhaps we'll pick some up together."

"She instructed me at home until my Uncle Steve—the grandest man in the world—taught me to fight with my fists, and to shoot and hunt, and such things. He and a few Indians, and rough trappers, and such fellows, you know, were my companions. Then my mother died, and I went into a store at Fort Bostwick. It was a rather wild place, I must confess, and I got into the habit of fighting my way with the quarrelsome clients. I didn't realize what I had been doing so casually, until one day the marshal called on me and told me that I would have to stop man—"

"Slaughter?" Nancy finished for me.

"How did you guess?" said I.

"Well," she answered, with her flashing smile, "I saw you drive down Cherry Hill, you know!"

"The marshal advised me to leave that section of the country for a time. I took his advice, used the money I had saved to pay for some of the damage I had done, and went to the Mississippi and got a boat traveling down the river. On that boat I met Charlie Granville, and in spite of my red hair he saw that we—"

"Red hair!" cried Nan.

"I'm sorry," said I.

"I love it!" she confessed. "And then—let me finish. He saw that you looked much alike. And with the changes that General Mcgruder suggested—a little dye—and a thorough posting on our family history—Oh, I begin to see it all! Charlie could disappear at New Orleans, and you come back in his place to fight Eustace Baring! How horrible! How shameful of him!"

I really couldn't answer that.

"On the boat," I took up the tale, "he saved me from a sneaking gambler who tried to knife me in the back—and then—"

"And Charlie used that for capital! Ah!"

I never saw such scorn and anger in any other face.

"And now you're going to fight another battle on his account. And the trouble at Mcgruder's house—that was a scrape that he worked up for you!"

"I've finished confessing," said I. "And I've shattered my oath to your brother into a thousand bits. Besides—it's nearly noon. And I have to go."

"To fight Archie Crosswick?"

"Yes."

"And when I see my brother again, I'll never be able to let him know that I understand what sort of a person he is! I'll stifle with it, Sam! But you shall not go to meet Archie!"

"I must. It's time to start now, and Palomides is waiting!"

"Sam, if you love me—"

She clung to me suddenly, pleading. It was very hard, very wonderful, too, to see that she really cared so much. But I had to break away and almost run for Palomides. I mounted and swept out of Granville House.

At the gate, I reined in suddenly. I had forgotten to kiss Nan!

Well, it was too late now. I galloped on again for the river and in the course of a half hour I came to the appointed place. I thought that there was no one there, at first, but afterward I saw the figures half lost in the shadow. Four of them. The doctor, Whitmore, Marston, and Archie Crosswick. And in the distance, Luke with the horses.

I rode up to them, dismounted, and shook hands with every one except Crosswick. He refused that ceremony.

I said to him: "Archie, I'm sorry that this has to be. Mind you, I tried to draw out of it, but you wouldn't have it so. I think that I can fairly put the blame for whatever happens on your head."

"You can't shake my nerve at the last minute like this, Mr. Granville," said he. "And if you have anything more to say, speak to Mr. Marston, if you please."

He was steady as a rock, this Crosswick lad. I could see that he was confident, with the confidence that comes of long practice. More than practice, too. As Charlie had

227

said, fighting was in the blood of that family. But what was his practice compared with that I had had at Fort Bostwick?

The doctor was Sumner Masson, a fellow with iron-gray hair, and iron-gray eyes, a man and a half, I can assure you. He made no effort to dissuade us from the fight, simply saying: "I'm not here as a moralist. I think that these affairs have to happen, and the youth of the land is all the better off for having blood let now and then."

Then he deliberately paced off the twenty strides agreed upon. We were posted with our backs to one another, a revolver gripped in the right hand. At the word of command, we were to turn and fire.

I took a long look at river, sky and trees. I would not leave these pleasant scenes. And I would not leave Nan. Crosswick must die!

Whitmore shook hands with me.

"I wish to God," he whispered, "that I could ever stand at the mark with such nerve as you've shown."

"Hold on!" cried the doctor. "There are some men riding in this direction. I'm afraid that we're discovered, gentlemen."

"The word! The word!" barked Crosswick, furiously impatient. "Let them find one dead man here. As for the other, our horses are all fast!"

"On your own heads," said the doctor, as cold as ice. "Gentlemen, I am about to give the signal!"

And then: "Gentlemen, fire!"

I whirled. I saw that young Crosswick was just as quick as I in turning, but he was swinging his hand up shoulder-high to take aim, and while that hand was still swinging, I fired from the hip, and shot to kill.

His pistol dropped from his hand. He clasped his body with both arms, then recovered himself instantly, and stood straight.

"Damn you, Granville!" said he. "You've killed me with your trick shooting!"

Marston took him in his arms and lowered him to the ground; and I, leaning over them, saw a crimson spot as big as my hand spreading on Crosswick's coat, just above

228

the heart. And I knew that St. Pierre would be a hot, hot place for young Charles Granville for some time to come.

Then I turned and glanced across the fields, and saw General Mcgruder at the head of a dozen men riding for all they were worth.

CHAPTER XXXIX

The Jig Is Up

WHILE I ran for Palomides, I understood perfectly why the general was afield. He could not forgive me for having foiled him in the morning. Besides, he was probably still convinced in his heart of hearts that I was no more Charles Granville than was he; and when he heard by chance some rumor of the duel to be fought with Archibald Crosswick, he had been tempted to interfere in the name of the law.

He was too late to use his authority to stop the fight. He was certainly not too late to hunt me across the country. And, if he could catch me, the end would be at hand. For it would not be two days before a rim of red would begin to show at the base of my black mustache. My hair grew so fast that I had to dye it carefully twice a day, working the stuff well into the roots, and yet not so close as to smudge the skin. It was a ticklish job and one that had caused me many an hour of cursing and anxiety. And, if I were lodged in jail on a manslaughter charge, and closely confined and watched, it would be impossible to apply the dye.

In the meantime, if Archie Crosswick were really a dead man, the authorities could bring a most serious charge against me. It might well mean a prison sentence. And if I turned out to be not Charles Granville but a mere interloper, then I could be sure that they would end by putting a rope around my neck.

I explain this so you will understand the serious necessity I was under of keeping myself out of the hands of the general. I swung into the saddle on Palomides, with Luke on another horse beside me, and we rode straight across country.

The general and his men only paused a moment by the spot where Crosswick was lying. They apparently found out all that they wished to learn, and then spurred after us as hard as they could come.

It reminded me of the flight from the general's house the other night, but there was a great deal of difference between being mounted on a picked-up nag and having beneath me the powerful loins of Palomides. Besides, the other horses had been traveling at a smart gait for some distance, while we had a fresh start. Away we went like the wind. I could rein Palomides into half his speed in order to remain with Luke, and even so, we drew steadily away from the pursuit.

When we were fairly out of sight in the woods, heading back in the direction of Granville House, as though I intended to go there for refuge, I swung off to the side again, and headed for the old mill on the creek. How often I had made that very spot my goal!

We rode harder, now that the general and his men were out of sight and sound; and when we came near the mill, I gave Palomides to Luke and told him to go back to the house by a roundabout way, and to answer no questions, except to tell the colonel that his son was safe, and that the duel had been a fair one. But, for that matter, Whitmore would be sure to report the details of the affair.

"What else can I do, sir?" asked Luke.

"Try to get to the old mill once every night," said I.

He told me that he would certainly be there every night at twelve, and would stay for an hour or more. Then he could give me news of what was happening; let me know whether or not Crosswick lived; and could tell me when it might be safe for me to venture out of the marsh again.

In the meantime, I hurried down to the edge of the creek, found the skiff at the usual place under the edge of the willows, and rowed hastily up the stream. I pushed the boat hurriedly through the water, and wound back and forth through the narrow passages and alleys of the marsh until I saw before me the shack which was our rendezvous. In front of the shack, seated on a stump and aimlessly whittling at a stick, was young Charles Granville.

He stood up with a yawn, and then started down to the water to meet me.

He had not shaved since leaving home. He was dressed in old clothes, of which there was always a stock at the shack, and, with a battered hat pushed far on the back of his head, he appeared reasonably unlike the heir of the Granville fortunes.

"What's up, Sam?" he called.

"Crosswick brought things to a head at noon," I told him.

"Hello!" said Granville, and whistled softly. "He wants to fight?"

"He has fought already."

"The devil! And—you dropped him?"

"He's dying, I think."

He struck his hands together with an exclamation of rage and impatient disgust.

"Then I'll have the rest of the Crosswicks on my trail as long as I live! You've done a pretty piece of work for me, Sam!"

That was his gratitude to me for having fought his fight for him.

I looked at him more closely, a good deal shocked by what he had said to me. I had felt for some time that he was deteriorating. The fact was, I suppose, that the ease with which he could drop through a trapdoor, as it were, and escape from every responsibility, no matter how serious, by leaving me to bear the blame, had been demoralizing. I thought, as I watched him now, that even his features sagged a bit; there was a taint of yellow in the whites of his eyes, and he appeared much more like a bit of poor white trash than the son of Colonel Granville.

My disgust was the greater because I knew that he was the brother of Nancy. I could hardly believe it. But the longer and the deeper I looked into his soul, the more I was shamed for him.

"You have an eye as cold as the eye of a fish, man!" said Charles Granville, scowling at me. "What's the matter? Oh, I'm thinking about my own hide, and not about the dangers that you've just been through. Is that it?"

"I've finished my business with you, Granville," said I suddenly. And what a great breath of relief I drew! "I've dropped Archie Crosswick, and you've given me your promise to let me go now and to release me from my oath to you!"

"Hold on—" he began.

But I said resolutely: "I'm finished, and I'm going to hold you to your promise. I have the right to. I'll just step into the shack and change from these clothes!"

I went inside and stripped myself of the finery which did not belong to me. I put on, instead, some slouchy, mud-stained, but comfortable clothes. And when I stood up in these again, I felt much better, you may be sure! Everything was more loosely comfortable for me.

The revolvers in their holsters beneath my armpits were easy to draw from that loosely fitted coat. The heavy bowie knife hung just left of center of the front of my belt. I had on old, strong boots, and a slouch hat whose limp brim hung down in a wave across my eyes.

Altogether as slouchy looking an outfit as ever a tramp wore, but I liked it better than all the finery of Charles Granville, because that did not belong to me, and I had a right to such clothes as these.

When I came out of the shack, I found Granville pacing up and down, extremely nervous.

I had a razor in my hand, and in my coat pocket was a bottle of weak acid which, with some water from the stream, would quickly remove the black stain from my hair and beard.

"Hold on!" cried Granville, as I went past him.

"I'll be back in a moment," said I, and went on down toward the river.

As I knelt by its edge, Granville's shout rang in my ears. There was real terror in his cry, and I stood up and turned to him. He had run down to me and now he pulled me strongly away from the water.

"Wait a moment, Sam," he gasped. "You gave me your oath. You're honorable. I hold you to your oath, Sam. By heaven, I hold you to it! You won't go back on me?"

He was fairly trembling, and though his terror rather sickened me, still I felt that he was right. I had given him such a binding oath that I could not recall it.

"Look here," he went on, "these Crosswicks are a dan-

233

gerous lot. A damned dangerous lot, old fellow. Always fighting. Always have been in no end of trouble and duels, you know. And now that you've stung one of them, the whole hornet's nest will be after us. After me, I should say. There'll be a dozen challenges in two days!"

"You won't be bothered," I told him. "I shot down Crosswick before he could so much as get his revolver up to the mark. And I think that he had a reputation for speed and accuracy."

"Yes, but I'm not you! I'm not you! There's a difference between us, and people feel it even before they sense that you and I are doubles and not the same person. I mean to say: You can carry things off with a high hand, very proudly and sternly, you understand, and men are afraid to offend you; but I'm more good natured and slipshod and careless—and—they quickly begin to take advantage of me. I haven't the iron in me. If you went back to Granville House, I've no doubt that not a single Crosswick would dare to tackle you. But if I went back, I would be a dead man inside the week! I know it, old fellow!"

It was an ugly moment for me, and I was turning the thing back and forth in my mind, when the prow of a boat pushed around the corner of the rivulet that passed in front of the shack, and there was General Mcgruder calling out in triumph, a thrill of victory in his voice: "I arrest you both for conspiracy and murder—in the name of the law!"

There stood Charles Granville. At his side stood another Charles Granville, and the general had proved his contention of that morning beyond a doubt.

There were two Granvilles, and not one!

Charles Granville recovered himself before I did.

"The jigs up! Run! Run!" he gasped.

And we whirled and leaped for the brush.

"Fire!" screamed the excited general. "Fire and shoot to kill! The scoundrels deserve nothing better!"

Behind us shotguns and rifles roared, and as we gained the brush, revolvers spat after us. But we had run past the line of fire, and every bullet missed us. We were safe in the green gloom of that little jungle.

CHAPTER XL

It All Depends on Me

DID I say safe? I mean that we were safe for the moment; but I've never seen such terror as showed on the wild face of Charles Granville as he turned toward me and sank almost to his knees.

"Oh, God, Sam," said he, "we're done for! The general will never stop now until he has both of us—and they'll kill me for—"

I was stunned by what had happened. After all our cleverness, our deceits, our tricks, our subterfuges, our patient study, our many rehearsals, we were undone because a foolish little man inspired by venom and hate had chanced to row into the marsh on a blind search! For that was exactly what had sent the general there. The devil inspired him. He hadn't an item of information about that shack to lead him.

I shook Charlie by the shoulder.

"There's no use whining," said I. "They'll be in this thicket in another minute and we'd better move!"

He nodded, but his eye was blank and rolling wildly. He was absolutely unnerved with terror.

I felt that to try to move on with him in that condition was worse than foolish. He would blunder through the brush and make so much noise that the general and his bloodhounds would easily find us. They would not be apt to search close at hand for a time. They would, I thought, first range to the far parts of the little island, combing the brush for us. So I whispered to Charlie that we would lie still.

We were in the densest sort of brush, which made a perfect covert, and in addition, a little rill of water trickled past us. I determined to use that water and the little time that was left us to do the only thing that remained to us to try.

I crouched by the stream, took from my pocket the bit of soap with which I had started from the shack for the river's edge, and worked up the fastest lather that you can imagine. Then I took my razor and shaved off mustache and beard.

I saw them (second "Charles Granville") float off down the little stream, while the noise of the searchers and their shouts resounded about us.

Then I ducked my head into the water, and Granville himself poured the acid over my hair. In half a minute the black was gone, and the red shone forth undisguised.

I dried my head as well as I could, and for the first time in many weeks, the true image of Samuel Cross looked back to me as I bent over the running water.

Charlie, trembling with relief, sat back and whispered: "They'd never know you, now!"

"They've heard my voice this very morning," I answered.

"Half husky from that caustic tablet," he reminded me. "But not your natural voice."

"Too near for them to mistake it, I'm afraid," said I.

"You've got to chance that," he said.

"What do you want me to do?"

"Go out of this ticket. I don't want you to be caught along with me."

"Walk out of this thicket and give myself up?" I asked, wondering at his simplicity.

"What else is there to do?"

I gave him no answer. I was too disgusted with his terrible selfishness. I crept down to the edge of the thicket and looked out. Before long the searchers and the keen general with them would come in from their hunt and would begin combing the thicket near the shack for us. If we were to do anything, we would have to do it quickly.

From the edge of the brush, I saw the general's long boat, with one man left to guard it. He was standing, rifle in hand, constantly watching the woods for a sign of game —human game.

I determined to hunt him just as he was trying to hunt us. I kicked off my shoes, slipped into the water under the

236

hanging boughs of a willow tree, and began to swim noiselessly.

The Indians had taught me the trick of it, and I thanked them for it now. Twice I dived, and, swimming under water, the second time I came up under the lee of the boat.

As I raised my head, my lungs were bursting for air. If I breathed, the noise would startle the watcher. I simply gripped the gunwale of the skiff and, jerking myself up, struck the man under the knees.

He fell with a startled yell, the rifle exploding and tumbling into the boat, toppled over into the water and struck off in blind haste for the opposite shore.

The noise had told Charlie Granville that something was up. Now he came rushing from the thicket, and was seated in the boat almost as quickly as I. Instantly the oars were bending half double under the strength of our combined pulling.

I tell you, the prow of that skiff fairly lifted out of the water as we sent the light boat leaping up the stream. And we had it well under way when the general himself rushed out into the clearing.

I shall never forget the scream of vexation and despair that he uttered when he saw us pulling at those oars. I had my head bent down so that he could not possibly see my face, and we swung the skiff quickly along the edge of the willows, cutting off his view.

He ran into the edge of the water, yelling for help, and so he got a view of us once more. But now we were several yards away, and every instant increased the distance. As luck would have it, he held only a shotgun. He fired, and the shot splashed into the water, short of us.

"Stop!" shouted Mcgruder. "Stop, or I'll fire to kill!"

He merely had wasted half a dozen very valuable seconds, and when he fired his second barrel, we were several boat-lengths farther off, Charles Granville moaning with pain at every stroke he made.

And what strokes they were! I saw the oars bending like switches under the sway of his body. Up the river we shot; and the second charge from the general's gun cut the water well short of us. He threw the shotgun to the shore and opened on us with a revolver. But the distance was considerable now; the general was apparently not a very good shot with that weapon; and he was disturbing his own aim by his constant shouts for help.

Help came to him at last—help in the form of three tall men, rifles in hand, who plunged out into the water until they were chest-deep.

They brought their rifles to the level, but at that moment we reached a cross stream, and drove the skiff strongly into it. The target was snatched away from before the eyes of the general's men. And the rifles vainly raked the willows with many bullets.

We still rowed on like madmen, making the boat leap through the stagnant marsh water, and drove it across the width of the low-lying district. When we came to the edge of the solid ground once more, Granville asked, trembling: "Now what, Sam? Now what shall we do?"

And he searched my face with vague, frightened eyes. I despised him, but I pitied him.

"Go straight home," I told him. "You're not fit for anything else just now."

"But when I get home—arrested for murder and—"

"Perhaps Crosswick is not dead."

"God bless you for saying that!"

"Besides, how could a Granville be hung for killing a man in a fair duel—when the other man was the aggressor?"

"But—remember, Sam, that that devil of a general saw the pair of us together. And his men surely saw us, too!"

"You can fix it up this way," said I. "When you rode away from the scene of the duel, you decided to hide in the swamp, you understand? And when you came to the hunting shack, you found that a tramp was in possession of the little house. An idea came to you at once—and the general himself had put that idea in your mind by accusing you of being the double of Charles Granville, and not your real self. You understand? The tramp was about your own height and build. You would pay him to put on a false mustache and beard—made of rope, simply, and blackened. Then he would start for the river, and let himself be

238

seen, in the dusk, heading in that direction. In the dim light he would not be taken for any one but Charles Granville. And the hunt would follow him. But if it came up with him, he could easily strip off the false beard and mustache. You understand?

"In the meantime, he would have acted as a decoy to take the hunt in a wrong direction, and you would escape."

"Clumsy! Clumsy!" said Granville, shaking his head.

"It sounds clumsy in the explaining," I admitted. "But perhaps it would go off better in the actual telling."

"And then what?" he asked.

"It chiefly depends upon Crosswick, of course."

"How?"

"If he dies, they'll have a legal hold against you, anyway."

"Yes, I know that."

"If he doesn't die, who can possibly put a hand upon you?"

"No, I hadn't thought of that. I simply feel like a hunted dog, Sam. With wolves after me!"

"You show it!" I couldn't help saying. "But, after all, it will be a great sensation when the general tells how he saw two Charles Granvilles standing side by side before the shack, and you'll have to have some sort of a story ready."

"If I tell that tale about the tramp—will any one believe me?"

"They'll have to believe you—unless they can find the fellow and prove that—"

"Well?"

"That he really had the same face, height, and voice as the second Charles Granville."

"Then it all depends on you, Sam!"

"Yes. I shall just have to disappear."

"Ah, Sam," said he, "you can do anything. And you'll do this last thing for me!"

"Have you any money?" I asked suddenly.

"Twenty-five dollars."

"It's better than nothing. Let me have it. And now, good-by!"

He held out his hand; it was shaking.

"Sam," said he, "you've seen me act the part of a hound. Before you're through with me, I wish that you could once see me act the part of a man!"

CHAPTER XLI

Gratitude

As to the possibility of Charles Granville ever playing the part of a man, I had my own doubts. But I kept them to myself. One thing was sure. Whether this thing finally turned out well or badly, I was near the end of my career of duplicity, and after to-day I could let the whole world know that I was Samuel Cross! I was anxious to see the last of Charles Granville, but he lingered for a time, though I urged him to go straight to Granville House at once. He was uneasy.

"You've rescued me from some nasty affairs, old fellow," said Charles Granville. "And now I'm wondering how I can possibly give you any reward."

"Why, I don't want a reward," said I. "It's sufficient reward to be able to be myself again, and to escape from the danger of being jailed as a criminal impostor."

He nodded, biting his lip a little. For you can see that I was swinging the lash on him.

"There's nothing that you can ask for?" said he.

"Tell me one thing," I replied. "Would you be willing to part with Luke for the same price that you paid for him? It was one thousand dollars, Charles."

He grew a quick red and said hurriedly: "Good God, man, after what you have done for me, would you hesitate to ask for a single slave? You should have a dozen, if you could use them and I had the authority to give them to you! I *have* the authority to send you Luke, and you shall have him. Tell me where he is to go?"

"I'll manage to send you a letter and I'll tell you in that letter where to send him."

"One more moment, Sam. Do you really think that I shall ever be able to face the general?"

"Yes," said I, "by flying into a rage whenever his name is mentioned. By storming up and down the room. And by drawing a revolver on him when you meet him and asking yourself aloud why you don't blow his head off. You must swear that he fired on you before you and your tramp friend moved a foot. He and his men will all tell one story. You must stick to another. And then I shall be produced. That will clinch matters!"

"And where will you go in the meantime?"

"Don't worry about me, man. Don't worry about me. I'm going to handle that matter without any difficulty."

He seemed a little reassured by what I said. He shook hands with me for the last time, and then, as he was going, I thought of another thing.

"A bit of black fur stuck on mouth and chin," said I. "That will be better than the story of the rope."

I watched him out of sight before I turned back into the marsh. As a matter of fact, I felt that both of the stories which I had suggested to him were exceedingly thin, and the general had already shown such keen insight that I did not see how Charles could make his tale convincing.

Nevertheless it was the best I could think of on the spur of the moment. It had to do for me, and for Charles, also, because his own powers of invention at the moment seemed to be nil.

As I retreated through the marsh, I kept a sharp lookout and when I finally found a little secure spot of dry ground, I beached the boat there and remained on the place until the darkness closed that day.

In the meantime, I had been turning over in my mind what I should do. The first possibility was to remain in the swamp, and, from that headquarters, I could hunt through the countryside and supply myself with provisions at night. However, without a horse it would be a precarious business. And I could not keep a horse in the marsh. It would be vastly better if I could get some more secure refuge. I considered the matter from all points and finally hit on a scheme which I thought would do.

I rowed to the edge of the marsh, left the boat there, and went across country until I came near Ransome's house. I scouted about the place, finally located his room, and clambered into it. There in a corner closet I waited until about midnight. Dick came up to bed. An old Negro lighted him, and turned down the covers of the bed; and after the Negro had left, I quickly stepped out of my place of concealment.

I knew that Dick Ransome was a ready man with weapons, so I took no chances. I covered him with a revolver as I stepped out. His back was turned to me, but the faint creak of the floor under my weight made him whirl about.

He threw up his hands at once. He was wonderfully cool and quiet.

"Well, my man," said he. "How the devil did you get in here? Ah, you've been hiding in the closet yonder?"

"You have good nerves, sir," I said.

He started a little.

"By gad," he cried, "I ought to know that voice!"

"Perhaps you've heard it before, sir."

"Yes, I think I have. Were you ever employed by my father?"

"No, sir."

"But still, I certainly know a man of your build, with just such a voice."

"You may have met me in a dream, sir."

"Hello! What's that?" said he.

"In a bad dream, sir," I added.

"By the Lord," said Dick Ransome, "I think I place you now! And if it weren't for your complexion, I'd call you Charlie Gran—hold on! Ten thousand devils! You're the general's double!"

It hadn't taken him long to strike the truth! And it made my heart sink.

Then he shook his head.

"No," said he. "You're bigger than Charlie. And your eyes are different! But—there's a confounded likeness. Tell me, man. Have I guessed the truth? Is the crazy old general right, after all, with his tale of the two men on the island in the marsh who were both Charles Granvilles?"

Already that story had crossed the countryside, then!

"I don't know what you mean," I replied.

"Ha!" said he. "That voice is still ringing in my ears— telling me to take the first turn into the woods—and keeping on in the open to draw the major danger after you. You are the man who played the part of Charlie Granville that night! Don't deny it!"

I put up my revolver.

"Suppose I say that I am?"

"By the eternal, it's the most amazing thing that ever happened! And you're the man who galloped down Cherry Hill. You shot Lipton and held off his men, and rescued Luke. You dropped Crosswick this morning, also!"

"How is he now?" I asked.

"You admit it all?"

I nodded.

He stepped up to me and wrung my hand.

"Thank God that I have a chance to thank you in person for saving me the other night! For bringing me clean off! Yet how under heaven you were able to pick me up like a baby and throw me on a horse—ouch! I'm still sore from the way you gripped me! The general swore that you had such an arm as never could have belonged to Charlie Granville! And I'll swear so, too!"

I was glad that I had come to Dick Ransome. He was a good deal of a rascal, but he was a whole-hearted fellow, too. I suppose he's not the first robber who was also something of a gentleman. He made me sit down, and then he walked round and round me. He was still exclaiming, when I asked him to talk more quietly.

"There are only two servants in the house," he said, "and they're both so old and deaf that they can hardly hear me when I stand in front of them and shout at the top of my lungs. You need not be afraid."

"That plaster on the side of your head, how do you explain that?" I asked him.

"Easily enough. I simply stumbled in the dark going down the cellar stairs, and a nail sticking out of the wall grazed my head. Besides, it looks so small one would never think that it was a bullet wound."

That was true enough.

"Now what are we to do with you—what's your name?"

"Samuel Cross."

"What are we to do with you?" Ransome repeated.

"I don't know. But I thought that you might be able to put me up."

"Oh, I'll manage it. Confound it, I'll manage the thing in some way."

"Have you any old shack back in the woods, say?"

"No. Not a thing. I have the woods on the place, but that's all."

"Very well. I've camped out in the open before."

"But look here, man. It isn't that I don't want to keep you, but it really seems to me that you had better clear out of this section of the country. Other people will recognize you as easily as I do."

"I would clear out," I told him, "except for two reasons. The first is that just now they'll be watching the river and every road away from St. Pierre for strangers of my build. The second is that I cannot very well leave until I'm assured that Charlie Granville is out of this tangle safely."

"Damn Charlie Granville!" said he with a black look. "I'm going to have something to say to him about this affair. He'll never be able to call himself a friend of mine again. Letting another man fight his duels for him—I never heard of such a cowardly piece of rascality in all my days!"

"That's done and forgotten," I insisted. "He's not really so bad. But weak. I owe him my life, Dick."

He nodded.

"Well, that's something. I think a bit better of him for that."

"I hope so."

"And of course, Baring was such a fighting devil. No wonder that Charlie tried to think of another way out. But what's the final decision?"

"I'll stay in the woods and make myself some sort of a shelter. Can you provide food for me?"

"Whatever I have is yours, so long as I live and have a penny, or strength to lift a hand for you, old boy. Other people may forget, but I never do. And I have something to remember about what you've done!"

CHAPTER XLII

The Contrast

So it was arranged in that manner. Ransome had a hundred and fifty acres of woodland and underbrush thick as a jungle; and he himself led me from the house and down a cattle path and so to a secure nook in the woods. I was supplied with blankets, and I knew that I could make myself comfortable enough.

There in the darkness I asked Dick to tell me the latest news about the general's story, and learned that Mcgruderdhad sworn that he had seen two Granvilles standing side by side. One half the countryside was doubtful, and the other half laughed openly at the report and said that the old general was trying to cover up his folly of that morning, when he had made such a strange scene in Granville House.

"But people are uneasy in their minds," said Dick. "Unless the general is quite crazy, it's hard to think that he would have invented such a fishy tale. Every one is in doubt, and it wouldn't take a feather's weight to turn public opinion one way or another."

I spent a restless night in the open. Not because I was uncomfortable, but because sleeping under the pines, and breathing the sweet open air, made me yearn for the plains with all my heart. There was my country. And whatever might be my fate, I wanted to live my life in the land where I was born.

Dick did not come to see me until the afternoon. He had spent the morning gathering news, and he declared that everything was going much better than could be expected. First and foremost, young Crosswick was, contrary to all expectations, rapidly recovering and was nearly past the danger point. I was heartily glad of that.

Second, Charlie Granville's tale of the tramp he had met was accepted, because it was known that a good many vagabonds and fugitives from justice resorted to the swamp in time of need. And the general's foolish declarations at Granville House were believed to have suggested to Granville the idea of disguise. It was also believed that the general and his men had fired first, and that Mcgruder made his followers swear that the pair had bolted before a shot was fired.

"Charlie and the colonel rode over to the general's house this morning," said Dick Ransome, "and it's said that Charlie turned his vocabulary inside out at the general. When he saw Mcgruder, he drew a revolver, and his father had to grapple with him and take it away from him. The colonel was somewhat heated himself. He denounced Mcgruder, and swore that he would make the country too hot to hold him. And from this point onward, I think that the colonel is so thoroughly identified with Charlie's cause that any one who doubts Charlie will have to doubt the colonel. And who wants to do that? Not I, for one! That old fire eater—"

He broke off with a half laugh. And I agreed with him. Colonel Granville was a power in the community and it would be folly to oppose him unless one was sure of one's ground. I suggested to Dick that he see Charlie and tell him where I was hiding.

That was done, and the following morning Dick came out to tell me of the next stage of the proceedings. The colonel had posted handbills all over the countryside, offering a reward to the tramp who had been with his son in the swamp, and stating that if the man would simply come to Granville House, he would be asked no questions and would be permitted to leave for any part of the country to which he desired to go; no one would be allowed to interfere with him, and he would be assured of a safe conduct.

"Charlie's idea," said Dick, "is that you will have to turn up. You're to confirm the story of meeting him in the swamp; of the disguise; of the way that you were to draw suspicion in one direction while he escaped from the swamp in another, and of the arrival of the general and his men which put you both to flight. And you're to swear that the general and his men fired before you ran!"

It was plain that there was a good deal of risk to be run in this matter; but it was a possible solution, and I determined to do my part toward ending the difficulty.

The next day I shaved clean, and Dick clipped my hair close to my head. The difference between a head covered by long, flowing locks like those of Charles Granville, and a cropped head like mine was wonderful. It seemed to change the very features of the face. And besides—to mention rather a silly point—it seemed to make my ears flare out from my head.

Then I walked straight across country, and in the middle of the afternoon turned in at the gates of Granville House and walked up the driveway. In front of the house stood Colonel Granville, directing some Negroes who were trimming the climbing vines that screened the face of the old manor.

"Are you Mr. Granville?" I asked.

He whirled around with a start when he heard my voice. Then he saw my head of glistening red hair, for I had my hat in my hand, and he blinked and recovered himself.

"I am," he replied.

"I got to see Mr. Charles Granville," said I, "about a reward—"

The colonel's eyes shone.

"You're the man of the marsh!" cried he.

"Yes."

"Ah, that's good! You'll never have to regret coming here, my lad! Walk into the house! Henry and George, go to the stables. Send out half a dozen of the boys to ride to every house between here and St. Pierre and bring back a representative from every household. Let everybody know that the man of the swamp has turned up! Confound General Mcgruder! I'll let him see for himself how he has been mistaken. Yes, send for Mcgruder in person!"

Then he hurried into the house, with me behind him, calling: "Mother! Nan!"

They came; and Negro faces peered curiously from the

248

doors toward me. There was a whisper running through the entire household. But my interest was centered on Mrs. Granville who came hastily into the room, with Nan behind her. I had replaced my hat.

"There," said the colonel. "There he is. There's the very man of the marshes that Charlie told about. Red hair—take off your hat, my friend, if you please!"

I took it off.

"This is—what's your name? You don't need to fear telling it to me. I'm your protector from this moment!"

"My name is Samuel Cross, sir."

I pitched my voice a little through the nose. Mrs. Granville did not seem to see the slightest resemblance between me and her son.

"But how could Charlie think that this man would ever pass for him?" she asked.

"Why, they're about the same height, mother. And the features are somewhat the same, and even the eyes—"

"Heavens, *Peter!*" cried she. "It's plain to see that you don't know your own boy! The eyes of my Charlie—oh, my dear Nan, will you see if there's the slightest resemblance?"

Nan, rather pale, looked at me with frightened eyes. No doubt I was a bad-looking object with my clipped head. And she had promised to marry me and go out to the plains with me!

"I never heard of anything so absurd!" said Nan.

And every one else who came that afternoon said the same thing.

Before they arrived, I related my story to the colonel. I told how I had met Charlie on the island; how he had made the proposal to me and paid me twenty-five dollars.

"Let me see the money. By the Lord, it's the very sum that I paid to Charlie yesterday! Who can fail to call this proof?"

When thirty people were crowded into the hall, the colonel had me brought out and placed at the side of his son. There was a great contrast, you may be sure, between his long, flowing black locks, neat beard and short mustache, and my red hair and smooth-shaven face. Besides, these few days of living in the sun had tanned my skin; though not, of course, to half the darkness it had had when I first came down the river to this wild adventure. Granville's long hair made him seem taller, too. And even if I had been dressed exactly as he was, side by side, the difference between us would have been apparent. It was only when we were apart that we seemd so exceedingly alike.

Then General Mcgruder arrived, and looked me over critically. He delivered his opinion loudly and boldly: "Dye this man's hair and let it grow long, and give him a beard and mustache like Charles Granville's, and you could hardly tell the two apart. Besides, I want you to listen to his voice. He hasn't spoken as yet, so far as I know!"

It was a critical moment, and fate alone saved me from a great embarrassment, for a man stood up in the rear of the hall—a man who had just entered—and cried: "There's no need to hear his voice. I recognize that rascal! He ain't the man that could of played double to Charles Granville. He's the man of Hardin! He's the man of Hardin! And I guess I'll just take him right back to the Hardin jail!"

That was a little more of an identification than I wanted.

The colonel's servants had been ordered to bring people of all kinds to Granville House, but they had worked a little too thoroughly. So that, by great chance, they had scooped up a man who had been across the river at Hardin on that day when I had visited the town. He started plunging through the crowd toward me. The general's argument that I could have been Charlie's double went unheeded.

"Keep back," ordered the colonel. "No one shall touch him. He's here under my protection!"

"The law has a right to that man, and the law will have him! He broke my brother's jaw, and he'll pay for that, goldarn him!"

Charlie Granville slipped me through a side door and led me up to his familiar room, and there was Luke waiting for us. His smile when he saw me did my heart good.

As for Charlie, he was in the seventh heaven.

"It's over!" he cried. "You've shown a clean pair of heels. I didn't think that you really could do it. I've been sick at heart. But you're wonderful, Sam. You're really wonderful!"

Their praise was not what I wanted just then.

I said: "Charlie, I have to see Nancy before I go."

"Why?" said he, very curious.

"For this once give me my way, and ask no questions."

He hesitated; then agreed. Ten minutes later I was standing before Nan in her little boudoir, while a reckless songbird, perched on the swaying tendrils of the vine that trailed in through the window from the balcony, poured out his heart in song.

Nan, very frightened, her face pale, her eyes big, stood near the window with her back to the wall.

"I wanted to tell you," said I, "that I understand. Of course, when I was here before, mine was a queer position. It was really very romantic, and I know it. And now that you've had a chance to see plain Sam Cross, without a beard and with a clipped head, you know what he really is. I understand perfectly, you see, and I want you to know that I don't expect you to remember what you said to me in the garden. I've forgotten it. We'll both forget. Goodby, Nan!"

I got through that speech to the very end in fairly good fashion, but when I came to her name, it stuck a little in my throat; so I didn't wait for any answer but turned to the door, rather ashamed of myself, and anxious to be away.

"Sam dear!" said a voice behind me.

I dared not turn around for fear that she was mocking me. I think that I was almost afraid to look at her.

"I never saw such a silly man," said she. "And if I was afraid of you—well, it was only because every girl likes to have her freedom as long as she can. But now I know that I can never be really free again, because I love you, Sam, and I shall never stop loving you so long as I live."

And still for another moment I couldn't turn toward her. I was too stunned with joy—too weak with happiness.

CHAPTER XLIII

Just by Chance

I MUST hurry to the end now.

In many ways life was hardly beginning for me. But I have noticed that a narrative which begins before a marriage usually ends with it. Because up to the point of marriage, the man and woman are free to make choices; afterward, to a certain extent, they shut out the world, and so the world has no more interest in them.

"What's become of Joe Smith?"

"Oh, Joe got married last year."

"The devil he did! Poor old Joe!"

You've heard people talk like that. And there's meaning under the talk. It means that Joe is no longer a restless spirit hunting for happiness; uneasy; stepping into the lives of others, showing them his heart, trying to find theirs; desperately seeking all the while for a contentment which he cannot find. While he is hunting, Joe is capital company; but after Joe marries, he is quieter. You will think that the keen dog has grown dull. No, it is only that Joe has his hands on real labor. He is too busy working to have much time for talk with even old friends. They fall into the background. A new life gathers him up to a new destiny.

Well, it was that way with me.

Nancy and I were not married at once. First, I went back to the West. And while I was there poor Charlie Granville came to the end of his days. A glorious ending for Charlie, I'm glad to say. After all, there was an inherent manliness about him which only needed to be developed. After the wild things that I had done in his name while I lived at Granville House, people began to expect something more from him than they had expected before. And when on a day the house of a Negro burned down in St. Pierre, and the little son of the slave—isolated on the roof by the flames—stretched out his arms to Charlie and screamed above the roar of the fire: "Mr. Granville! For God's sake! Help! Help!" he did not appeal in vain!

Oh, I should have liked to see Charlie Granville then, tearing the ladder from the hands of the firemen, planting it against the side of the house, and running up it as far as he could go through the branches of jutting flame. Standing there in the fire, Charles took the boy from the roof and carried him to the ground. The child was badly burned, but he lived. Charlie Granville was quite badly burned, and he died.

A letter from Nan told me the pitiful and beautiful story just after I reached Fort Bostwick.

After all, if you believe in heaven, you will say that it was really nothing to weep about, an heroic death like that!

The day following, while Chandler was begging me to come back to my old place in his store, Marshal O'Rourke walked in and found us together. He took me outside at once.

"Young man," said he, "I'm glad you're back. After I had that letter and that money from you, I took the privilege of changing my mind about you. I think that you're the sort of timber out of which proper Westerners are built. But don't go with Chandler again."

I told him that I would not, and I kept my promise.

Instead, I went out with Uncle Steve, gray and a little bent, but hardier and wiser than ever. That winter we did the most profitable trapping that had ever come his way. In the spring we split the profits. And in June Nan came out with a party of friends "to see the West."

Just by chance, she came to Fort Bostwick. Just by chance, she met there the same vagrant who had been with Charlie Granville in the swamp. And, again, just by chance of course, a sudden romance sprang up between them.

We were married that fall.

Yes, there was trouble with the colonel because his daughter had married so much beneath her proper station in life. But for two years Nan and I worked things out together, and life was for us a glorious procession of joys.

Then we went back to St. Pierre on a visit.

And my second meeting with the colonel in my true rôle of Sam Cross was not at all difficult. He seemed to take a liking to me. He still wore mourning for his heroic son. As for Mrs. Granville, she said suddenly and softly as we sat one evening before the fire: "Peter, it's almost to me as though dear Charlie were back with us once more!"